You're About to Become a

Privileged Woman.

INTRODUCING
PAGES & PRIVILEGES™.

It's our way of thanking you for buying
our books at your favorite retail store.

— *GET ALL THIS FREE* —
WITH JUST ONE PROOF OF PURCHASE:

◆ Hotel Discounts up to 60% at home and abroad

◆ Travel Service - Gua... airfares plus 5% cas...

◆ $25 Travel Voucher

◆ Sensuous Petite Par...

◆ Insider Tips Letter with sneak previews of upcoming books

◆ Mystery Gift (if you enroll before 6/15/95)

You'll get a FREE personal card, too.
It's your passport to all these benefits– and to
even more great gifts & benefits to come!

There's no club to join. No purchase commitment. No obligation.

D1711788

As a *Privileged Woman*, you'll be entitled to all these *Free Benefits*. And *Free Gifts*, too.

To thank you for buying our books, we've designed an exclusive FREE program called *PAGES & PRIVILEGES*™. You can enroll with just one Proof of Purchase, and get the kind of luxuries that, until now, you could only read about.

Big HOTEL DISCOUNTS

A privileged woman stays in the finest hotels. And so can you—at up to 60% off! Imagine standing in a hotel check-in line and watching as the guest in front of you pays $150 for the same room that's only costing you $60. Your *Pages & Privileges* discounts are good at Sheraton, Marriott, Best Western, Hyatt and thousands of other fine hotels all over the U.S., Canada and Europe.

Free DISCOUNT TRAVEL SERVICE

A privileged woman is always jetting to romantic places. When <u>you</u> fly, just make one phone call for the lowest published airfare at time of booking—<u>or double the difference back!</u> PLUS—

you'll get a $25 voucher to use the first time you book a flight AND <u>5% cash back on every ticket you buy thereafter through the travel service!</u>

FREE GIFTS!

A privileged woman is always getting wonderful gifts.
Luxuriate in rich fragrances that will stir your senses (and his). This gift-boxed assortment of fine perfumes includes three popular scents, each in a beautiful designer bottle.   <u>Truly Lace</u>...This luxurious fragrance unveils your sensuous side. <u>L'Effleur</u>...discover the romance of the Victorian era with this soft floral. <u>Muguet des bois</u>...a single note floral of singular beauty. This $50 value is yours—FREE when you enroll in *Pages & Privileges* ! And it's just the beginning of the gifts and benefits that will be coming your way!

$50 VALUE

FREE INSIDER TIPS LETTER

A privileged woman is always informed. And you'll be, too, with our free letter full of fascinating information and sneak previews of upcoming books.

MORE GREAT GIFTS & BENEFITS TO COME

A privileged woman always has a lot to look forward to.
And so will you. You get all these wonderful FREE gifts and benefits now with only one purchase...and there are no additional purchases required. However, each additional retail purchase of Harlequin and Silhouette books brings you a step closer to even more great FREE benefits like half-price movie tickets...and even more FREE gifts like these beautiful fragrance gift baskets:

L'Effleur ...This basketful of romance lets you discover L'Effleur from head to toe, heart to home.

Truly Lace ...A basket spun with the sensuous luxuries of Truly Lace, including Dusting Powder in a reusable satin and lace covered box.

ENROLL NOW!
Complete the Enrollment Form on the back of this card and become a Privileged Woman today!

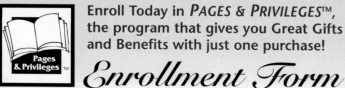

Enroll Today in *PAGES & PRIVILEGES™*, the program that gives you Great Gifts and Benefits with just one purchase!

Enrollment Form

☐ *Yes!* **I WANT TO BE A *PRIVILEGED WOMAN.***
Enclosed is one *PAGES & PRIVILEGES™* Proof of Purchase from any Harlequin or Silhouette book currently for sale in stores (Proofs of Purchase are found on the back pages of books) and the store cash register receipt. Please enroll me in *PAGES & PRIVILEGES™*. Send my Welcome Kit and FREE Gifts -- and activate my FREE benefits -- immediately.

NAME (please print)

ADDRESS   APT. NO

CITY   STATE   ZIP/POSTAL CODE

PROOF OF PURCHASE

Please allow 6-8 weeks for delivery. Quantities are limited. We reserve the right to substitute items. Enroll before October 31, 1995 and receive one full year of benefits.

**NO CLUB!
NO COMMITMENT!**
*Just one purchase brings you great **Free Gifts** and **Benefits!***
(See inside for details.)

Name of store where this book was purchased_____

Date of purchase_____

Type of store:

☐ Bookstore   ☐ Supermarket   ☐ Drugstore

☐ Dept. or discount store (e.g. K-Mart or Walmart)

☐ Other (specify)_____

Which Harlequin or Silhouette series do you usually read?

_____

Complete and mail with one Proof of Purchase and store receipt to:

U.S.: *PAGES & PRIVILEGES™*, P.O. Box 1960, Danbury, CT 06813-1960

Canada: *PAGES & PRIVILEGES™*, 49-6A The Donway West, P.O. 813, North York, ON M3C 2E8   PRINTED IN U.S.A

Guy had never spent a longer night.

He was remembering the bomb she'd dropped earlier. She hadn't *acted* like a virgin. Then again, what did virgins act like?

She'd acted like Mary. That was how he thought about her, witch or not, virgin or not—she was just Mary. The same Mary he'd hung around with as a kid. The same Mary he'd already become dangerously fond of since returning to Stagwater.

When they were kids, he'd felt vaguely responsible for her, being both older and the boy. He'd felt responsible for Lazare, too, and look where that had got him. He didn't want to feel responsible for anyone anymore. It scared him that she had almost let him become not just her lover but her first. And it scared him a lot more to realize how much he wanted her.

Dear Reader,

You've embraced the first two titles in Evelyn Vaughn's miniseries, The Circle; now indulge yourself with number three. *Beneath the Surface* is a haunting tale of years-old tragedy and passion as new as today— and far more dangerous than you can imagine. This miniseries keeps getting better and better, as I think you'll agree once you've dipped into this shivery tale.

In months to come look for Lindsay Longford's welcome return, with the eerie and passionate *Dark Moon*, as well as an exciting new werewolf trilogy, Heart of the Wolf, from top-selling author Rebecca Flanders. As always, we here at Silhouette Shadows are dedicated to taking you for a walk on the dark side of love—and bringing you back alive!

Enjoy!

Yours,
Leslie Wainger
Senior Editor and Editorial Coordinator

Please address questions and book requests to:
Silhouette Reader Service
U.S.: 3010 Walden Ave., P.O. Box 1325, Buffalo, NY 14269
Canadian: P.O. Box 609, Fort Erie, Ont. L2A 5X3

EVELYN VAUGHN

BENEATH THE
SURFACE

Published by Silhouette Books
America's Publisher of Contemporary Romance

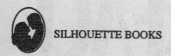 SILHOUETTE BOOKS

ISBN 0-373-27052-6

BENEATH THE SURFACE

Copyright © 1995 by Yvonne Jocks

Books by Evelyn Vaughn

Silhouette Shadows

*Waiting for the Wolf Moon #8
*Burning Times #39
*Beneath the Surface #52

*The Circle

EVELYN VAUGHN

has been a secret agent, a ghostbuster, a starship captain, an elf, a prince and a princess. When not involved in role-playing games, she teaches junior college English and is an unapologetic television addict. She lived in five states before settling in central Texas, and has traveled most of the United States and Europe. She has been writing stories since the first grade. Although she has not yet found Mr. Right, she is enjoying Mr. Write with every book!

On the completion of this book, I owe thanks to my editors Leslie and Melissa; to Honey Island Swamp Tours (Pearl River, Louisiana) and Caddo Lake State Park (Texas); and to a whole slew of fast-reading and big-hearted critique mates: Pam, Cheryl, Toni, Nancy, Jodi, Judy, Doniece and Cousin Erin.

Thank you.

I dedicate this book to the beloved memory of my cousins, Kellie Boyce and Kim Roy, and my sister, Linda Jean Jocks.

PROLOGUE

"Some people," muttered Clem Maddox as he stared at his TV, "can be so greedy."

The evening news superimposed weather statistics—humidity, temperature, barometric pressure—over footage of Mardi Gras parades in New Orleans. Masked attendants on glittering floats hurled handfuls of beads and "doubloons." High-stepping bands danced over the booty. Excited revelers jostled each other to catch all they could, some even raising upside-down umbrellas to provide larger targets while they shouted to the floats.

"Throw me somethin', mister," Clem said, mimicking the revelers and flipping a doubloon in his own hand. This coin, however, didn't gleam—and it weighed much more than the parades' aluminum currency.

Liking the heft of it, Clem tossed it again. He had a lot more to celebrate tonight than Mardi Gras. He and his two buddies, Earl and Bobby Lee, had made yesterday's paper with their recent discovery of decomposed remains in the Louisiana swamp. They'd been searching for a local man whose car went off a bridge last week; instead, they'd discovered a skull, a hipbone, and maybe a thighbone, with scraps of cloth and a nylon belt. Pretty cool.

Better yet, they'd found a dirt-encrusted plastic wallet, like the kind kids carry, with three gold coins spilling out.

Of course, they hadn't told the authorities about the coins. The man who had gone off the bridge—later found drowned—had owed Earl money. They figured they deserved what they could get.

The curtains of Clem's living room window burst bright with lightning, while a simultaneous thunderclap shook the earth—one mother of a storm out there. Clem glanced back at his TV, which now displayed the weather map. Storms covered southern Louisiana and Mississippi. Even if Earl and Bobby Lee did get here this century, the parties wouldn't last long.

Another boom of thunder struck the air around him with a flash. The lamps, the hum of the fridge and the TV all faded out.

In the sudden, dark silence, something hit the front door.

Clem nearly jumped out of his skin, then snorted at himself. "Wuss." Find a few moldy bones, and he turns into an old lady.

Thud! Thud! Thud! Not so much a knock as a deliberate, sludgy pounding. The door shook under each blow... but then, it was a cheap door. It went with the cheap apartment.

"Keep your pants on!" Clem called. Probably Bobby Lee and Earl, laughing their butts off. He reached for the door.

It waited.

He snatched his hand away as the door shuddered beneath another knock. "Damn it, I said—" But when Clem did yank open the door, his protest caught in his throat.

Between the blackout and the steady downpour, he could hardly see the figure—taller than Earl or Bobby Lee—filling his front stoop. That wasn't what scared him, though. Something seemed weird, wrong, about the shape before him.

He noticed a dark smear on the front of the door. "Aw, man..."

But with the next explosion of lightning, Clem saw what was *really* weird about the guy on his stoop.

It struck.

He didn't get a chance to scream.

Yesss...

As Clem's body slid down the mud-slick door, the doubloon fell from his suddenly lax fingers. It bounced, rolled into a puddle, vanished beneath the coffee-colored, rain-pocked surface.

Then the lights flickered back on to show nothing on the stoop but muddy footprints, smeared where Clem's corpse had been dragged across them. The drumming rain quickly washed the mud away, too.

The wind picked up, became the tormented moans of lost souls. Too late, always too late. Then they, too, vanished.

In the background, muffled by the steady tattoo of the downpour, sounded the jazz strains of Pete Fountain's Half-Fast Marching Band...and a cry of "Throw me something, mister!"

CHAPTER ONE

Drinkin' in the dark. And it didn't get much darker than this, mused Guy Poitiers, leaning against a thin tree trunk. Even if there were a moon tonight, which there wasn't, heavy cloud cover hid the sky and sprinkled misty rain. Oh, well. Louisiana, with its thick vegetation and tall, top-heavy loblolly pines, wasn't exactly known for its big sky.

From the dampness floated the mournful hoot of a wood owl. "There are," Guy drawled at the portent of death, "certain benefits to not giving a damn." He crushed his empty beer can.

Only the crickets, the cicadas and the banjo frogs made any comment. Them, and his belated conscience.

"I mean a darn," he muttered. Vaguely curious, he tipped the flashlight on his belt loop far enough to click it on and see his watch. He clicked it off again, let it dangle again from his hip. He'd agreed to give up swearing for Lent. Here it was eight minutes into Ash Wednesday, and already he'd sinned.

Had to be a new record.

Well, heck, he hadn't observed Lent for years, anyway. He wouldn't have given up anything, had he not returned to the old homestead, with its memories of a more religious childhood—and with his devout aunt, desperate for comforting. Guy didn't fully approve of his lapse back into religion, even so. He didn't like people counting on him, not for his beliefs or anything else.

Just in case he started to give a...darn.

He crouched down to the cardboard box at his feet to trade his empty for a refill. He had to do it by feel, since turning on the flashlight had destroyed what little night vision he had. The wet spring night, thick with the fragrance of new growth, was a black void around him. A void with an owl.

He didn't normally drink like this, but he could find his way around a twelve-pack. Now an eleven-pack. No, a ten-pack, he thought as his hand closed around another cool can, and he lifted it in memory of nights when he'd snuck out here with his brothers—and in memory of the cousin who should have lived to sneak out with them. "Happy Mardi Gras, Lazare," he muttered at the nothingness around him. *"Laissez les bons temps rouler."* He didn't really speak French, but his parents and grandparents did; he'd picked up a few useful phrases. "Let the good times—"

And then he heard the giggle.

Guy blinked, and immediately doubted the sound. A giggle? Not a lady's giggle, but a kid's? He replaced the unopened can and hefted the cardboard box. It seemed pretty full.

He tried to chuckle, but it came out more as a wary "Huh." And he realized the banjo frogs had quit their prideful croaking. The cicadas' endless drone stumbled into uncertainty.

Another giggle bubbled at him from the trees, thin and distorted, and Guy slowly rose to his full height, sans beer. He tried to shake off the sense of morbid familiarity that sped his pulse—a familiarity even less conceivable than the giggle.

Then, through the thick pines, a faint voice called out. "Gilly?" And Guy—Guillaume—felt his breath leave him as solidly as if he'd been tackled by four very large defensive linemen. No one had called him Gilly since...

He swallowed, hard, and decided to go back to the house and check on Tante Eva. Party over.

"I can't be drunk yet," he protested, stepping high over a snarl of honeysuckle vine—even in the blackness he recognized the sweetness of a few early blooms. "I only had one—" His deep voice cracked, as if ten years had been stripped from him.

No, eleven. Eleven years, this summer.

The giggle echoed around him again, and a hushed whisper. "Gilly, I found it."

Guy stopped, midstride, because he *did* recognize the voice, and not just because of the human remains some Mississippi men had found in the swamp a few days back.

The remains that had brought him and Tante Eva home.

"Lazare?" he called, slowly turning to face the thicker wood, the slough and the swamp. "Lazy?" It occurred to him that, if this was a sick joke, he'd played right into it.

It occurred to him that nobody in Stagwater was that sick.

"I found it," chanted the voice, singsong, and Guy caught a movement in the depths of the wood. No, not movement—light. A faint, half-visible bluish green, like spots of brightness struggling through the misty rain. "Come see," prompted the voice, coy, from the same direction. "You gotta come see."

The light—will-o'-the-wisp?—bobbed closer. A sober corner of Guy's mind labeled it swamp gas, only to be ridiculed by his adrenaline-shot imagination. Swamp gas didn't move—or giggle.

He fumbled to unclip his flashlight from his jeans. *Feu follet* came his papère's unbidden label. *Couchemal.*

Don' go inna that swamp at night, boy. Couchemal gonna get you, that's a fact.

There! Let there be light. He aimed the beam directly at the hovering greenish glow. It vanished with another giggle.

Guy crossed himself, backing toward the road to keep his eyes on . . . well, on the dim circle of yellow light where whatever-it-was had been. Pinecones, needles and dead twigs crunched soggily under his boots. Something snagged his ankle and clawed at his jeans—blackberry vine. Even in the dark, he knew those briars. He tore loose and kept backing up. Then he paused, unwilling to leave it at this.

He killed the light. "Hey, cuz." Talking to nothing, alone in the woods, he felt like an idiot. But he'd feel worse if he tucked his tail between his legs without even trying. "Um...what're you doing here?" *It's you they found, isn't it?*

Again, the sickly light pulsed closer. Guy's hand stiffened around the flashlight barrel. He could smell menace in the heavy, silent air. He could taste death.

"I found it." The words echoed in the moonless, misted night. "I found it."

"I...uh...Lazy, I hate to be the one that breaks this to you, but—" When Guy took another step backward, the ground dropped away beneath his heels and he tumbled into a sudden void—then sprawled into the overfull drainage ditch that paralleled the road. Dark water sloshed over his legs, waist, ribs. Something skittered by his submerged hand as it gooshed into soft mud. Crawfish? He scrambled to his feet. The light hovered, too close to him, reflecting disjointedly off the disturbed water.

His fingers slipped as he fumbled to turn on the now muddy flashlight, aimed at the *couchemal* like a weapon. There!

Nothing happened. It had shorted out. Cheap piece of—

"I'll show ya, Gilly. Follow me. I'll show ya. *Follow—*"

"No!" The misty light shrouded him, colder than a corpse, colder than the drowning depths of a bayou. Guy shielded his eyes with a dripping arm and stumbled from the water. He felt blacktop beneath his muddy boots. *No, Lazare, you're dead!*

At the sudden wail of a horn, Guy lowered his arm to stare into the glare of headlights—and again broke his Lenten vow.

Mary Deveraux slammed both feet on the brake pedal and yanked the steering wheel in the opposite direction from where the man dived. Her headlights streaked by a confusion of pine trunks and undergrowth, and the reflective green dots of a startled animal's eyes farther back in the darkness. She felt a lurching weightlessness while the engine sped and her seat belt tried to cinch her in half. A horrible jolt knocked her feet from the brake and bounced her sack purse off the dashboard. Everything tipped off kilter. . . and stopped.

She grew aware of stalled silence, a whimpering sound she suspected might be her own, and one headlight shining on the muddy waves of a disturbed, overfull drainage ditch. The other light shone beneath the brown surface, an eerie, watery glow.

She fumbled with her seat belt. Had she hit him? When she managed to undo the belt, she started to slide toward the passenger seat, due to the pickup truck's sickening angle. She grasped the steering wheel, her feet finding purchase. She had to get out, had to check on him! She'd always feared the day she would hit a squirrel or rabbit—or, Lady forbid, someone's pet—but a human?

The door handle wouldn't work. Then remembering, she unlocked it. It flew open, torn from her hand, and she screamed.

A shadowy figure splashed back from her cry. Then it—he—spread his arms to show harmless intent. She sank back against her lopsided seat with relief. Just a live, uninjured man.

Just a man? As opposed to what, the Honey Island Swamp Monster? Even standing thigh-high in ditch water, in the near-dark, the shadowed, broad-shouldered figure looked big, rangy. But swamp monsters probably wouldn't wear denim.

And, actually, Mary wouldn't have wanted to make road kill out of even the Honey Island Swamp Monster.

"You okay?" His resonant, deep voice sounded vaguely familiar, if a bit shaky. She could understand only the latter.

"Better than my truck, I'd bet." But an old truck—even hers—seemed a fair trade for a life. Trucks could be fixed. Even knowing first aid, and other assorted healing arts, she didn't want to take chances with people. "You?"

In answer, the man took a sloshing step toward her. She belatedly considered that this could be a carjacking ploy—not that her truck made much of a prize, even on land. She dismissed the idea. If he meant to harm her, she'd have sensed the déjà vu by now—that sickening realization that she'd already dreamed and forgotten this very scene. Mary dreamed, in advance, nearly every important thing that happened to her. Rarely did she retain those too-subjective premonitions, at least not in time to prevent them. But even if she'd dreamed and forgotten her own attack, this was about the time she would realize that she had seen this movie before, and hadn't liked the ending.

No such sensation. The shadow's extended hands spoke more of chivalry than of menace. When she tried to collect her keys, her awkward fingers surprised her further. If she'd tried to climb out herself, she probably would have flopped into the rain-swollen ditch. With cautious gratitude, she swung her legs out the door and braced herself on the man's broad shoulders, her hands splayed atop damp denim jacket. Nice deltoids.

He circled her waist with big hands, lifted her as easily as he might have a child, and carefully lowered her to the soggy grass edging the ditch. Again a sense of familiarity trickled through her, this time at the solid warmth of his palms on her waist. She didn't know him from premonitions of the future, but . . .

"I can pull out your truck in the morning, check the damage, get it fixed." His low drawl sounded local, maybe Cajun. That could explain the familiarity of his voice. But what about the familiarity of the touch that slid belatedly from her hips? "My aunt's staying half a mile north of here. You can call someone from there, or I can give you a ride. You sure you aren't hurt?"

She ignored the last question. Nothing stood just north of here except her parents' house, where she'd celebrated Mardi Gras tonight. Her parents', and the old Poitiers place.

The Poitiers place? In the indirect illumination of her headlight, she stared at the man beside her. He glanced nervously toward the even darker woods across the road, while she discerned bits of profile. Chiseled jaw—not merely handsome, downright chiseled. Nice nose. Tousled hair. Only a Poitiers boy could, half-hidden, look so damned good . . . but after all these years! Ralph? TiBoy?

No; the tingle his hands had left against her meant the past had caught up with her, whether she felt ready for it or not. "Guy?"

He cocked his head toward her. Now she recognized blunt cheekbones; full lips parting in astonishment; eyes so blue they glowed in the shadows. *Guy?* She must be mistaken. Stagwater, Louisiana, did not produce men this gorgeous. Not even Poitiers.

But then he bent closer, and his mouth stretched into a broad, if distracted, smile. "Mary?" The distraction left his smile; he caught her at the waist again, swept her high into the air and spun her around with a splash. "Hey, Mary Margaret!"

"Hey yourself," she murmured, nearly drowning beneath a wave of déjà vu. She *had* seen this movie before...and though she couldn't remember the ending, it felt like a doozy.

"You cut your hair." His eyes still readjusting after having been caught like a deer's in her high beams, Guy had somehow expected Mary Deveraux to fit his memory's clear picture. Still little; when he set her back on the bank, she'd barely reached his chest. Still elf-faced, with those big golden eyes and that uptilted nose and that generous mouth, though she'd finally grown into the features. Still blond, even. So the first obvious difference that had struck him was her short hair, the same hair that used to hang in a messy braid down her back.

Next he noticed that she'd gotten curvy. Not like some of the top-heavy girls about whom they'd compared notes on walks home from the school bus. Mary Margaret wore some kind of tight leggings, and a flowing, oversize blouse that hid most of what she did have, but he had developed an eye for these things. Besides, his hands still spanned her tucked waist. The girl had grown up—well, grown—thoroughly female.

Suddenly embarrassed, he wrenched his gaze back to her impish face, glad he'd noticed and blurted out his surprise over her hair first. He let his tardy hands fall free.

"Don't call me Margaret," Mary chided, grinning.

Son of a . . . gun. Eleven years fell off him. Here he stood on the Old Slough Road with Mary Deveraux. A fall of little silver stars from her ears, bracelets that jangled like chimes at her wrists, and a cluster of otherworldly symbols on her necklace—a crescent, a crystal, a five-pointed star—somehow gave the impression of moonlight and magic. *She* reminded him of magic. If he hadn't already touched her, he'd have feared she'd waver and vanish like a reflection in a pool of water, or a particularly nice memory. Or a ghost.

The warm fuzzies of old-home night faltered as he remembered what—who?—he'd seen. He caught her hand; she still didn't vanish. "Come on, let's get you out of, uh, the weather."

She jumped the ditch easily. What kid from Old Slough Road couldn't jump a ditch? He had to yank his own feet free from the mud, and he sensed from the weight as he splashed to dry land that he'd probably gotten an inch taller in the mud while he stood there, poleaxed.

"What about the weather?" Mary asked as he towed her up the road, wary of any threat. But surely not the ghost of a nine-year-old boy! Lazy couldn't be evil, not even dead.

A *couchemal*, though? Guy's grandfather would say *couchemals* were bad omens, lures to death. Then again,

Papère barely spoke English, and was a tad superstitious. Guy briefly considered telling Mary. There'd been a time he could tell her anything, and she'd always had her own direct line to the unknown.

Then he remembered that his cousin Lazare hadn't drowned alone, eleven years back. Tossing dead relatives into the conversation this quickly seemed kind of tacky, even for him. And despite looking much the same, she might have changed.

He certainly had.

He cleared his throat—had she asked a question? Oh, yeah, the hurry. "Could be it's going to storm."

"Could be you lie like a rug." She easily kept up with his long-legged stride, like always. At the rumble of distant thunder, Guy couldn't resist a told-you-so grin. So far, nothing had jumped out at—

Light caught the edge of his vision. Stepping quickly between it and Mary, releasing her hand to free his, he realized he'd overreacted. *Dumb as a duck.* This was plain incandescent light from the living room window of the two-story rental house, past the clearing. His parents owned it. He'd grown up here with his brothers and parents, his cousin Lazare, and sometimes, when their Nonk Alphonse got wild, with their tante Eva.

Had he imagined the giggle? *I'll show ya, Gilly.* He almost wanted to go back, to double-check. For Lazy.

The hand that touched his arm, light as the mist but deliciously warmer, dissuaded him. "You okay?" Mary Margaret appeared by his elbow, her golden eyes searching his. He lost himself in them for a moment. Better than in thoughts of ghosts.

Much better.

The bulk of his memories protested his reaction to her nearness—*Mary Margaret?* But another memory stood out in defense of his attraction: them on the bayou, bare feet sinking in the mud. They'd both worn cutoffs, him bare-chested, her in a tank top that skimmed her then-boyish figure. They'd been tanned brown, her dark-honey braid bleached gold from the sun. He had awkwardly suggested maybe he could take her to a dance, when she started high school that fall. She had shyly accepted. Both instinctively understood the implications, that their lifetime relationship hovered on the verge of momentous change. Her golden eyes had gazed up at him with thirteen-year-old expectation as he licked his lips, then leaned closer...

And jerked away, embarrassed, when he heard his brother's truck approaching. She'd looked embarrassed, too, but hardly displeased by this new sensation. They'd held that excited self-consciousness between them for as long as possible before looking away to their interruption. And then TiBoy had leaned out the truck's window, asked them when they'd last seen Lazare and Joey—and Mary's tanned, elfin face had gone white. Guy had known that look. It meant she'd remembered something. She'd dreamed something would happen, and when TiBoy asked the question, she'd remembered it, and it had terrified her.

That alone had terrified him.

Lazy's tragedy—Lazy's and little Joey Deveraux's—had stolen that long-ago moment. Now he stared into those same eyes by the dim light that meant his tante Eva was waiting up for her nephew, since her own son was long dead... though maybe not as dead as they'd thought.

"I think maybe you're drunk," Mary said with a patient smile, innocently skimming her palm down his arm to take his hand in her small grip and tugging at him. "Why don't we get you inside, where your aunt Eva can tuck you in, eh?"

"Me? I'm not drunk," he protested, overtaking her in two strides and passing her with the third. Wasn't *he* supposed to be getting *her* safely inside?

Wasn't he supposed to not give a darn?

"How many beers have you had?" she asked him challengingly.

"Not enough, *chère*," he groaned, holding open the screen door to the porch for her, then ducking past to open the front door, too. "Tante Eva! See who I found!"

He wished he hadn't left the rest of the beer in the woods.

Stepping inside the familiarity of her onetime best friend's home, Mary braced herself against memories of his family's departure. The past had lurked for a long time, ghostly at the edge of her vision, but she'd skillfully avoided it—until one of its denizens darted out of her memory and into her pickup's path, in full living color. Bigger and better and more handsome than before, Guy had grown into a hunk.

Not that it mattered. She'd once missed him, of course, missed him terribly. But that was the past, trying to suck her down like a deadly undertow beneath placid waves.

Like the unexpected current in a flooded bayou.

The Mary she'd been at thirteen missed the Guy he'd been at fifteen. But they'd gone on, become other people... really good-looking people, in his case, but strangers nevertheless. They'd found other lives, and he wouldn't likely stay in hers for long. He'd probably only returned because of the human remains some men from Picayune, across the state line, had found in the swamp. Lazare's remains, she knew, identification pending or no.

He'd only returned because of the morbid past.

"Guillaume?" Miss Eva's voice trembled; when the older woman stepped from the nearly bare living room into the front hall, Mary tried not to stare. Eva, who couldn't be much past forty, looked sixty! More than faded hair and sunken features had aged her. The woman looked scared, as if she'd been scared a long time.

Mary smiled gently. "Hello, Miss Eva."

Miss Eva did not smile back.

"You remember Mary Deveraux?" prompted Guy, resting a warm hand on Mary's shoulder. "Mr. Al and Miz Maddy's second daughter from down the road? Her big sister Anne used to date TiBoy."

Miss Eva said nothing—but Mary thought she did remember them. After the accident, Mary's family had found little Joey's body. Eva had not gotten even that comfort. Yet. But from the moment Mary heard on the news about the grisly discovery, she'd known it was Lazare, finally Lazare. "Miss Eva—"

"Get out," said the older woman.

Mary blinked, startled. Guy's fingers tightened on her shoulder. "But—I think you should know something."

"Get out of my sister's home. You practice your black arts somewhere else, and leave my boys alone."

"What are you—?" Guy stopped his protest when Mary raised her fingers to his own. He dropped her a sulky glance, but let her defend herself. Yes, she wore a pentagram—but not the inverted pentagram of a satanist! The woman was way off.

"If it puts you at ease, Miss Eva, I'll leave. But you needn't be frightened. I don't do evil. Guy and his brothers are no longer boys. And—" She swallowed that last one just in time. *And they aren't yours, anyway.* Definitely not something to tell a lady who'd lost her only son. So Mary shut up, shrugged off Guy's grip and got out.

She did, however, let the screen door slam on her way down the front steps. Black arts! *Leave my boys alone!* As if—

A chill worse than the spring mist settled over her, and she raised her hands to her mouth in dismay. Miss Eva couldn't think she'd had anything to do with Lazare's death, could she? Not when Mary's brother had died in the same accident! The bayou had been at a record high, a level not repeated until this spring. Lazy and Joey had apparently climbed onto a drifted tree wedged against the bank. A stupid, childish risk. An accident!

Everyone knew it was an accident.

Only as she blinked away hot wetness did Mary notice tears in her eyes. She fiercely wiped them away with the back of her hand, aware of Guy's raised voice—his new, deeper voice—inside, and Miss Eva spewing something back in rapid French.

If only she could smear away the unwanted memories as easily. Joey and Lazy, that was past. Eleven *years* ago! It had been tragic, and she still missed her little brother now and then, but life had gone on. *She'd* gone on.

She hiked across the lawn, from the oyster-shell drive toward the bordering woods, with their darkness and their drone of cicadas. She'd take the old shortcut across the slough to her parents' place, sleep on the couch, and get a ride home tomorrow. There she could think about her kid sister's upcoming wedding, her older brother's pregnant wife ... the happiness of the future.

She'd barely escaped the glow of the porch light before she heard the hollow slap of the screen door behind her.

"Mary!" The squelch of Guy's boots and the rub of wet denim mixed with the crunch of shells. Remembering the mud, she allowed herself a single petty smile, and hoped he'd tracked it inside. "Mary, wait up!"

She glanced over her shoulder and got a full-length view of the man loping toward her. Who would have thought the runt would become the pick of the litter? Look out, women of Stagwater.

"Where are you going?" he asked, his voice thick with... embarrassment, she guessed. "Don't let Eva run you off."

"I'm not," she insisted; it didn't lessen the concern shadowing his bright eyes. "But it's late, my parents are probably already in bed." She started to turn away.

He dodged around her to block her path. "The shortcut must be grown over by now. And it's dark."

Actually, between her younger sisters and her older nephews, she suspected, the path had remained more or less passable. He was sweet to worry, though. "I'll be fine." She patted his rain-damp arm comfortingly as she went around him. Nice biceps. Triceps, too. "It's no darker than the road."

She didn't get suspicious until he ducked in front of her again, then leaned with feigned nonchalance against the branchless trunk of a tall pine. "Let me give you a lift."

"No way. You've been drinking."

"One beer, *chère*." His hundred-watt grin washed over her, tickling her stomach. "Come on, Mary. I help trash your truck and get you accused of satanism in one night. Good luck comes in threes, you know." When the grin didn't work, he raised his eyebrows entreatingly. "I'm sober as a clam."

She didn't fight the smile that pulled at her mouth.... No harm in a good smile now and then. "I thought clams were happy."

"I don't know—are they?" Guy's voice almost cracked; he was trying so hard to be casually charming, he practically vibrated with it. In truth, she doubted he could exude all this high-frequency energy if he was the least bit intoxicated.

Still, she had another way to check him out, so to speak, and raised a practiced hand to his cheek. His eyelids fell, heavy with suspicion, but except for instinctively tipping his head back, he held still. His facial muscles didn't feel lax. He shifted his weight from one foot to the other, then slanted his brows apologetically and tried to hold still again. The pulse at his temple, beneath her fingertips, beat steady and quick, too. Soft stubble brushed her thumb. If she spread her hand, her thumb could reach that lower lip of his...

Hold up—this was *Guy*, childhood buddy turned complete stranger! She dropped her hand, flustered, a moment before her investigation became a caress. "I could examine your eyes or make you walk straight lines and touch your nose to kingdom come," she said quickly. "None of that's really trustworthy."

Guy finally stood completely still. His eyes had, in fact, softened as they focused on her mouth. He extended one big hand, index finger raised—and as his eyes cleared and his smile returned, he touched it to the tip of *her* nose. "Trust me. I had one beer. And that was one gho—" His cough sounded fake. "One good while ago. C'mon, *chère*. Let me drive you home."

Trust him? The man acted as crazy as a jaybird. But her instincts insisted he was also sober as a...clam.

He could take her to her own home. Even her parents' house embodied the past. "I'll need a ride to work tomorrow if it's raining," she warned. "If I stay with my folks, someone could—"

"I'll give you the ride," he promised, clearly relieved by her decision. "Maybe I'll have news on your truck. Deal?"

She cast one more glance at the dense woods beyond him, tangled with twining creepers and trash brush, where they'd been inseparable as kids. In the distance, lightning flashed, illuminating more snarled growth, deeper. She shuddered.

Someone walk over your grave?

Before she could try sensing the area for anything truly spooky, though, Guy's big hand had swallowed hers, and he was steering her back from the dark woods to the lit carport—and from the confusions of their past toward...

What?

CHAPTER TWO

She lived on a houseboat.

Leaving his motorcycle at a dead-end dirt road, Guy followed Mary down a tangled path that cut through piney woods, past moss-draped granddaddy oaks. Part of him savored the rightness of the two of them trekking through nature. Another wondered how often she walked this path alone, and disapproved.

A light, too high to be a porch light, beckoned to them through swaying tree limbs. Then the woods abruptly ended, black willow and tupelo gum trees crowding the bayou bank for open space, and he saw the house. The house*boat*, rather, anchor light mounted on top. Not a cabin-cruiser houseboat like well-off families keep for fishing jaunts into the Gulf, either. No, this was a shack-on-a-raft deep-South houseboat. All it lacked was trotlines, crawfish traps, and maybe a bathtub on the porch.

Guy would be shocked to find a Deveraux living in a decent mobile home, but a houseboat? He expected better for Mary.

"Guess you didn't become a doctor after all, huh?"

She glanced over her shoulder, amused. "I did a couple of years at Tulane, but med school wasn't...me." Before he could protest—she'd *always* planned to go to med school!—she picked up on his "This-Is-Your-Life" theme. "So what about you and your football scholarship? Have the Saints picked you up yet?"

Yeah, right. She'd done better with her life than he had, at that. "I...um...went to LSU."

"The Fighting Tigers, eh? What'd you major in?"

He never *could* lie to her. "Partying."

"I see." Tactful response. He relaxed at the acceptance in her hazel eyes, the lack of scorn on her cute mouth. She could figure out for herself why neither the Saints nor anyone else had picked him up. She just didn't seem to mind.

"I do a lot of carpentry," he offered, shoving his hands into his jeans pockets. "Construction, too." He almost mentioned his on-again, off-again idea of starting his own contracting business—more than one boss had told him he had what it took. But Guy knew better. A man had to think ahead to make something like that work, and he didn't much trust the future.

That sense of his own transience—his own mortality?—felt a lot heavier after what he'd encountered in the woods. He shook it off. "I worked the oil rigs for a while, two weeks on, one week off. Real good money, but I didn't much like it."

"Not enough parties?" she asked teasingly, and he felt even easier. She had no reason to disapprove of his lifestyle. They were just friends. Still. Like no time had passed at all.

Spreading his arms, he flashed her his most charming grin and lowered his voice. "Not enough women, *chère*. Not enough women." He half expected her to chuck a handful of mud at him. Instead, she ducked her head, and when she looked back up from beneath her bangs, a pretty smile pulled at her generous mouth. The expression woke something deeper than friendship within him, something warm and pleasant, and far too fragile to be disturbed after so many years. Oh, my. He hadn't known his own power. Sure, his grin worked on the ladies—but this was Mary Margaret!

Her eyes sparkled; her little nose had wrinkled with her smile. She was too honest to be coy. Guy quickly looked away to the houseboat. He pulled his hands from his pockets, then didn't know what to do with them. Time *had* passed, whether he'd wanted it to or not. She was proof of that.

He glanced back at her, and offered an awkward smile. How'd they gotten so uncomfortable all of a sudden?

She shrugged amiably at his unasked question, cocking her head so that the silver stars dangling from her ears lapped at her bare neck. The cicadas, tree toads, crickets and banjo frogs sang their little hearts out, filling the swamp night with noise and life. Something splashed downstream. He could hear a faint lapping noise against the side of the big raft that held Mary's . . . house. He could feel her nearness, barely two feet from him after years apart. The whole moment seemed eerily familiar.

Distant lightning strobed the southern sky, like a nudge from the heavens—how late was it, anyhow? "Let me get your number, so I can phone you before I come out." It sounded like a line *I'll call you sometime*. But he *had* promised.

Mary spread her hands. "No phone."

"You're joking." Instead of agreeing, she narrowed her eyes, like he'd just double-dog dared her. "You live in the boonies, and you don't have a *phone?* Do you know what kind of weird—?"

"I know. But I'm fine." She planted her hands on her hips with a jingle of bracelets; the cuffs of her oversize shirt swallowed them. "I'm not still thirteen. A lot has changed."

No kidding.

Another distant pulse of lightning threw the trees, the water, into weird relief. The memory of an otherworldly giggle hovered too fresh for him to feel right leaving her without a phone. Maybe he should tell her about the *couchemal*.

But maybe he should tell her in the daylight.

Thunder echoed the lightning, another divine admonition. "I'll be here in the morning, then," he said. "Nine, right?"

"Sure."

He backed away several steps, stopped again. Then he lit on a reason to have stopped. "Will you need a ride to mass, too?"

Her mouth dropped open; what, she'd forgotten Ash Wednesday? "I don't go to mass anymore, Guy. I haven't in years."

Which shouldn't bother him, since he hadn't been in a year himself. But the Mary he remembered had attended church regularly.

"Oh. Okay. I'm just giving my aunt a ride..." Now, that was a fine idea; put Mary and Eva in a car together. Another flicker of lightning prodded him. *Say good-night, Guy.*

"See you tomorrow, then," she said, but continued to hold his gaze—or else he held hers. A good six feet stretched between them, since he'd taken those steps, and yet he could feel her presence, smell her sweetness, as strongly as if they stood toe-to-toe. Just like when they'd almost shared that first kiss.

They never had shared it. It still waited for them.

Guy swung away from Mary with a half wave and headed down the now very dark path, toward his motorcycle. He practically had to feel his way along, and considered going back for a flashlight that worked—but no. He had to escape the intensity, good and bad, that hovered between them. Through the first half of their lives they'd created a sort of bond, but he suddenly dreaded its reemergence, after nearly as many years apart.

There wasn't a thing he'd touched in the last ten—eleven?—years that he hadn't somehow messed up. No relationship. No job. Certainly not his football career! He had no future. The best thing he could do for Mary Deveraux was stay the hell—the heck—away from her.

He only wished he had a better track record for doing the best thing.

* * *

Mary hopped from the weedy bank onto the deck, ducked through her screen door, then sank back against the doorframe, hugging herself. Wow.

She'd thought, for a moment there, that he meant to kiss her. They would see each other again, so he still might try. Not that she had to wait for him to try anything—if she wanted a kiss, she could just kiss him. She was a self-sufficient woman of the nineties, after all, albeit a tad inexperienced in the romance department.

But she hadn't kissed him. So she must not have wanted it...even if her pulse still raced, and her stomach still flip-flopped. Had he not kissed her for the same reason?

Her stomach sank, and only then did she make the connection between herself and some teenager getting asked to the prom. She frowned at the direction her thoughts, or at least her body, had taken. But—wow. Straddling the motorcycle behind Guy had given her personal experience with his terrific lats, which matched his impressive delts and biceps and triceps and...well, she assumed, other and sundry admirable musculature. Guy's body was a massage therapist's dream—and she was a massage therapist.

Yeah, that was it: professional interest.

"Tell me another one," she muttered, boosting herself toward the bedroom before she could completely melt into a little puddle on the floor. She didn't bother to light any lamps. The glow from her anchor light reflected off the water and, faintly, through her open windows, and she prided herself on conserving energy...especially since her electricity ran off a deep-cell battery that would cost *beaucoup* bucks to replace. Besides, she wasn't afraid of the dark. Especially not in her sanctuary.

The boat would never have made *House Beautiful,* even in better days. It listed slightly, the roof over the sink leaked, and she suspected one whole wall was rotten. When she'd inherited it from her crazy uncle Jean, she'd surprised everyone by mooring it on a stretch of her father's land and actually moving in—but she loved it. She'd painted the walls pale blue and hung fishing nets across the wall, and she lived close to nature, and rent-free—the only way she could afford her own place on the money she made at the Wellness Club. Who needed more than a bedroom, a head, and a combination living room–galley?

She wondered how jack-of-all-trades Guy Poitiers managed to keep *his* own place . . . and for the first time noticed that he hadn't mentioned whether he did. Well. She'd always figured that any man too rich, too handsome or too famous was a major jerk risk; apparently Guy was only one for three.

And Catholic? Not a bad thing, of course—but she wasn't anymore. She'd lapsed long before finding her current beliefs. But she knew her family, though tolerant, worried that she'd turned from the church only when she became Wiccan—a witch.

She did not, she decided, stripping to her underwear, need the strain of getting involved with anyone who thought similarly. No matter *what* his nearness did to her resting heart rate. Besides, Guy reminded her of a past she'd rather forget. She had a terrific life now, with friends, family, work . . . and magic.

She slid into bed, pulled cool cotton sheets and a soft azure blanket to her chest, lay back and closed her eyes. No, becoming a witch hadn't turned her away from the church; she'd been a witch her whole life, felt the magic her whole life, but only in the past few years had she learned to identify it. Now, if she spread her hands and concentrated, she could sense the magic, even at this ebb of the dark moon. It hovered over the water like a silver fog. It saturated the spring air. It fluttered through her room like an improbable breeze, pulsing with wonder and possibility, and she thought that if she reached out, she could grab a handful of it and hold it close to her as she slept.

And then a huge jolt of it exploded through every channel of her—and she sprang halfway out of her bed, eyes wide, muscles tight, as disoriented as if by a blaring horn or a flash of bright...

Of bright light. A roll of thunder explained the burst of energy that had disrupted her meditation. She should have known better than to reach out, unshielded, near an electric storm. All of nature exuded power, but not all of that power was as soft as the still night air or the slow current of the bayou. Some of it, like lightning, could be downright dangerous in its strength.

Sinking back under the covers, she said a quick thanksgiving for having avoided hitting Guy Poitiers. She wasn't sure whether to be thankful for his brief return in to her life. She hadn't suddenly gotten her best friend back, after all. They were different people now, and she had other best friends.

Not a single one of whom could speed her metabolic rate the way he had, with that sexy smile and those shoulders...

She groaned, blamed her frustration on spring fever, and pulled her covers over her head.

A dog's howl floated from the woods past the yard, warbled, then faded into a whimper. Not much could sound sadder than a hound. Guy glanced toward the sound, but the animal wasn't showing itself. Probably some stray that got left off the highway.

The storm had passed overnight, and this morning a steady mist fell, clinging to his eyelashes and glazing his hair as he returned to Mary's truck, parked beside the carport. The mud would never wash off at this rate.

Guy could have waited till later in the day and borrowed a tractor; instead, he'd called a wrecker, which cost more but had gotten the truck out of the ditch before it could scare Mary's family. That hadn't left him much for parts and labor, especially since he was using this week to reshingle his parents' old house, at cost. Financial planning played a very minor role in his current life-style.

But this was for Mary Margaret.

He ran a hand over the slimy tailgate, clearing a patch of pale blue, and slopped the resulting handful of goo to the ground. He looked almost as bad as it, having volunteered to get in the water to hook the tow chain to its axle. *What does this picture remind you of?* Dirty ex-jock, broken-down truck, even a hound dog. All he needed was a gimme cap and a bottle of beer to complete the good-ol'-boy image.

And he'd had the nerve to flirt with Mary Deveraux?

He'd even dreamed about her...not the kind of dream he could ask her to analyze, either, though she'd once had a knack for that kind of thing. Its meaning had been erotically plain.

Maybe he should go to mass after all.

The dog whined. Guy considered getting some scraps to feed it, but didn't want it to think it belonged here. In another week or so, whether Lazare's remains had been found or not, he and Tante Eva would go their own ways and the house would go up for rent again. Eva surely wouldn't want a stray, and Guy knew himself better than to take responsibility for it. A dog? He wasn't even sure he could get the truck fixed before—

Before what? Again the sense of a deadline loomed, stronger since he'd returned to Stagwater, stronger still since he'd seen the *couchemal* last night.

I'll show ya, Gilly.

The hair at the back of his neck stood on end. No, he hadn't imagined that. Few folks would believe him, but he knew what he'd seen . . . and heard.

Mary would believe him. At least she would have. Once.

The hidden dog howled again, lonely and sad, as Guy went to the outside wall faucet and crouched to wash the worst of the mud from his hands. When he saw his cleared watch face, he swore, then regretted swearing. Had someone mentioned responsibility? He had to leave now, mud and all, to pick up Mary on time.

Good thing he had no business romancing his onetime friend . . . 'cause he wouldn't have a hope in hell.

In heck.

What an oppressive morning. On her deck, in the soft fall of mist, Mary shuddered from more than the chill air. When she looked down the bayou, its café au lait water, shadowed by overhanging trees and vines and tattered drapes of Spanish moss, looked more ominous than beautiful.

But she'd gotten out of bed spooked. Coming face-to-face with the past last night hadn't helped. Then she'd thought she saw Lazare's face reflected in her glass of water this morning, though she'd closed her eyes before she could be sure. And she couldn't remember her dreams, which she hated, since that most often happened with dreams—premonitions—she wouldn't like.

She glanced through her living room window at the clock. Something about her personal energies stopped every watch she tried to wear. Guy should be here by now. She skimmed a hand over her mist-dampened hair and the blue gauze of the oversize empire-waisted dress she wore. Then she realized she was primping, and decided to wait for him at the road.

She heard the car's approach even as she walked the overgrown path, rogue branches and weeds painting dampness on her skirt, bare legs and tennis shoes. She found herself hurrying—toward him, or away from the dismal atmosphere of the bayou this morning? Either way, she made it to the dirt road even as the engine died and a car door shut. Guy Poitiers rounded the front of an uninspired brown sedan, and she got her first good look at him in the overcast daylight.

Oh, but he did look good. Football, construction, carpentry—she could believe it all. His hair, once blond like hers, had darkened to a tousled, tawny brown with bronze highlights. Whatever sun had highlighted his hair had also browned his handsome face, his muscular arms and big hands. Okay, so he also looked grungy. Mud splattered his clingy black T-shirt, coated his faded, tight-fitting jeans and completely obscured the boots he wore. He'd scrubbed his hands and arms, his face and hair—which looked like he'd run his hands, if not a comb, through it. He'd *attempted* to clean up. If she'd disliked mud, she'd have never made her home on the bayou. Even grungy, the man looked real good. When he caught sight of her and raised a hand in greeting, his clear eyes made up for the lack of blue in the sky.

She hoisted her canvas duffel bag onto her shoulder and hurried toward him, and away from the tangled path behind her. "Hi there! Either you haven't changed clothes since last night, or you've been busy this morning."

"I pulled your truck out," he admitted in that wonderfully deep, throaty voice, stuffing his hands in his pockets and shrugging. "Don't know the damage yet, though."

"And here it is nine in the morning? What have you been doing with yourself?" She poked him in the chest before she could catch herself—some folks didn't like touchy people, which she was, but that damp shirt over those pecs just begged for it.

His grin relieved her. "I've got a reputation to protect, *chère,*" he drawled, opening the passenger door. "A man starts working, next thing he knows, folks expect it. Can't have that."

She laughed at his obvious posing as she got in; while she fastened her seat belt, he came around. It had to be Aunt Eva's vehicle. The car's interior was, if possible, even more boring than its exterior, except that Guy had draped a now mud-smeared sheet across the driver's seat. Yet once Guy shut his door against the morning wetness, the sedan felt like its own protective oasis, boring or not. Its engine started, smooth and sure, and Mary relaxed into her seat, feeling safer than she had since waking.

Guy pulled a U-turn and headed toward the main road, toward civilization. "Um, Mary? About last night?"

She let her eyes drift shut, at ease. "What about it?"

"The reason I acted so strange..."

She opened her eyes again to warily search his expression.

"I, uh...saw a *couchemal*," Guy admitted, not taking his eyes from the road through the encroaching woods. Not quite the "I find you really attractive" she'd half expected.

"*You* know..." he started to explain when she said nothing, so she quickly nodded.

"I know what a *couchemal* is." In this part of the country, folks usually called swamp lights *feux follets*, or "crazy fire." But sometimes they used the darker name of *couchemal*, because French superstition considered them the angry ghosts of unbaptized babies who "slept badly." It warned of death. But... "I don't buy into negative omens," she stated, drawing her sneakered feet onto the seat to hug her knees. "Something bad might not—"

"Something bad already happened when I saw it," Guy insisted, and glanced quickly to her and back, squinting a bit in distress. "It called me Gilly."

So much for feeling at ease. The knots in her stomach reminded her just who *had* called Guillaume Poitiers "Gilly." *It couldn't be. Except*, she knew such things *could* be.

Pulling onto the two-lane blacktop, Guy continued to tell his experience. He'd been near the slough. He'd heard giggling.

She didn't want to listen; didn't want to know.

He'd seen a strange light.

She stared out the fogging window at the woods crowding the roadside drainage ditch. If he'd truly seen Lazare's ghost, that meant Lazy hadn't gone to...wherever. Heaven, or Summerland, or his next incarnation. It meant Lazy's spirit was stuck. Which could mean her baby brother Joey might also be soulbound, despite what little comfort she and her family had wrung from the idea of him going to a better place.

Lazy had wanted Guy to follow him. Guy's words pounded at her; she wanted to raise mental shields against them. That, or cover her ears and hum. Lazy had found something—

"Why are you telling me this?"

Guy glanced from the road to her, his eyes widening at her defensive tone. "Old habits die hard, I guess." He looked back at the road, shrugged. "Didn't mean to burden you."

She studied his profile, surprised at how much his disappointment mattered. Because *Guy* mattered—or used to, in the dark recesses of her memory. Somewhere in the past, she'd missed him too much to think about. Now, when he finally did show up, the specter of death hovered over his shoulder.

She made herself relax—well, try. It wasn't his fault that he awoke bad memories. And it wasn't his fault if ghosts found him companionable; he was a companionable kind of guy.

"Death isn't my favorite conversational topic," she admitted, through discomfort that bothered her as much as the subject matter. She believed in natural cycles. Usually.

"Oh." He cast her an apologetic glance. "I forgot about Sneezy Bunny."

She didn't want to discuss her onetime inability to handle a pet's demise any more than dead family members; luckily, he dropped it at that. His considerateness, and the fact that he didn't continue his story from last night, encouraged her to make more of an effort. "I tried to tell your aunt. I have a feeling it's Lazare they found in the swamp."

He sighed. Disbelief? Annoyance? Then she recognized his slumped shoulders as acceptance; the weight of prolonged ignorance ended. He believed her, as surely as if the medical examiner had called.

She almost missed the turn into the Wellness Club, for staring at him, but he compensated for her last-minute warning skillfully. Shells crunched beneath their tires as he pulled up to the double-doored entrance. Then he dropped his hands to his grungy thighs and sagged back in his seat, letting the car idle. The intermittent swipe of the windshield wipers punctuated the drone of the engine. "At least we'll be able to bury him, huh?"

Bury him. Against her will, she thought of something. "If his remains were disturbed, couldn't that explain—?"

"Why I heard him last night?" Only then did he look over at her, his blue eyes haunted, hopeful. "So maybe if we bury him proper, he'll be okay."

A fond warmth melted the rest of her unease; she resisted the urge to cup his face in her palms, to promise him it would be all right. This man wanted to take care of his baby cousin, even after that cousin was...

Well. She gathered her duffel bag onto her lap. "If it really was Lazare," she said cautiously.

He frowned. "I didn't imagine it, Mary Margaret."

"Spirits can lie." Besides, she didn't want it to be Lazare. "It's been known to happen with Ouija boards," she pointed out, when he continued to scowl. "Some spirits can be very convincing."

His raised eyebrows clearly asked how she might know. Maybe she should tell him she was a witch; it wasn't a secret. She wore her pentagram in the open, and a silver goddess ring on her middle finger. But she'd been learning, slowly, the value of discretion. Some things, like religion or sexual preference or state of health, just shouldn't be blurted out. Not to people just passing through.

"I hear things." She unfastened her seat belt, unlatched the door. "Just don't follow it anywhere, okay?"

He widened his eyes in a teasing challenge. "I thought you didn't buy into negative omens."

"I don't." But she had a bad feeling about this, anyway. "Can't hurt to be careful, right?" As she slid out of the car, Guy leaned across the seat and grabbed for her hand. He got her arm instead, and his callused fingers, muddy from his jeans, slid down to her wrist. They should have felt cold, dirty. Instead, they felt warm and strong, and too disturbing for this already disturbing morning.

"You need a ride home tonight?" he asked, half lying across the seat. His handsome face was tipped entreatingly up at her.

She found herself smiling back, despite her unease. *I'd love a ride home. Let's do dinner—no ghost talk allowed.*

"I've got plans," she admitted, surprised at her own reluctance. *Witch plans.* Once her friends heard about her truck, she'd have no shortage of help. "I'll be okay."

He nodded and released her hand; *now* it felt cold and dirty. Seeing the smear he'd left, he threw her an apologetic look from beneath hooded eyelids. "Thanks for listening, anyway."

She wanted to say *anytime,* but she wasn't sure she would mean it. While she shut the door, then opened and reshut it because she hadn't pushed hard enough the first time, he levered himself back into the driver's seat.

And then he drove away, and the coolness of mist on her cheek felt like a lonely, ghostly caress.

Ghosts and church, decided Guy, do not mix.

He ducked through wooden double doors into the solemnity of Ste. Jeanne d'Arc Catholic Church, then stood against the stream of departing parishioners, their foreheads still smudged with ash. He spotted Tante Eva's slump-shouldered form kneeling by the votive candles. She'd probably lit one for Lazare's soul.

Guy shouldn't have asked her, on the way over, if Lazy had ever been baptized. She'd looked stricken, murmured something about Nonk Alphonse not liking the priest—and now she lit candles. Thank God he hadn't let on just what kind of limbo Lazy's soul might be in.

She took out her rosary; he'd be waiting awhile. Guy tried to look inconspicuous between the holy-water font and a statue of the Madonna. He didn't feel inconspicuous. He didn't belong.

The richness of incense, melted wax and furniture polish awoke memories of weekly attendance. The glitter of candlelight, stained glass and the high-beamed ceiling all reflected a time when things had order. Baptism. First communion. Confirmation—he'd decided at thirteen that church wasn't cool for a guy, but he remembered Mary's, even the virginal white dress she'd worn. Family weddings. Joey Deveraux's funeral, and Lazare's memorial, too. Things had a proper cycle, here. You were born, you lived, you died, and your soul went to heaven, hell, or purgatory.

Except maybe for Lazare. At least Guy had left the fold of his own accord. Lazare couldn't have helped not being baptized—or dying. That had been other people's responsibility, not his.

Tante Eva still fingered her rosary by the votive candles, bright stars of light in their blue glass holders. Surely God wouldn't hold something like that against a nine-year-old boy. Even lapsed, Guy couldn't believe that of his God.

Still, he had to get out of here, away from the church's old-world scent and the deceptive comfort of its memories and its order. He fished his keys from his pocket, deciding to pull the car around and wait for Eva outside. He preferred Mary's explanation of the *couchemal:* that disturbing Lazare's remains had reawoken his spirit, and that burial would bring him peace.

Then at least one of them would be at peace.

CHAPTER THREE

"What do y'all think about ghosts?"

Mary's three best friends—her circle—looked startled at her abrupt question. The four of them sat in wrought-iron chairs around a matching table behind Cypress Bernard's house. The freshness of the rainy night, beyond the deck, mingled with the scent of melted wax from a snowy pillar candle on the table, but Mary's mind hadn't been on their ritual, either. Now that they'd finished celebrating the beginnings symbolized by the new moon and settled down for wine and cakes—in this case, juice and cookies—Mary had decided the only way to get past her obsession with Guy and his *couchemal* was to confront it.

She probably should have led into it a bit more smoothly.

Still, her friends adapted quickly. "Don't know any personally," quipped Cy, pouring the juice into thick glass tumblers. Usually the epitome of corporate image, the black-haired, jet-eyed woman had changed into an embroidered tunic that fell to her tawny calves; a large golden ankh around her neck completed her metamorphosis into mixed-tradition magic user.

Fiery-haired Brigit Peabody said, "I hate 'em." Five months into her first pregnancy, she raised a protective hand to the front of her new maternity jeans. Brie came from a long line of Celtic witches, and hoped her daughter would continue the tradition. "This is just idle curiosity, right?"

"It *would* be awfully coincidental," Sylvie Garner agreed, retrieving tissue-wrapped cookies from their bakery bag. The slim brunette was about as new to Wicca as Mary, but Sylvie had a degree in folklore—and she ran the bookstore where they'd all met over a year ago. Brie, Sylvie's sister-in-law and onetime teacher, had engineered the meeting. The women's complementary interests, backgrounds and abilities had done the rest in forming their circle.

After years of feeling like the blond changeling Gram always called her, Mary finally knew people as different as she.

"No such thing as coincidence," Cy teased, accepting a cookie before turning again to Mary. "But considering the craziness we've seen this past year, I'd have laid odds against you having yourself any close encounters."

"I didn't," admitted Mary. *And I'm glad.*

Brie leaned back in her chair. "Thank goodness!"

Cy pursued it a bit further. "You're just asking because—?"

"A friend of mine thinks he did. And since he saw the ghost of a relative, and he's a good Catholic—well, a Catholic, anyway—it's especially upsetting."

Sylvie raised an eyebrow. "As opposed to the average agnostic running into the ghost of a stranger?"

Mary grinned at that. "It's just…I find it upsetting, too. I know that death is part of the natural cycle, and I thought I believed in reincarnation, but this really bothers me! Why would someone's spirit hang around after his death?"

"Guilt," suggested Brie, and downed her glass of fruit juice as if she wished it were two shots of bourbon. "We reap what we sow. What goes around comes around."

"Or revenge," added Cypress dramatically. "Like in that knock-knock story about the girl's ghost going after her evil uncle. Or a lust for gold, like Jean Laffite's ghost lurking in the bayou where he hid his pirate treasure."

"I thought Laffite was a smuggler, not a pirate." Sylvie ducked from the cookie crumb Cy threw at her.

"Thank you, Teach. Even if he hid something, it surely wouldn't be this far north, unless he was a river pirate. We're *brainstorming* here." Cy rolled her hands to simulate their mental interaction. "We're doing a *focus group.* Run with it."

Sylvie ran. "Sometimes ghosts don't know they're dead. Sometimes they've left unfinished business. Or sometimes they do need to right a wrong they committed in life. How's that?"

"But it's so sad!" Mary could see right off that Brie didn't completely agree; Sylvie and Cy withheld facial comment. "This is the ghost of a little boy, and the idea of him all alone in the swamp, for years and years..."

Cy opened her mouth and started to raise a hand. When Mary caught her eye and shook her head, ever so slightly, her friend reconsidered both actions and busied herself with her juice. Of the circle, only Cypress had lived in Stagwater back then. Four years Mary's senior, she probably remembered the details of the boys' drowning more clearly than even Mary did.

"Damn," admitted Brie grudgingly, her other hand finding her lap. "Yes. Okay. It's sad."

"But ghosts may not experience time like we do." Sylvie leaned forward, getting into her topic. "It may be years for your friend, but for the ghost it could still be the day he died—assuming he even knows he's dead. Quantum time."

Mary already knew that theory—maybe everything happened all at once, and the illusion of time just let people view it in acceptable pieces. It helped explain how she could see possible futures, anyway, and how they could cast magic circles—spheres of timeless, placeless energy wherein they could work spells before releasing them into their world. "So maybe this boy's soul is safely where it should be, even if he's floating around the swamp. I can buy that. Maybe even Guy—"

And for the briefest moment she froze, as if saying his name would summon him into their midst. In a way, it did.

"Guy Poitiers?" exclaimed Cypress, breaking a cookie in half in her surprise. "Ralph and TiBoy Poitiers's brother?"

"TiBoy?" repeated Sylvie, who was a Yankee.

"Means 'Junior,' sort of," clarified Cy with a wave of her hand. "*Petit* Boy. You're saying the Poitiers are back in town?"

Well, wasn't she Ms. Enthusiasm? "Just Guy, and his aunt Eva," Mary admitted, and immediately regretted her guarded tone—it wasn't like *she* had any special claim on them.

"The body those Picayune boys found in the swamp." Cypress nodded at her own deductive skill. "The Poitiers must think it's that little cousin of theirs who..." Then she noticed something in Mary's expression, and shut up.

"Who..." prompted Brie; neither she nor Sylvie knew about Joey. Mary hadn't planned on it coming up, either. The announcement would only stir unpleasant memories and invite uncomfortable sympathies, eleven years too late.

Lest Cy tell more than necessary, Mary answered, "He drowned." She felt Cy's hand capture hers beneath the partial cover of the table for a comforting squeeze; Mary squeezed back before getting up and escaping to the shadowy edge of the deck. The lawn smelled of wet mint. Water streamed from the eaves, inches past her nose, and beyond that the rain continued to fall in a steady hush. Her friends were doing their best to put the idea of ghosts into perspective; why didn't she feel comforted?

"One fine-looking set of brothers," Cypress added, neatly steering the subject away from the drowning.

"Oh, really?" Brie said with a laugh, a moment before Mary, turning to stare, could ask the same thing.

Instead, Mary said, "I didn't know you knew them that well."

"Ralph Poitiers and I...um...dated. Briefly." Cy didn't try to hide her wicked grin. "He was a wild one—caused quite the scandal at Stagwater High. Oh, my! I haven't thought of the Poitiers in a long time."

That made two of them ... didn't it?

"Speaking of fine-looking boys," Cy continued brightly, with less subtlety this time, "how are your menfolk doing?"

Sylvie laughed as she answered—Mary didn't quite hear what she said about her new husband, Rand. Instead, she took advantage of the momentary privacy Cy had bought her. Leaning against a wooden post, she reached out to catch a handful of water. She shouldn't try to censor Cy's reflections, she knew. But her own emotions, particularly about the boys' deaths—and about Guy Poitiers—seemed awfully unstable. On the one hand, she felt immediate and instinctive affection for the man, despite not having seen him in years.

On the other hand, she didn't completely trust him . . . or at least she didn't trust her feelings where he was concerned.

She glanced at the small puddle of water she cupped in her palm. Suddenly, without trying, she was watching him in its reflection, almost as if she'd been drawn. She immediately recognized the tall, broad-shouldered figure descending steps in dark rain. She recognized the stairway, too—it ran from the upstairs of the Poitiers house to the backyard.

Behind her, Brie said something about her husband, Steve, and their plans for the baby. Mary, moving slowly, added her first hand to the second and caught more water from the roof. Guy rippled, then reappeared on the lawn, his sweatshirt plastered to his chest, his hair dripping down his cheeks. Handsome, even via premonition. He pressed his lips together, looking for something low. He said something she couldn't hear.

Then his head snapped up.

Mary caught her own breath and watched him lope to where tamed lawn met encroaching woods. She leaned closer, as if that would help. She could see only him, the lawn, and the house behind him. If only she could see through his eyes! She could almost feel his racing pulse; when he raised a hand to wipe dripping hair from his eyes, only to have the wet curls slide right back, she nearly reached out her own hand to repeat the motion for him. He squinted . . . but at what?

Then she saw how, even in the darkness, his eyes shone. Normally a clear blue, they now glowed aqua. In fact, an unnatural light bathed the front of him.

The *couchemal!*

Her blood chilled; her stomach twisted. She had a bad feeling about this. She had to know more, sense more. If she could see it, just once . . .

Maybe she could.

Fighting to regulate her breathing and maintain her trance, she carefully shifted her point of reference from Guy toward whatever he was watching. The water blurred again, as if fogging over. She immediately missed the comfort of his image.

She also immediately realized what a stupid idea this was—and to see nothing? Or was a glow filling her palms, thickening the blue-green water? Her hands felt suddenly dirty; the sensation seeped up her wrists—

When a hand touched her shoulder Mary spun, bumped against the support post, tried to dodge the water that flew from her opened hands as if it were acid that might yet destroy her . . . and found herself staring blankly into Cypress's concerned face.

"I called your name, girl," Cy explained gently, and rolled her eyes toward the others. They had also stood at some point, and now hovered near her. "What were you doing?"

Mary looked at her hands, then back to her friends, feeling a shudder building within her, knowing she couldn't keep it back. "I . . . I need . . ." She took a deep breath, tried to ground herself. It didn't keep her voice from wavering. "Please, I need a ride to my folks' neighborhood!" *To Guy Poitiers.*

She didn't know what she'd seen, but it definitely felt dead. It felt wrong. And it felt . . .

It felt as if it knew she was looking at it.
It felt as if it had looked back.

Guy had worked on the truck as much as he could while rain turned the yard into a marsh. Now, with nightfall, the rain wasn't letting up any. And Lazy was out in it somewhere. Maybe.

Dry and warm in his old bedroom, Guy stared out the water-veined window. He wondered if ghosts got wet, caught colds. Then it occurred to him that the stray dog he'd given in and fed could. Sh— Shoot.

The old house wasn't all that old; Guy's parents had built it when they married, just over thirty years ago. Still, they'd given it a few traditional touches. East-west hallways cut through the middle, to make breezeways of sorts. The older Poitiers couldn't have meant the upstairs to become a *garçonnière*—they couldn't have known they'd have only boys—but the separate entrance and outdoor stairway served much the same purpose as in the old Cajun homes in the French parishes. Their sons could come and go without disturbing the rest of the family.

Stepping back from the window, Guy decided against his denim jacket. It wouldn't shed water worth jack, anyway, not in this. He flipped on the outdoor light, took a deep breath and stepped out into the downpour. Wet grass below him sparkled, off-color, in the pool of lamplight; he could see the rain cutting through the air where the light hit it. Outside that pool, though, darkness reigned. He could barely differentiate between the treetops and the sky.

He tried to descend the wet-darkened wooden steps quietly, and waited till he'd crossed the yard to whistle. By then, his hair already lay flat on his head, and rivulets of water ran down his face. He heard nothing but the patter of rainfall, loud against plentiful leaves. So he whistled again. Then he tried calling in a hoarse whisper, "Hey, pooch!"

Like the dog would hear that. Then again, dogs could hear—

The giggle.

Guy tensed, then loped toward the woods. Another distorted giggle bubbled out at him, and he slowed to a walk. Hair dripped into his eyes as he searched the tangled, rain-blurred scrub that edged the yard. When he tried to push the lock away, it only slid back again, so he made do with squinting.

"Gilly?" Lazy's voice drifted toward him, clear as it had been the day he died. But did it sound sadder? Weaker? Did it sound cold? "I found it, Gilly."

"Wha—" Guy's normally low voice cracked; he cleared his throat and took several steps in the direction of the voice. "What did you find, Lazy?"

"Follow me!" Another giggle bounced out of the blackness ahead of him, neither weak nor sad. Guy had reached the very edge of the yard, the start of the woods. Black-berry brambles coiled at his booted toes and tangled in the brush beside him. If he tried wading blind into that, he'd be facedown in the briars in seconds—and probably disturb a snake or two doing it.

"I need a light." The sudden cold that he sensed, colder than the rain, colder than winter, drew his attention up from his feet to a blue-green glow that hovered maybe ten yards into the pine woods. "I meant a Bud Light," he muttered, his voice shaky despite the halfhearted attempt at levity. The giggle, and even Lazy's pleas, had raised the hair on the back of his neck, had churned in his stomach. But the *couchemal* scared him spitless.

Just don't follow it anywhere. He didn't need Mary to tell him that. Wasn't that the whole point of *couchemals?* They flicker, victim follows, they flicker some more, victim falls into a nest of water moccasins, or runs into a pack of feral pigs, or . . . drowns. Then the *couchemal*—

"Follow me!" Lazy laughed again, from nowhere—a nowhere past the curtain of off-lit rain.

Mary had said their old shortcut past the slough was navigable. Assuming he wanted to navigate it. He most definitely did *not* want to navigate it. Only an idiot—

"I found it, Gilly! Wait till...you...see..."

"Tell me what it is you found," Guy demanded, torn.

"I'll show ya!"

"Damn it, Lazy, you little—" Oh, Lord, he was standing in the rain, bickering with a ghost! "I'm not following you."

He half expected to get called a fraidy cat. He didn't have to; he already felt like one. This was Lazare! Somehow, impossible or not, this *was* Lazy—still little, still annoying...still wanting his attention.

Attention Guy wished to God he'd paid eleven years ago.

And here he stood, a full-grown man, hesitating to enter the big bad woods. What did he have to lose?

Unbidden, he remembered Mary Margaret this morning, huddled in the passenger seat of Eva's car, clutching her duffel bag like a teddy bear. *Don't follow it.* Yeah, he knew. But she'd thought he cared about stuff like personal safety, or the future.

He had nothing to lose. He'd kept it that way.

The light pulsed, morbid, across a narrow break that marked the path. "C'mon, Gilly!" Then the voice, the horribly familiar little-boy voice, said something truly frightening. "Pleeeease!"

And Guy waded into the wet darkness and the crowded trees, taking small steps to keep from tripping on the snarled creepers that caught at his feet. "Okay, Lazare," he called, low. "It's okay. I'm coming."

Idiot.

Idiot!

Mary barely waited for Cypress's car to make a complete stop on the shoulderless Old Slough Road before she pushed the door open, slid out and jumped the ditch. She heard her friends call after her, but couldn't wait for them...the scent, or in this case the *sense*, was still warm. It might not stay that way for long.

Through the veil of rain, she could see lights in the Poitiers house as she ran past it. Eva would be no help. Too important that Mary follow the impression of Guy. Too important that she find him before...she didn't know what, but she dreaded it.

She hit the path running, wet, leafy vines grasping at her ankles. Brambles bit at her legs and tore at her gauzy skirt. Roots tripped her. Branches from trash saplings—whole bushy boughs—smacked at her chest and her face, despite her outstretched hands. She skidded in mud; at one point she slid into a pine and scraped her hands on bark, clutching the branchless trunk to keep her feet.

And she couldn't see a thing. But in the same way she could find lost rings or guess where someone was, she knew where to go. This was how Guy had gone after the *couchemal*.

The idiot!

She hadn't taken this path for years. Before she was ready, the ground sloped gently from beneath her. She fell on her butt in the mud, and so slid, rather than dived, into several inches of dank-smelling water; even as she splashed to her feet, she recognized, remembered, where she was. Low ground made a natural slough, sometimes little more than a filigree of near-standing water threaded around hillocks and tree trunks. Tonight the water reached from one end of the slough to the other, ankle-deep, knee-deep, almost thigh-deep at one point as she splashed across, her feet sinking into soft bottom mud. She tried not to think about fish eggs and snakes before scrambling quickly up the other side, a rise almost too gradual to be called a bank. She paused to get her bearings, searched for the psychic trail that had drawn her this far—

And knew only that he'd left the path to head for the swamp.

"Guy?" She took a tentative step in that direction, bubbles gurgling around her toes inside her sneakers, but something felt wrong. More wrong than charging into the Louisiana woods at night—in the rain, yet! It felt . . .

Anomalous. Unnatural. Dead.

Undead.

The rain had been washing the *couchemal*'s own trail clean. Now that she was closing in, the stench of undeath muddied her sense of Guy's path. She blinked rain from her eyes—for all the good it did—and stepped slowly, carefully, across a stretch of ground where heavy pine straw inhibited the worst of the undergrowth. She stubbed a muddy toe on a root, then against a clay crawfish mound. Then she walked facefirst into a wet thicket of what smelled like honeysuckle.

She reared back just as quickly. The impenetrable snarl of vines and leaves grew higher than her. "Guy?"

Suddenly the distinct stench of undeath overwhelmed even the perfume of rotting vegetation, the sweetness of a few early honeysuckle blooms. Threat filled the disorienting darkness.

She took a step backward, then another. It sensed her here. It knew she'd been spying. It had her alone, alone except for—

"Guy!"

"What?" His husky voice, so close, drew a startled shriek; then she spun to face where she could sense him standing. She could hear from his panting—over her own panting—that he'd fought an equally losing battle against Mother Nature. She could even feel the heat off him. But she couldn't see a thing.

Rain drummed leaves and mud and slough water, slower than before. It slicked her hair to her scalp, ran off her nose, dripped off her hands and joined the sodden mess of her skirt.

"Mary?" Guy demanded, his voice aimed slightly over her shoulder. He obviously couldn't see, either. "What the heck are you doing out here? Are you crazy?"

She judged exactly where he was from the sound of his voice—and whacked him across his washboard stomach.

"Stop it!" Guy fumbled at Mary in the darkness and blindly managed to catch her arms before she could hit him twice more. He adjusted his hold, wrapping his fingers around her small wrists. It kept her from smacking him again... and it gave him physical, tactile proof that he was no longer alone with a specter. Mary was real, warm flesh and steadily pulsing blood, a faint, beachlike scent of perfume, and a voice.

"Idiot!" That voice, especially in her annoyance, sounded equally real. "I told you not to follow the *couche-mal!*"

"I didn't follow the *cou*—" He held on when she tried to pull loose. He didn't want to be alone again so quickly. "Not directly, anyhow. I followed Lazy. What are *you* doing here?"

"Saving you, you stupid—"

"Don't call me stupid." But he couldn't muster his usual anger at such an accusation, for savoring her voice. Almost as much as the warmth of her rain-slick skin beneath his fingers, her voice made a comforting contrast to Lazy's surreal giggle and haunting pleas. Mary's voice had called him back. Now, holding her very real wrists, he wondered if she'd just saved him... or merely aided his own irresponsibility.

Sooner or later, he *would* have to finish this.

He heard, sensed, her shudder. "You cold?"

"Scared," she admitted, even as he released one of those small wrists to loop his arm over her shoulders. He drew her to his side, rubbing her wet sleeve to help her circulation.

"It's gone now," he assured her. "It went on without me."

Her hand covered his, on her arm. He stilled and waited a breath. And another. It really *was* dark out. The night warmed and thickened as the rain slowed.

Mary shook her head—the wet ends of her hair brushed his chest and arm. "Gone *now*. What if it doesn't stay gone? Doesn't the idea that it's even out there bother you?"

Maybe she couldn't see him, but he squinted at her anyway, taken aback. "That's why I was *following* it!"

"Oh, never mind. Come on." She stepped away from him. The hand that had gently covered his own now gripped it to lead him back. He didn't question her directional ability; she'd gotten this far, right? And she'd always been terrific at blindman's buff, when they were kids. Soggy pine straw and leaves scrunched beneath his boots, between patches of mud. Rain trickled down his neck; he'd long since reached the saturation point.

Something hard slammed into his face.

"Ow!" When he raised his hands to protect himself, he scraped his knuckles on the same pine tree he'd walked into. Damn, damn...dang. That *hurt!*

He still didn't doubt Mary could find her way back...but he now knew she couldn't lead worth jack.

"What?" She'd asked as soon as his hand dropped hers.

Unwilling to answer at first, he leaned against the attack tree and tested his nose with wet fingers. Not broken, but he'd probably scraped it pretty bad, and bruised his forehead, too.

"Guy!" Her hands found his fleece-covered elbows and felt their way up his arms to his wrists. "What happened?"

"I hit a tree." He scowled at what could have been a giggle.

"And it hit back, eh? Let me see."

"Good luck," he muttered, letting her searching hands pull his away to gently probe the throbbing scrape. Déjà vu...hadn't she done something like this last night? "Ow!"

"I bet the tree looks worse," she said teasingly, and he had almost thought of a comeback when something really odd happened. Odd . . . and poignantly familiar.

The pain started to fade into her fingers.

One minute he was clenching his teeth against the throbbing, sure that the ache would only increase as his surprise wore off. Then, beneath her ministrations, the jolts of each hurtful throb calmed to small waves, then to a faint pulse of sensation. The sting that had indicated a scrape grew intensely hot, then cooled, as Mary's fingers drew across it.

The rest of him got warm and stayed that way.

Magic Mary. He knew she used to do this, with childhood cuts and bruises, sprains and bites. But after years away he'd suspected his *belief* in her had actually healed those.

Did he still believe in her so very much as that?

As the pain faded, he grew aware of her touch elsewhere. She'd leaned into him to reach his face. Her damp front molded against his, from the softness of her breasts all the way down, past her firm tummy and her firmer thighs, to her knees. He pictured the filmy dress she'd worn this morning.

He pictured it soaking wet.

She lowered her spread hands from his face, bracing them against his chest, still leaning on him. It sapped her strength, this healing thing she did; he remembered that, too. He raised his hands to her back, holding her to him, pretending it was so that she wouldn't fall. The warmth of her undermined the coolness of her wet dress; he found himself spreading his hands wide so that his pinkies rested in the dip of her spine, and his thumbs slipped beneath her arms, toward the softness of her breasts. He didn't want to lose the feel of her against him like this.

The rain had stopped, taking most of the chill with it, leaving the air dense and heavy with expectation. Somewhere nearby, an *ouaouaron*—a bullfrog—croaked its name. He wanted to kiss her. Oh, God, he wanted to kiss her. He'd wanted to, ever since that first almost-kiss the day Lazy and Joey died. He'd felt guilty about wanting it, too— felt it was selfish, compared to the tragedies of that day. But he couldn't help himself, any more than he could help responding to the soft, soothing reality of her. He wanted. . .

He slipped one hand upward, into her short, damp hair, and found her head already tipped toward him. Cradling her, he leaned closer, blindly seeking her mouth with his own.

He connected on the first pass; they didn't even bump noses.

Her lips tasted of water from the spring rain, fresh and pure. He drank her in, the familiarity and the newness of her. She caught him behind the neck with one hand, tasting him back, curious and passionate. He drew his hand, the one under her arm, forward to capture her breast in his palm. As he gasped surprise—she wasn't thirteen anymore!—she breathed a sigh against him. Right, so very right. He felt like he'd come home . . . and it had nothing to do with Stagwater.

Mary . . .

She shrieked into his mouth and pushed away from him.

CHAPTER FOUR

"What? *What?*" He'd never had quite this effect on a woman. Had he moved too fast, insulted her—or had something *else* scared her? He tried to find her again, blindly catching her shoulder. "Are you all right?"

"It's...okay." Her voice shook. "It's gone now."

"*What* is?"

"Something..." She paused, caught her breath in an almost-giggle. "I think something licked my ankle."

He crouched to feel the ground around her feet; his hand touched wet leaves. "Don't look at me, *chère*," he murmured. She couldn't look at him in the darkness. As he straightened, he slid his arm back around her. "*My* tongue was busy."

She smacked him again; if she'd had the slightest chance of hurting him, he might have found that annoying. "I'm not kidding!"

"It was just a vine," he said, then paused. "Listen!"

Even as he heard Mary's name called more clearly, he saw the bobbing light. For a moment his stomach clenched. *Not Lazare, not again!* Then he recognized the light as a hand-held flashlight.

"Here!" returned Mary, her call uneven—from the kiss, or her scare? His palms still tingled for want of touching her. His blood pounded through him; his legs felt weak. All from that kiss. He hoped her shaky voice meant she felt the same way.

Then the flashlight beam caught him in the eyes, like a police spotlight. "There you are!" announced an unfamiliar, female voice, while he blocked the light with his arm.

A second person said, "You had us worried, girl!"

"We're safe." While Mary also squinted away from the light, Guy saw her for the first time since she'd called him back from the *couchemal*. She looked drenched, muddy, raggedy, and so attractive that he had to make fists to keep from grabbing her to him again. "Shine that thing on the ground, and we'll get out of here faster," she advised with a laugh, and her friends complied.

Mary caught Guy's hand in her own again. It didn't feel the way her touch had moments before; it was neither passionate nor curious. It felt like Mary Margaret and Guy at four and six, eight and ten, eleven and thirteen.

Twenty-four and twenty-six had its benefits.

This time he led the way, weaving around trees and fording the mucky slough, and he tried not to resent her friends for being here when he wanted to kiss her again. After all, they hadn't interrupted. That had been . . .

A low whimper caught his attention. He glanced down, and saw the glow of animal eyes in the brush. The stray dog that he'd fed. It must've followed him—and maybe licked Mary's ankle? He grinned as it vanished into the weeds. Good taste.

"Guy, this is my friend Sylvie Garner," said Mary as they came abreast of the woman with the flashlight. "Did y'all leave Brie in the car?"

The tall brunette named Sylvie nodded. "She took cellular-phone duty, in case we got lost, too."

"You might remember Cypress Bernard," continued Mary, turning back to Guy. He studied the dark woman she indicated; the name sounded familiar, but . . .

"I knew your brother Ralph," Cypress prompted. Yeah; he sort of remembered that. "What's he been doing, anyway?"

Mary's hand slipped away from his, and he instinctively recognized the official end of their brief intimacy. So maybe he sounded a bit peeved when he answered, "He's a priest."

But that didn't explain why Cypress's jaw dropped.

* * *

He'd kissed her. She'd kissed him. They'd kissed each other. That was *not* what she'd meant to happen when she chased after him. There were easier ways to get kissed.

But maybe not kissed like that.

Following the others, trying to keep up light conversation, Mary relived the kiss, once, three times, five times. He'd seemed to know just how to move his lips over hers, neither demanding nor hesitant; seemed to know just what she wanted, and on deeper levels than she herself knew. She'd felt off-balance, adrift in the overwhelming sensation of him, yet he had been her anchor.

Proceeding single file down the overgrown path, she caught herself watching the faded pockets of her anchor's jeans. *Warning: rampant-hormone alert. Anchor? Guy?*

The man who had majored in partying?

By the time they reached the road, her reason had rapidly closed her emotions' lead. Of course she enjoyed kissing him; she felt comfortable with him, attracted to him. But did she want to get involved with a man who chased *couchemals* into the swamp?

Even as her sinking stomach indicated a major score on the side of reason, Guy, who'd waited up for her, caught her elbow and detoured her away from the others. His rangy height sheltered her from the dripping trees as he bent nearer for privacy.

"Mary Margaret, I..." What very blue eyes he had, especially with his eyebrows raised and eyes wide with sincerity. "I'm sorry if I upset you tonight." His low voice scored *beaucoup* points on the side of emotion. Tonight had definitely been worth the upset.

"Just don't go after it again?" She laid her hand over his. He blinked. "Huh?"

"The *couchemal.*"

"I wasn't talking about—" He stopped himself, frowned. "I may have to go after it, *chère.* It's Lazare."

He hadn't been talking about the *couchemal?* Then he must have meant the kissing! "Why would that upset me?"

"You just said for me not to—"

"No...I mean why would what we did..." The rest of his argument caught up with her. "You don't know that."

He looked fully confused. "That—?"

"That it's Lazare. It's stupid to risk your life on the word of an apparition." Bad choice of words; he straightened up.

"It's my life to risk."

And she couldn't think of an answer to that. "I've kept my friends out too late already," she offered weakly.

He let her change the subject, shoved his hands in his pockets. "You need any more rides? Tomorrow maybe?"

"I'm fine, thanks. I'll see you later, though?"

"Sure." He shrugged. "I've got your truck."

"Well...goodbye, then." She went back to the car, jumped the ditch and opened the passenger door.

"Yeah," he said, before she could shut him out. Maybe she shouldn't have kissed him tonight. She'd let him awaken a hunger in her, let him promise, albeit not verbally, to fulfill that hunger. But someone that suicidal had no place making promises.

And she had no place believing them.

Living in a mobile home during a downpour was like living inside a drum. But the pounding on the door wasn't rain.

It waited.

Earl Singleton let an empty beer bottle fall from his fingers to join the pile on the ratty tan carpet and tried not to hear the door. Thunder, he told himself. Nobody would be at his door this time of night, in this weather, right?

Thud. Thud. Thud. The trailer shook under sludgy blows.

It waited. Need.

Earl opened his minifridge and, seeing he'd finished the beers, fumbled for a wine cooler. He was acting like a baby. If Bobby Lee or Clem could see him now, they'd laugh their butts off.

Except Clem had disappeared the other night.

It waited. Hunger. Thud. Thud. Thud.

The wine cooler had a twisty top—thank God for small favors. Earl wasn't sure he could handle a bottle opener, what with how his hands shook. He'd never been this bone-deep scared in his life. He wished South Central Bell hadn't disconnected his phone over those 976 calls. He'd sure like to talk to Bobby Lee right now. Nothing scared Bobby Lee.

Earl didn't even know what was out there, and it scared the living daylights out of him.

Rain rattled on the aluminum roof. Lightning lit the trailer—the electricity had gone out in the storm—and a moment later thunder crashed against it.

Thud. Thud. Thud. Thud. Whatever waited in the dark storm outside was losing its patience.

Earl drained the wine cooler and dropped the bottle; it clinked against the others. He should still have some Jack Daniel's, too, somewhere. It'd give him a hell of a hang-over tomorrow, but he wasn't even sure he'd *see* tomorrow.

After what seemed like an eternity, the drumming on his roof started to slow. He got his last wine cooler, fumbled off the twisty top, sucked it down. He wasn't falling for this. Something waited out there.

It felt them *approach. No!*

A new noise caught Earl's heightened awareness, a moan like voices, like wind before a hurricane. But this wasn't hurricane season. He listened as the moan howled past him, louder and then fainter, like a passing truck or freight train. He shuddered, 'cause he didn't live near a highway or rail-road track.

He drained the second cooler, then searched out the Jack Daniel's.

Only the next morning did Earl dare open his trailer door. Sunlight pierced his bleared eyes and pounded through his head. Humidity wrapped itself around him. And sludgy, thick mud coated the wooden steps he'd built. It streaked

down the textured front of the door, too, despite the overnight rain.

Earl felt sick, worse sick than the hangover, worse sick
than when he and his buddies had found those old bones in
the swamp.

He reached into his jeans pocket and curved his fingers
around his lucky gold doubloon for comfort.

Mary reached the concrete side of the pool, turned, and
launched herself through the water in the other direction.
The Wellness Club, where she worked, gave her access to
weights, step machines, stationary bikes—but she most
loved the indoor pool. Swimming laps relaxed her, like
meditation. Usually.

She hadn't seen Guy since Wednesday night.

She reached the other end, pushed off and started back.
Grampa Deveraux had bought an aboveground pool for the
family the year after Joey...well, ten years ago. He hadn't
wanted anyone to fancy themselves afraid of the water. He
needn't have worried—the luxury of a real swimming pool,
even one with fiberglass sides and a blue plastic bottom, had
won them over. Mary had gone on to get Red Cross certifi-
cation, and had worked as a lifeguard at summer camp. She
always went on—

The boots on a level with her eyes, when she reached the
other end of the pool, looked familiar. So did the ankles of
the jeans that covered them. Letting her feet drift to the tiled
bottom, still clutching the edge of the pool, Mary looked up
past those jeans to a broad chest, to a strong jaw and blue
eyes—to Guy.

Her memory of their recent kiss hadn't faded at all.

He stared back for a long moment, wavery light off the
water playing across his face. "They said you were in here."
He swallowed, then flashed a teasing grin. "Nice job you've
got."

Instead of explaining that she had no more appointments scheduled today, she laughed. "You should see what they pay me to lounge in the hot tub."

"I can see *why* they—" He cut himself off too late, as if he'd gone into flirt mode automatically and only now remembered who she was to him. Whoever that was.

He probably did have an awfully good view of her cleavage, even when he crouched to close the distance between them. And her line of sight to his face included how well his jeans fit. She drifted back from the edge several feet, to change the angle, but she still felt exposed, even in a one-piece; she couldn't remember ever feeling more aware of her body. And she liked it. "So, what brings you here?"

He rested his forearms on his knees. "A couple of things," he admitted, serious. "I never did thank you for coming to my rescue last week. Whether I needed rescuing or not."

The corner of his mouth turned up at the qualifier, but she decided against splashing him, or pulling him in. Childish ideas, in light of their less-than-childish attraction. "And?"

"And to give you this." His extended hand dangled a key.

"It's fixed?" Her relief echoed off the walls around them, along with the splash of water she made reaching up, between his knees, for the key.

He didn't let it go, and his warm, dry hand brushed hers. "Where are you going to put it, Mary Margaret? You haven't got any pockets, have you?" He leaned closer, as if to check, and his gaze grew sleepy—no, fascinated.

She fell back into, then under, the water, before he could lose his balance. Or kiss her—not that he'd meant to. When she resurfaced, he'd settled himself on the floor, back from where water had splashed the concrete—and a safer distance from her.

"I'm sorry it took so long," he admitted. "Until the weather cleared up, I thought it would never dry out. I pulled off the tires and cleaned the dirt and mud out of the wheel bearings and brake linings. The wiring looks good. I checked the steering knuckles and kingpins, and your tie-rods and frame are okay. So . . . she's gassed up and waiting for you outside."

That sounded like a lot of work. "Did it cost anything?"

"Don't worry about it." He stood and, making sure she saw, laid the key on her towel. "It's the least I could do." He meant to leave? But he'd just gotten here!

She dived for the edge of the pool again. "Have you heard anything from the medical examiner?"

He cocked his head at her, probably surprised at her interest in so morbid a topic. "Not yet. There wasn't all that much left to—" Blessedly, he cut off that train of thought. "Anytime now." When she nodded instead of cringing, he added, "I saw the *couchemal* again. Twice."

And he was standing here to tell her about it? He'd taken her advice after all! "You didn't follow it?"

"Yeah, I did." He didn't seem to notice her disappointment. "It went too far into the swamp. I lost it both times. I'd have needed to get a boat to keep going."

Her sense of foreboding returned, in spades. "Are you?"

He shrugged. "Haven't decided. It seems like a lot of planning and effort for something as crazy as a ghost. Look, you don't want to hear this. I'll let you get back to your laps."

"Let me make you dinner." She made the offer before thinking it over—was she asking him on a date? He'd made it clear he wouldn't be around long. Maybe someone like her friend Cy could use that to emotionally divorce herself from him, and just enjoy the company and conversation—and scenery. Mary knew herself better. She got emotionally involved in minute-long greeting-card commercials. She had no armor against this.

But she had to do something to keep him from going.

He looked as surprised as she felt. "Dinner?"

Which gave her a chance to laugh. "Yeah, to eat. Tonight. You need a ride home, anyway. And I owe you for the truck."

He shook his head. "I owe you for trashing it."

"Then you have to accept." Ha! She had him there. She levered herself out of the pool, braced herself with a knee—then felt big, warm hands circle her, lift her from the water and set her onto her feet. Guy radiated dry warmth, and the smell of fresh earth and air from outside. The scent soothed her chlorine-stripped sinuses. The warmth drew her chill body as his callused palms slid to her hips. She wondered what the contrast between her soaking swimsuit and his dry, warm T-shirt and jeans would feel like—but he stepped back before she could find out.

"Then I accept," he said with a good-natured shrug.

"I'm—I'll get dressed." She felt his gaze follow her to the dressing room, as warm and sensual as his hands. If this was a date, it was probably a mistake.

She couldn't wait.

This was not, Guy reminded himself for the umpteenth time that evening, a date.

He'd reminded himself while he watched her in her kitchen—her galley. She'd fixed red beans and rice for dinner, with no meat, and not just because this was Lent. She didn't eat animals, period. That reminded him of her at eight, sobbing her heart out because Sneezy, the runt of a litter of motherless rabbits they'd rescued, died. Remembering her as an eight-year-old definitely helped this not be a date.

He'd reminded himself again over dinner, when she finally told him what she did, which was give full-body massages. It shouldn't bother him, and not just because, as she'd pointed out, "Bodywork is a healing art, not a sexual technique." They had no business judging one another's lives.

It wasn't as if they were dating.

But he had the hardest time remembering it wasn't a date after she'd cleared the dishes and poured them both another glass of wine. She'd looked so attractive in a fluffy pirate shirt and jeans, her short, tousled hair drying naturally, that he suggested ghost stories as a distraction before he remembered that she didn't like death. She used to love ghost stories.

To his surprise, she still did—fictional ones.

"So then it floods," he said, gesturing out the living room window at the misty bayou that flowed slowly past. Mary, on the floor by the coffee table, leaned forward as he continued the story. "And since the uncle had been too cheap to give his niece a proper tomb, and the graveyard was on low ground, the coffin washed up. It floated to his house, where water had risen past the porch, and it bumped against the door. Thump." He softly kicked her scratched, stained coffee table for effect. "Thump."

Mary shuddered, but smiled as she did. Nothing to get someone's mind off real ghosts like pretend ones.

At least, he *hoped* his papère's legends were pretend.

"After the flood, neighbors found the open coffin on the porch. The niece's corpse, smiling—and her uncle, dead of fear."

After the appropriately eerie pause, Mary asked, "Would you do me a really odd favor?"

"Depends on the favor."

"Would you hold my feet?"

He glanced down. Her bare feet looked cute and clean—and vulnerable, one trying to hide beneath the other. "Okay."

She crawled over to sit on the other end of the sofa and swung her legs up, so that he could pull her feet onto his lap. He liked the feel of her cold feet in his hands. From the way she arched her back and closed her eyes when he started rubbing them, it seemed she liked it, too. "Mmm..." She sighed.

This wasn't a date, right? They *were* just old friends.

She opened her eyes. "Okay, my turn. We haven't done the pirate Jean Laffite's curse yet."

"You mean how he haunts the bayous, luring folk to his hidden treasure?" They'd had this problem all evening; coming from such similar backgrounds, they knew the same legends.

"Because his curse is to forever protect in death the money that he gathered in life," she agreed. "And if he can get someone else to take it, he'll be... mmm... free."

He'd warmed her feet; now he began to pay attention to each individual toe. *This little piggy went to market.* "Except you'd think that, as long as it's been, he'd be free by now, and whatever fool he'd lured over would do the haunting." He stole a glance at her rapturous expression; with her eyes closed again, she couldn't see him absorbing how pretty she was. "The legend of farmer Joe Smith's curse doesn't sound so good, though, eh?"

"Did you know Jean Laffite wasn't really a pirate?" Mary asked, kind of breathily, moving her feet in his lap.

He stopped rubbing them and swallowed, hard. A few inches higher, and this foot-holding thing would get real erotic. *Not* something that happened with most of his friends.

She opened her golden eyes and blinked sleepily at him; her now dry hair fell over her face, and he wondered suddenly what she looked like after sex. He tried not to wonder about that. But her flowing shirt and loose jeans couldn't disguise her curves. Even if they could, he remembered what she'd looked like in that bathing suit well enough to fill in any blanks. He fought the temptation to draw her feet those extra few inches himself. He'd done that with a woman's *hands* before... but this was getting weird.

Wasn't it? He tried to remember why they shouldn't date.

"How about I tell you the one about the werewolf?" she suggested, obviously unaware of his inner battle. "Or about the possessed husband?" She drew in her feet to prop against the side of his thigh, but he'd already passed sensory overload.

He moved his gaze to her wall, which held numerous photographs of her family. He remembered her parents, and her big brother, and her as a seven-year-old. Oh, yeah; that was why. "You got a deck of cards?" he asked, almost desperate.

"Sure do." To his relief—and disappointment—she swung her feet to the floor and padded off in search of them.

Since she didn't have a dining room, much less a dining room table, they played on the coffee table—and cheated shamelessly. He couldn't remember being this easy with someone, or having this much fun, in a long time.

"I'll raise you two." He put down two aluminum "doubloons" from past Mardi Gras parades. He had a full house.

"Look at this," Mary said, laying down her hand.

Guy squinted at the cards. Four spades—and a heart. He grinned at her. "Wanna play strip poker?"

He'd meant it as a joke, but his imagination latched on to the idea with vehemence. *Mary, taking off her earrings and her otherworldy necklace. Mary, slipping off her rings. Mary, wriggling from her jeans to play just in her panties and that fluffy shirt, and then putting down a trash hand...*

She stretched her denim-clad leg out beneath the coffee table to nudge his, breaking his trance. He glanced quickly toward her family portrait for strength. He wasn't the sort of person who did well with relationships; Mary Margaret deserved better than his transient interest.

"I think these cards are a warning of some kind," she said.

He scooped the doubloons, and the wooden penny she'd anted with, over to his side of the coffee table. "It's a warning not to play strip poker, *chère.*"

But Mary gathered the deck and began to shuffle, glancing at him as if to judge his reaction. "Playing card suits developed from tarot. Cups became hearts, wands became clubs, pentacles became diamonds, and swords became spades. Understand?''

Magic Mary knew tarot? It didn't surprise him, and she obviously wanted to show him her stuff—so to speak. He nodded.

She laid the cards out, facedown, one across another, in the middle and one at each quarter. ''This is a Celtic-cross spread.'' Her hands hovered for a moment over the bicycle patterns, her eyes closed, and he suddenly remembered what Tante Eva had said about Mary practicing black arts. Ridiculous. She'd always been able to do stuff like this, right? She'd just never used props.

Still, concern encroached on his interest as she flipped the first card in the middle to show the King of Hearts plunging a dagger into his head—the suicide king. Then she turned the card that lay across it, revealing the Jack of Spades.

''These are the situation card and the cross card,'' she explained. ''I'm almost positive they're indicating you.''

Concern made sudden headway. ''The suicide king?''

''In tarot he wouldn't be a suicide king, just King of Cups, crossed by the Knight of Swords. The King of Cups is a fair, responsible man, but his own recklessness—the Knight of Swords—is getting in his way.'' Her gaze, golden in her low-wattage lighting, lingered on the face of the suicide king.

Guy leaned forward, drawn to her reading, and to her, against his better judgment. ''What's wrong?''

''I'm wondering if maybe it should be the Queen of Cups. I mean, the Queen of Hearts. That usually symbolizes me.''

Always your best bet. The words from a song. He wished it *were* her at the center of the reading; more than the idea of tarot, the idea of seeing his own future seriously bothered him.

He looked away from her reading, tried to find distraction in the room around him. Mary obviously took good care of her simple home, but couldn't compensate for its construction. The steel drums that floated its foundation were, he suspected, beginning to rust through, which explained the list. Constant exposure to the damp had rotted some of the wood in the walls, and warped them around the window frames.

The fog seemed to be waving for his attention through one of the windows.

"In the immediate past," Mary murmured as he rose and went to the window, looked out. Nothing except water and fog. Across the channel of the bayou, Spanish moss dripped in ghostly tatters from cypress trees. "Six of Hearts, childhood memories."

No kidding. He pulled the shade, and turned back.

"In the immediate future..." He didn't like that she hesitated, didn't want to hear bad news—yet he looked. Two of Hearts. She merely said, "It means, um, friendship." Which seemed odd—hearts meaning mere friendship?

He didn't want to know bad enough to challenge her.

"In the distant past," she continued, "Five of Hearts, or Cups. Disillusionment, or maybe the loss of a friendship."

Like eleven years ago? He sank belatedly onto the couch, staring at her. She could be making this up, of course. She knew how Joey's and Lazy's deaths had stolen their childhoods.

But the way she gazed at the spread before her, looking at it and past it at the same time, told him she wasn't faking. She'd never faked in the past, when she would warn him about a pop quiz or a surprise rain, and she wasn't now that she used cards. Her earnestness made it all the more eerie.

"And for the overall future—"

But Guy put his hand over hers before she could turn the card, before he even realized he meant to. "Don't look, *chère.*"

She raised her gaze to his, confused. "But it's been pretty positive so far. I thought we'd see more Spades. Swords."

"Let it go." He didn't understand the panic that had seized him, but he did *not* want to see that playing card.

"Does this bother you?" She looked from him to the spread, then back, suddenly vulnerable. "I'm not channeling this from anyone or anywhere else. I'm not fraternizing with spirits here."

No, *he* was the one who fraternized with spirits. He still didn't move his hand.

"It's more like..." She managed to tug her hand free from beneath his; thankfully, the card remained. "Like the psychic part of me already knows the future, and can tell what card is which without looking. It's like my subconscious deals the cards so that they'll tell me the right story." She said it so earnestly. And it made sense, as much as he understood that sort of stuff. Nothing dark or dangerous about Mary Margaret.

So what the hell—heck—scared him?

He leaned back in the sofa, away from the card, hoping she wouldn't turn it. One of the window shades flapped in a surprise breeze; storm coming. The air through the open windows felt heavy and lush, ancient and expectant. The sound of water against the bank, though, and the creatures in the woods beyond, had turned ominous in the week since he'd seen the *couchemal*.

"Most of the future is changeable," Mary said finally, pulling herself up onto the sofa beside him. She didn't turn the card. "So even if I saw something we didn't like, it might be a warning to stop it from happening."

What a lovely philosophy; he didn't believe it for a minute. "You couldn't stop Joey and Lazare."

"Maybe I could have." Her voice fell softer as she looked down at her hands. "If I'd been better at precognition, or if I'd known tarot back then. Maybe."

He didn't want to crush her optimism, but he put a hand on her shoulder and gently turned her toward him. "But you *did* know, Mary. You dreamed it and then you forgot, just like you do all the other bad stuff. You've got the ability to forget—it keeps you sane—but I don't. I don't *want* to know the future.''

''But you don't have to fear it—''

''I think I do.'' He hated his own certainty; thanked God that he wasn't psychic, that he could be wrong. ''We all die, *chère*. You can't say if, just when. And what good does that do? A girl at school got sick with toxic shock syndrome and died at sixteen! After graduation, a few buddies went out joyriding and didn't look crossing the railroad track—the accident took all three of them. In college—'' He could see in her eyes that he was hurting her. The last thing he'd wanted was to hurt her.

He gentled his voice, raised his hand to her hair as if he could soothe away this kind of anxiety with a mere caress. ''What I'm saying is, the present was all they had. Knowing the future would have just got in the way.''

She shook her head. ''Maybe if they'd known a clairvoyant, your friends would have looked both ways at the railroad track.''

''And the girl who got sick?'' He brushed honeyed strands from her defiant eyes. She wasn't going to believe him. ''The *present*, Mary. Right now. That's all we've got, all I've—''

She leaned forward on the sofa, her elfin face frightened and stubborn, familiar and new—and she kissed him.

CHAPTER FIVE

He physically overwhelmed her.

Guy had been pummeling her with dark words and ideas, like rising waters against a stressed levee. Mary had wanted to make his hurt better; wanted to make him shut up; wanted, actually, to kiss him—and so she did. Even as she pressed her lips to his she felt him tense, saw his eyes widen, then warm—

And in an instant, Guy had slipped an arm around her and taken charge of that kiss. He wove a hand into her hair and teased her lower lip with his own. Defenses evaporating, she let her head sink back into the cradle of his palm. Her eyes fell closed as pleasure melted through her in direct response to his attentions. Oh, Lady bless . . .

She had started to fear she'd imagined their attraction.

Not according to the way his lips moved against hers, charming and inviting, coaxing hers to part. Not according to the way she willingly opened her mouth to him. She—no, he!—licked her lips, and she liked the sensation of that, and the way it sent more trickles of shivery warmth down her spine. She tried it on him. He groaned, and then his tongue played into the intimacy of her mouth, and she whimpered happily.

He drew her closer against him, even as he leaned forward and she leaned back. His size filled her dazed vision. His ragged breathing echoed around her. The wine taste of him and the fresh-air smell of him overwhelmed her. She couldn't differentiate between the gentle sway of her houseboat and her own restlessly shifting weight beneath him, or her spinning thoughts. Sensation surfing. Emotion diving. The newest daredevil sport... Mmm... Magic.

Guy kissed the corner of her mouth; she felt herself sinking beneath him, onto the seat cushions. She dazedly raised her hands from where they'd clutched handfuls of his shirt, to his shoulders, to hold herself up against him. His nose rubbed across hers as he transferred attention to the other side of her mouth. *Like Eskimos.* She panted for a moment against his moist cheek, then turned her head to take *his* mouth.

He didn't seem to mind at all when she tried his tongue technique. In fact, *he* whimpered, deep in his throat.

She felt hot, so wonderfully hot from the way they pressed together, moving anxiously and hungrily against one another. Her body wanted to do what their mouths were doing.

That realization burst through her with surprise, excitement—and rightness. Oh, yes, it felt very right. Not sure how to get his opinion on this—not while kissing him—she dropped one hand from his shoulder to his waistband, then slid it behind him and into his back jeans pocket. The perfect home.

He made a gasping sound, but neither of them was breathing normally—it was more like buddy breathing—so it didn't sound distressed. And he then illustrated surprising new depths to the tongue technique, and, oh...

She was floating, drowning, melting, boiling. Light flickered at the edge of her vision, as if she were going to faint. A flash of power surged around them, into their own energy, then ebbed out of it. Actually, fainting wouldn't have surprised her at this moment, but it surely would have disappointed her.

The rumble that rippled through her on a subsonic level— *that* surprised her, but only for the moment it lasted. Then she started chewing, ever so gently, on Guy's lower lip.

He moaned something that almost sounded like an attempt at speech, but it sank back into a moan. His muscles—glutes—flexed intriguingly beneath her pocketed fingers. She raised one blue-jeaned knee between his thighs, delighting in the awareness of her arousal against the hardness that must be his.

Their breathing had turned into successive gasps that they tried to inhale around. This time, when lightning strobed in around the drawn window shades, she saw it through the veil of her lashes. This time she understood the rush of power that charged their own building energy. Still they kissed. Thunder shuddered through them, a bass harmony to their lovemaking.

And then, unbelievably, Guy drew his mouth from hers, levered himself off her and gasped, "I've got to go."

He couldn't mean it. Why? She followed him upward to kiss his mouth, the corner of his mouth, his chin. Somewhere in the back of her mind, she registered his ragged gasps as he sat completely up, drawing her into a sitting position with him.

When she returned to his mouth, he kissed her back, once, twice, but then he shook his head, depriving her of more. "I've got to go, *chère.*" He groaned the words.

"Uh-uh," she protested, tightening her arm around his waist, pressing her cheek against the top of his chest, tucking her head under his chin. His shirt had come open, just a bit, so she kissed his collarbone, then licked it. He gasped.

"Uh-huh." The equally nonverbal insistence rumbled gently in his chest, like the distant thunder. Did he know his chest was heaving? Such an overused term, but she kind of liked it. "Now. Really. While I can."

Oh—*now* she understood; he was trying to protect her. He feared compromising her virtue, not being able to stop if they went much further. *Not a problem,* cher. *Stay here tonight.* She could say that. This was the nineties. This was Guy.

He winced. "I'm sorry. I'm...sorry." And he stood.

Her hand slid from his pocket, and she shivered. "Guy?" Now she would invite him into the bedroom. Or back down onto the couch. She could be flexible. So to speak.

Yet she couldn't make the words come out, couldn't completely give in to instinct. Tonight she didn't want him to ever leave...but sleeping with him tonight wouldn't stop him from going away later.

It *shouldn't* stop him. Not for its own sake.

She tried not to shudder in withdrawal as Guy backed toward the door. Her need for him ached, forlorn like her. And there he stood, hands spread, ready to leave yet again.

Again? A disproportionate wave of misery washed over her, churning her confusion and disappointment and bone-deep frustration to unbearable depths. She felt as if she should have expected this of him, and she didn't know why. Maybe, instead of wanting her too much, he didn't want her enough.

Maybe he never would.

Guy swallowed in discomfort. "It's going to rain, *chère*." She stared. This was Louisiana. It always rained.

He tried again. "The *couchemal*. It likes the rain. I've got to go." So that he could try to boat into the swamp after it? He didn't even know what he'd be facing! And since he wouldn't let her turn that last card, neither did she.

She got up herself, managed to say "Thanks for fixing the truck" without bursting into tears, and escaped into her bedroom.

Guy flinched when her door slammed shut—and not just because it wasn't set properly in its frame. Thanks for fixing her truck? Had she just been through the same electrifying experience he had?

Thanks for fixing her *truck?*

Maybe that hadn't been her on the couch. He'd imagined kissing her before, of course, but not like that! Not Mary Margaret. This had been like some incredibly passionate stranger had taken over her sweet little body. Maybe she *had* been possessed during her tarot reading, normal cards or no normal cards. Or maybe he was really reaching here.

He barely noticed the flash of lightning this time, but he could feel the rumble of thunder. He hesitated, uncertain and *incredibly* uncomfortable.

He should talk to her, though not in her bedroom. If he went into her bedroom, it would take more than a dead cousin to get him back out—and he had to get home before the rain hit. What if the *couchemal* came to him again tonight? What if it came to him at Mary's?

He shifted his weight, clenched a fist and willed his body to catch on to the fact that the show was over. The *couchemal* scared Mary... and he thought maybe he did, too. He couldn't make her have to handle them both at once. Besides, Lazare had known her, too. What if he tried to lure *her* into the swamp?

Guy should definitely leave.

But only a pure-dee jerk would leave her like this. Lightning flared over the trees to the south, and Guy compromised by calling, "Hey, Mary Margaret, you okay?"

"I'm fine!" she yelled back. "Peachy!"

He detected a note of sarcasm. "You sure?"

"Of *course* I'm sure! You have to go. Go! Take the truck!"

There he had it. The lady said go.

And lightning flashed, closer.

Guy ignored Mary's offer and hiked the three-plus miles back to his childhood home—up the muddy track, then along the highway to Old Slough Road and down that—in record time. He could hear the rain approaching, sounding like a heavy wind as he reached the yard, and he barely outran it to the front door. He wouldn't have gotten damp at all if he hadn't stopped to stare at the little hound dog that stepped into his path from the shadows, whining and ducking its head.

Because Guy took the time to open the door and whistle the little drifter dog onto the porch, bringing in the food bowl he'd set out earlier, they both got caught in the mist kicked up by the downpour. The dog hid under a camp stool, so Guy went on in.

He took off his muddy boots in the front hallway, wondering, as he had all the way home, whether Mary was madder at him for taking liberties or for not following through. He doubted she'd disliked the liberties—she'd kissed him first. Wow, had she kissed him! He leaned back against the paneled door and closed his eyes for a moment. He'd definitely done the right thing by leaving. This was Mary Margaret! But remembering the painful passion of those kisses, he could imagine what it might be like to—

"Guillaume?"

His eyes flew open: "Holy sh—" Tante Eva couldn't have startled him more if she'd snuck up and bit him. He readied a deserved apology for his jumpiness, but saw no censure in the older woman's expression.

In fact, she looked pale, shaken. In two strides, Guy reached his aunt's side, catching her frail arm, leading her toward the living room. "Eva? What's wrong? What happened?"

She looked up at him with lost eyes, and his chest seemed to implode. He couldn't breathe; his legs threatened to collapse. Was this what Mary had almost seen in the cards? "Did Mama call? Oh, God—someone's dead!"

"Lazare." She slumped onto the couch. *"Mon petit Lazare."*

She'd seen the *couchemal?*

Then she said, "It truly is him, Guillaume. They called this afternoon. Just after five. Did you know they might call after five? They said it's my baby they found. They..."

"Shhh..." As his aunt started to sob, he gathered her into his arms and held her. Funny; she'd stayed with them so often through his childhood, he could remember being maybe five, crying in *her* arms. Now they'd traded places. It didn't seem right.

Neither did it seem right to send a quick thank-you prayer heavenward, but he did so. No one *else* had died. Yet.

If only he could feel he'd been pardoned, instead of just given a stay of execution.

Mary eyed the unturned card.

It lay there, an inanimate piece of cardboard with a bicycle design on it, pregnant with possibility.

She sniffed, almost snuffled. She'd actually let Guy's departure make her cry; she cried too easily, anyway. Though she'd since recovered herself and reclaimed her living room, her sinuses weren't letting her forget that childishness.

Turn it. Nothing to be scared of; no reason to fear the known future. Only the unknown could ambush a person. Right?

She turned the card—and stared. She'd forgotten the Joker was even in the deck, and so hadn't expected to see it—certainly not upside down. *Reversed,* she'd call that in a tarot reading.

In telling Guy where playing cards came from, she hadn't explained that only the fifty-six-card Minor Arcana, the second half of the tarot deck, had made that conversion. Minor Arcana cards generally signified possibilities, outcomes that could be changed. The twenty-two-card Major Arcana, though, represented larger life events, heavy-duty future events, probabilities instead of possibilities. And only one Major Arcana card had made it into the modern deck.

The Joker. In tarot, the Fool. Reversed, that meant someone setting out on a dangerous course of action.

She looked back at the original two cards, the King of Hearts crossed by the Jack of Spades, which she'd laid out before kissing Guy tonight, before he kissed her. Before her emotions got so very tangled up in him.

She suspected he wasn't the only fool in this reading.

*   *   *

Guy opened his eyes, stared into the darkness for maybe a ten-count—then, awake enough to move, he crossed himself. After playing funeral director over the telephone half the night, he'd expected to dream of Lazare, or the Grim Reaper himself. Instead, he'd dreamed he was making love to—passionately making love to—Mary Deveraux. She'd wanted it, too, screamed out her pleasure... until suddenly she'd become thirteen years old again, sobbing in terror, her white confirmation dress torn and muddied—by him.

Just a nightmare, thank God. His heartbeat was just starting to slow when rain blew against his window, like someone drumming his fingers across the glass.

Just rain. Just—

"Giiiiillllly!"

Oh, no. He recognized the giggle that burbled at him from the yard. Tendrils of bluish green light seeped around the edges of the miniblinds the last renters had left. No.

"I found it, Gilly! Just wait till you see!"

Guy slumped back in his childhood bed. Not again. He'd tried to follow it, but he couldn't navigate the swamp on foot. Besides, he'd already done his duty by Lazare tonight. While Tante Eva had hunched miserably at the kitchen table, he'd talked to his parents and brothers, Father Dreyer of Ste. Jeanne and Nonk Alphonse, even to someone working the night shift at the morgue.

They would bury Lazare this Saturday.

Another giggle teased the rainy night. "Come on, Gilly!"

He couldn't risk Tante Eva waking up to this. Then he remembered his aunt downing a second sleeping pill before she shuffled off to her old bedroom, downstairs. Waking Tante Eva tonight would be about as easy as waking... the dead.

"Aw, Gilly, you gotta come!"

"No." He wanted to shout it, but didn't bother. Lazy hadn't responded to anything he'd said before...why should that change tonight? He only had to survive three days, and his cousin's soul would finally be put to rest. Mary had as much as said so. And Guy suspected that Mary, with her healing fingers and her tarot cards, should know.

Lazare would find peace, and maybe, then, so would Guy.

Though he had to wonder what could be so important—

No! He dragged a pillow over his head, unwilling to watch the play of the *couchemal*'s malignant light through the blinds any longer, unwilling to listen to the ghost's cajoling.

Three days. He didn't know if he could last.

"You're drunk," Earl said from the passenger side of Bobby Lee's pickup, his voice slurred. "Y'oughta let me drive."

Bobby Lee Picou laughed at that, because Earl was just as drunk, maybe drunker, and besides, nobody was going to drive his pickup but him. Storm or no storm.

Rain sheeted over the windshield. Even crawling along, Bobby Lee couldn't see as far as his headlights—not that they did much good. Whenever he felt the tires veering off the asphalt, he compensated. So far, they'd stayed out of the ditches.

Earl said, "It was raining like this the night Clem disappeared." Dumb Earl held the crazy opinion that they were cursed. Which was dumb. And crazy.

Bobby Lee lifted the mouth of a beer bottle to his own, and took a long draw. Some rug rats had found Clem wedged facedown in a culvert. That was why he and Earl had gone out drinking: in memory of their buddy Clem.

"You think something got him?" Earl asked.

"What could of got him?"

"Whatever got Frank." They'd been looking for Frank when they found those bones instead.

Bobby Lee couldn't swerve his truck fast enough to miss knocking Earl's mailbox over—he hated when that happened. "Frank drowned," he snarled, bringing the vehicle to a halt. "He got high, drove off a bridge, and drowned. Now we ain't gonna see none of that money he owed us."

"Something got them," repeated Earl, barely audible over the sound of the engine and the rain. "And it's gonna get us next."

It waited.

Earl shook his head mournfully. "I'm getting out of here, Bobby Lee. I ain't staying around for no monster to get me."

"Ain't no monster going to get you."

It waited. Need.

"It was outside my trailer the other night! I could feel it. It's what got Clem, man." Earl looked like he was going to bust out crying or something.

"Look." Bobby Lee leveled a finger at him, realized he was pointing at the rearview mirror, and adjusted his aim. "What happens, happens. Like that song says, 'Don't Fear the Reaper.'" So much for his store of wisdom. "Get outa my truck."

Earl gave him one last basset-hound look, then obediently unlocked the door and poured himself out. "Think what you want. You, me and Clem made something madder than hell, and—"

It struck.

A muddy, skeletal arm caught Earl around the mouth, muffling his scream as it dragged him out of Bobby Lee's view and into the storm-tossed darkness.

Yesss...

Whoa. Bobby Lee blinked at the open door where Earl had been just a second, two seconds, three seconds ago. Then he yelled, and floored the gas pedal. The truck kicked shells as it leaped away from the crumpled mailbox, from Earl, from...It.

The passenger door, still open, flapped like a broken wing. Bobby Lee didn't slow down. A fog swirled toward him, forms and faces diving at his headlights. A palpable misery brushed the edges of his pickled brain—moans, howls—before he left that behind, too, still accelerating. Hell! Earl had been right? Dumb, crazy Earl had been *right?*

Bobby Lee wondered what to do. Then he reached the main road going too fast, overshot it, and flipped the truck into a tree.

Then he didn't have to worry anymore.

Organ music thrummed into the sunshine from inside the church. Yet another car pulled up in front. Yet more dark-clad people climbed out, the women gripping their purses, the men adjusting their suit coats. Mary knew some of them. She'd already seen her friend Cypress running block-ade between Cy's dark-skinned Granny Vega, who used a walker now, and her regal Grandmère Bernard. Mary had already seen her own family, and Guy's. Most of the people she knew stopped to say hello, or give her a hug, and tried to draw her in with them, but she declined.

The people she didn't know gave her confused looks as they climbed the church steps, as if her staying outside in the sunshine seemed odd. Staying out *here* was odd?

When the wooden double doors into Ste. Jeanne opened behind her, loud organ music swelled out to shiver across her nerves. She'd only once made the mistake of looking in, seeing the little coffin up at the front of the church. She'd quickly looked back at the street and the parking lot, scanning the people who got out of their cars. Her breathing exercises began to fail her. She would start shaking in a minute. She couldn't do this.

Another car turned in from the street. She stood on her toes, squinted to see who was in it. She watched it park, watched the people get out, recognized the Duprey family.

Her stomach sank.

Familiar. That was the problem. The music. The smell of flowers from inside the church. The little coffin. The community support. She'd gone through it all before, and she'd never wanted to remember. But how could she not, with it replaying itself down to the last detail?

She nodded at the Dupreys as they passed her; shook her head when Miz Delia beckoned to her to come in with them.

Down to almost *the last detail,* she reminded herself. At Joey's funeral, she'd been in shock. She'd gone through the previous two days in a listless daze, allowing grown-ups to tell her what to wear, when to eat, where to go. They hadn't even been *her* grown-ups, since her own parents had been as bad off as she. Her daddy had even cried, and she'd never seen him cry before.

So she couldn't remember much. But she remembered balking at the front steps of the church. It hadn't mattered that she had on brand-new funeral clothing; hadn't mattered that Mama and Daddy had already gone inside; it suddenly hadn't mattered anymore what anyone wanted her to do. She would *not* go into that church.

Her big sister Anne had called her a baby; her aunt Elsie had pleaded with her; her little sister Elizabeth had started to cry again. Her big brother Simon had gone inside by himself. But she'd shut her eyes, not about to budge.

And then a hand had closed around hers, and she'd opened her eyes, and fifteen-year-old Guy had been there. His bloodshot eyes had said he'd been crying, too, but that hadn't scared her, because she'd seen him cry once or twice. Somehow Guy had gotten her to go in. She'd clung to him as the only constant in her life she felt, at that moment, she could be sure of.

It occurred to her now that she'd been wrong.

In front of the same church, eleven years later, Mary looked up with a gasp when a hand closed around hers.

"Sorry I'm late," Guy Poitiers said apologetically, just as if she hadn't slammed her bedroom door in his face the last time she saw him, just as if she'd expected him. From the way her strained nerves eased at his sudden presence, she realized she had. Guy was here, tall and washed and handsome, in what was obviously another new suit. He would get her through this.

And maybe, she thought, noting his tired eyes and set muscles, she would get him through it, too. Even if they weren't meant to be lovers, they could still be friends. And in a situation like this, a friend was worth twenty lovers.

He slid her hand around his arm; she leaned against him, thankful for the comforting, callused hand he laid over her own.

Together, they entered the church.

CHAPTER SIX

By the funeral's end, Mary had vanished.

Guy turned in a slow circle by the grave site, scanning the sunny cemetery and departing mourners. People distracted him, offering condolences or saying they'd be by the house later.

No Mary. That worried him.

Despite his concern, she'd survived the mass, though he'd sensed she was maintaining her composure only through extreme effort. Somehow, the old tragedy that had buffeted them all had struck a particularly deep, permanent blow against the oversensitive changeling of the Deveraux clan.

He'd felt guilty even leaving her, but he'd been one of the four pallbearers; what could he do? And now she'd vanished.

Could anything happen to her in a cemetery?

He remembered Lazare's giggling voice, and the pulsing glow of the *couchemal,* and he decided not to look at the still-open grave behind him. Now that they'd put his cousin to rest, he'd never know what Lazy had wanted him to see.

He felt kind of guilty about that, too.

Guy cast one last glance at the rapidly emptying parking lot, and could tell by Mary's truck that she'd not left.

What *could* happen to her in a cemetery?

With a groan, anxious to change out of his go-to-meeting clothes, he went looking for her. If anything *could* happen to her, he'd rather not find out the hard way.

* * *

Ste. Jeanne d'Arc sat atop fairly high land for this area; its cemetery held as many ground-level graves as raised tombs. Joey's resting place lay flush with the land, a marble angel watching over it, a jar of azaleas at her feet. A gnarled oak sheltered it and other plots with curtains of gray Spanish moss.

Mary sat on the grass, most of it still winter brown, but some emerging in patches of green, and she looked at the grave and tried to remember. She reached out one hand and traced the lettering at the marble angel's base: *Joseph Francis Deveraux,* and the too-close dates of his birth and death. She could remember eleven years ago. Hadn't she barely fought off replay after replay of Joey's funeral, while enduring Lazare's mass?

As a healer, she knew that whatever caused pain deserved attention—she should face her unwillingness to think back. And she was already at the cemetery. She might not have the guts to make herself come again. It was time to remember.

She closed her eyes. They'd been a large family. Joey was the youngest, the one everyone else had to watch out for.

Like a blow, the image of Guy's family moving away hit her. *A big moving van in front of the Poitiers house. Guy explaining, again, how Tante Eva and his mother needed to get away, how his father's home office back in Assumption Parish needed help anyway, how he would write her, how maybe they would come back.*

She clawed her way out of that memory; this should be about Joey. She took a deep breath, tried again.

The year after the funeral. Her first year of high school; she didn't know anyone very well except other freshmen. Her friend Susie asked if she was going to the fall dance, and she started to cry. Passing students pretended not to notice.

She surfaced again, frustrated. Dwelling on the wound of Guy's absence wasn't helping. She wondered if she even had the fortitude to risk the pain of a third look back.

"Hey there."

For a moment, trapped between the past and the present, she felt a rush of joy flood over her at the familiar voice. He'd come back! But the Guy she opened her eyes to was older than the one who had left Stagwater, who had written maybe three awkward letters before giving up on the unnatural attempt at being her pen pal, who had drifted away from her. That Guy had been shorter, skinnier, cockier—and far more comfortable with her.

Then again, the suit probably explained some of Guy's fidgety stance. And even in this newer incarnation, he'd helped her as surely as his younger self would have. She wasn't sure she'd have been able to face this funeral without his warm hand and steadying presence. But his very presence foreshadowed his future absence. She should find out when he planned to leave again, needed to come to terms with it, yet she hated to ask questions when she didn't want to know the answers. It was enough that life, which had stopped for little Joey and Lazare, had continued for the rest of them. With the one exception of this funeral, she'd managed just fine without Guy Poitiers to count on.

Counting on him again would be as foolish as an alcoholic agreeing to *just one drink.*

"Hey yourself." Her response felt automatic, habitual.

He stepped around a nearby raised tomb and leaned against it with an apologetic glance toward the name inscribed. Then he nodded toward Joey's grave. "Shame we couldn't bury them beside each other, huh? They really were inseparable."

"Hey, Joey! C'mon!" Black-haired Lazare ran backward, taunting the smaller, golden-haired boy who chased him.

She blinked, surprised, the image gone as quickly as it came. "They weren't the only ones."

If he got the connection, he didn't say so. Instead, he shifted his shoulders beneath his suit jacket, and looked at the mason jar of early-blooming azalea branches by the grave. "You bring those?"

No. But she knew exactly what bush they'd come from. "My mom does. Every Sunday, after church. At least she used to. I don't attend anymore."

He took a fortifying breath, cocked his head. "Why not?"

Don't ask questions you don't want to know the answers to, either. She met his serious blue gaze. He'd admitted he didn't go to church much himself, but it still obviously ate at him that she didn't, either.

"I'm not Catholic anymore." But he knew that. What he didn't know was how long it had taken her to find her own spiritual path. First, she'd had to lose her faith in God, as surely and tragically as she'd lost her faith in Guy Poitiers. "I'm not Mary Margaret anymore. I'm—"

A movement behind Guy caught her attention. When he realized that she was looking beyond him, he turned.

A golden-haired man, about Guy's age, approached them along a shell path. He wore torn jeans and a T-shirt with a cigarette-company logo—obviously not funeral dress—and his arm, swathed in a plaster cast, hung in a sling. He looked nervous, determined.

"Some funeral, eh?" The stranger asked it the way he might of a party, or a concert, but his eyes flicked between them. "Um...either of you kin?"

Mary stood and brushed off the blue-black silk of her skirt.

Guy asked, "You mean, to Lazare?"

"What else would I mean? Kin to me? Or maybe to each other... ." He paused after saying that to look past Guy, at her. She narrowed her eyes at the slimy feel of his appreciation.

Guy stepped closer to him. "I am. Why?"

"Then I've got something for you." The stranger dug into his jeans pocket with his good hand. "I was gonna leave it on the grave, but I, uh, had to be sure, you know? Think fast."

And something arced through the air, glittering. When Guy caught it, one-handed, a chill ran through Mary. *Déjà vu.*

Guy started to ask, "What *is*—"

"It's your problem now, that's what it is." The stranger started to back away from them with a wary shrug.

Psychic memory superimposed over the reality of the moment. The coin—she'd dreamed a coin—flew through the air. Guy caught it, good with his hands like always. The beginning of something bad. Worse than the *couchemal.* Worse than him leaving again.

Guy started to follow the man, and she trailed Guy. Maybe she'd imagined this. If she'd forgotten dreaming it, perhaps she hadn't dreamed it at all. She had to see. She caught his arm, took several more steps before he slowed down enough for her to look. She clutched his wrist and turned his hand; he opened it for her, even as he watched the departing stranger.

It *was* a coin—a doubloon. No aluminum Mardi Gras doubloon, either. Despite dulled age, it looked like gold; she could make out a woman's profile, with a halo of what looked like stars.

She heard an engine start, glanced up to see a battered red sports car pull away, and remembered that from the dream, too.

"Who *was* that?" muttered Guy under his breath, turning the coin. The other side showed a faded eagle. "The funeral fairy?"

How did the dream end? Damn it, she knew the coin frightened her, but she couldn't remember how the dream ended. A bad sign. Maybe Guy *should* go, and soon. No matter how easily—how foolishly—she could come to care about him again, he would be better off away from Stagwater... because she rarely dreamed things that happened as far off as Assumption Parish.

And, Lady bless, whatever she had dreamed about this coin frightened her deeply.

"Whoa, there!" As Guy headed down the house's outdoor stairs, he had to dodge one of his nephews, and two little girls he didn't know. Then he realized there must be thirty people gathered on the back lawn—a postfuneral family reunion. He spotted his parents immediately, and Papère in a lawn chair, speaking fluent French to another old man. He as quickly recognized his brothers, Ralph and TiBoy, and saw TiBoy's wife helping set up one of several long tables, calling to her older son as she did. The other people must be the Deveraux clan.

As his booted feet hit the lawn, Guy reached into his jeans pocket, where he'd transferred the coin after changing out of that suit. He and Mary had agreed during the ride over not to upset the families by mentioning their strange encounter. At the time, he hadn't felt sure of their decision. But the faces of strangers, pseudostrangers, confirmed it.

At one time, the Poitiers and Deveraux families had been so close, the younger children could get confused about who they actually belonged to. Guy recognized Miz Maddy and Mr. Alcee, Mary's parents—eleven years hadn't changed them much. But the fellow talking with TiBoy, the one with a slight beer belly, wearing glasses, was that Simon Deveraux? A woman stood toward the back of the yard, yelling into the woods at some children in a voice he recognized, despite that her hair seemed the wrong color and she carried a lit cigarette. Anne? Mary's big sister Anne?

"Excuse me—are you Guy?" A young woman tapped him on the arm; he looked away from the sea of semifamiliarity. She was a darlin', her jeans and Tulane jersey hugging all the right curves in just the right way, her brown hair flipped back from hazel eyes. When he nodded, she laughed. "You don't remember me, do you? I'm Elizabeth! Betsy? I'm here with my fiancé."

Betsy? Mary's kid sister Betsy? This well-built collegian did *not* connect with his memories of eleven-year-old little Betsy-who-threw-up-easily. No way. And she was *engaged?*

"You want a beer?" he asked, hoarse. He would never have imagined offering alcohol to bitsy Betsy, but she looked old enough for it—and he needed a drink.

"Nah, just wanted to say hi. You should've seen your face!" She gave him a quick hug, then ran back toward her...fiancé?

He went inside, and when he saw Mary working in the overly hot kitchen, he could have kissed her just for being familiar. Well, maybe *not* just for that. But her presence, the recognition on her elfin face when she caught sight of him, seemed to slow the rapid change of his world. Maybe the rest had turned into other people, but even dressed in a grown-up ankle-length dress of some black material so shiny it reflected patches of blue, and even with her shorter hair, Mary was still Mary. Wasn't she?

"Make yourself useful, Poitiers." She handed him a bowl of potato salad. "We're feeding an army."

"I need a beer," he told her, accepting the bowl.

She smiled at him, that sweet and familiar smile that knew him so well, and retrieved a brown bottle from the fridge, tucked it under his arm. "I know. A lot of memories out there, eh?"

Which spoiled some of the familiarity between them, because it wasn't the memories that bothered him. It was that things hadn't stayed the way he remembered.

Setting up dinner took something resembling a bucket brigade for food. His brothers, TiBoy and Ralph, and Simon and—was that little Luke Deveraux?—joined Guy in carting the heavier pots and stacks of dishes. At least he recognized the food. Along with a cooler full of beer and sodas, they set up two huge pots of iced tea, sweetened and unsweetened. They had crusty French bread, and corn bread, too; boiled shrimp and crawfish and crab; creole and gumbo—"I made a little without meat, for Mary," said his mother as she bustled by, to explain the extra dishes of those—and "dirty rice" to dribble into each.

"No meat?" asked TiBoy, catching Mary in the kitchen at the same time Guy came back for another load.

When the fair-haired Deveraux daughter only rolled her eyes at his big brother's teasing, Guy explained for her. "Mary doesn't eat meat."

"Sneezy Bunny, eh?" Guy laughed at TiBoy's guess. Mary scowled at them both, just as she had hundreds of times in the past, and Guy escaped with a pecan pie before laughing harder. Maybe some things hadn't changed.

But more had.

By luck or plan, most of the original families ended up at one of the big folding tables, while most of the in-laws occupied a second table. And among the original family, the conversation centered on changes in everyone's lives. Anne Deveraux Landry had two children, a third on the way. Simon Deveraux had a business degree. Luke played in a zydeco band.

Guy listened, ate, noticed clouds massing to the west, and shared his relief with Mary, in sidelong glances, that they wouldn't bring a *couchemal*.

Then his mother said, "So, Mary, what do you do now?"

Luke Deveraux laughed. "Mary thinks she's a witch."

Guy wouldn't have believed so many simultaneously talking people could fall silent so fast. He stopped chewing. He looked down at Mary again, realizing that he should have already connected that word with her. The healing touch in the woods. The tarot cards. Her truck even had a bumper sticker: *My Other Car Is a Broom.*

He'd thought that meant something domestic.

"Really?" asked Guy's mom, too brightly. Most of his family looked uncertain. Most of her family looked vaguely amused, as if they'd gone through this before and had decided to let her handle it. Only Tante Eva actually frowned.

"I don't *think* I'm a witch, I *am* a witch," Mary said carefully, raising her chin. "A Wiccan, anyway." And yet, for all her proud body language, Guy could sense discomfort from her. Did she not want to be a witch? Was she ashamed of it?

Or maybe having two full families all focused on her was a mite distressing.

He didn't know what a "Wiccan" was, just that she didn't used to be one. But he didn't like her feeling outnumbered and uncomfortable, either. Beneath the table, he slid his hand onto her lap, and felt hers slip gratefully into it.

"So what's Wiccan?" he asked, trying to sound easy. Her hesitancy at his question didn't bolster his desire to know.

"I've read about Wicca," said his brother Ralph, helping himself to a piece of French bread. "It's sort of a resurgence of old European nature religions, right? Pass the butter."

Guy passed the butter, and glanced again at the woman—the Wiccan?—beside him. She blinked, surprised, at the priest. "Right. Some people say it's a continuation. Most don't care."

"I met a Wiccan from CUUPS, the Covenant of Unitarian Universalist Pagans, at an all-faith conference. He was an okay guy." Ralph grinned. "Except for not being Catholic, that is."

Guy leaned back in his chair, unsettled by the conversation. His hand still encircled Mary's, but he increasingly realized that he didn't know her. *I'm not Mary Margaret anymore.*

"There were Catholic witches," added Papère, from the head of the table. "Mary, she is *une sage femme,* eh?"

Mary laughed. "Does that mean a wise woman? You know, that's what the Anglo-Saxon *wicce—w-i-c-c-e—* means." She paused, comfortable enough now to take a sip of her iced tea. "I work at the Wellness Club, so you could say I'm a healer."

"Like a treater!" Guy's mother looked happy to be able to file Mary into an acceptable Cajun category. "Isn't that what they called the old healers, Papa? The ones who used herbs?"

"Une traiteuse," agreed Papère with a wink.

Guy could see Mary liking this more and more. Damned if it didn't fit her, too. The calm woman in the black dress, at least, with her dark golden hair and silver jewelry, looked like what he guessed a healer or a good witch might.

But she looked less and less like his old Mary Margaret. He squeezed her hand, then let it go.

"An angel maker!" Tante Eva's less-than-flattering translation cut through the growing pattern of interlacing conversations. "The old midwives, they were abortionists."

Mary met the older woman's glare. "They delivered babies, too. But I don't do either."

Yeah, Mary could handle herself.

She could feel it, when Guy started to draw away from her. It flared through her, like a panic. Too many memories crowded around her for her to confront alone.

On the other hand, she had no hold on him, and for good reason. TiBoy had already mentioned something about a job waiting for Guy, back in Assumption Parish. She knew he'd only returned here to see Lazy buried. Well, Lazy was at rest now. The *couchemal* that had thrown her and Guy together in the first place should finally stop wandering the bayou.

As for the strange doubloon...she hoped he would get rid of it, sell it, give it away. If he took off for home tomorrow, or even tonight, that would pretty much end her involvement there, too.

Maybe their lives could continue as they once had been.

That sense of finality, of closure, depressed her, despite the Poitiers' acceptance of her chosen path. She couldn't savor their familial indulgence, not with Guy excusing himself from the table while pie was being served. Twisting around in her chair, she saw him take the same path they'd followed after the *couchemal* last week, and her stomach tightened. One of TiBoy's sons started after his uncle Guy, but TiBoy called him back. "Hold it, boy—it's getting dark and going to rain," he warned, dragging the child onto his lap to tickle him. "You don't need to go wandering those woods. Swamp Man gonna get you!"

The little boy laughingly protested that there wasn't a Swamp Man, but Guy's papère, and Mary's own grampa, jumped into the story with relish. No swamp man? The children gathered around their great-grandparents. Anne shook her head to warn that the stories shouldn't get too scary until the little ones went *do-do*, to sleep.

Grampa launched into the story about how the lobster's long and hard journey, after the Acadians' exile from Nova Scotia, wore it down into a crawfish. He used a gruff, husky voice for the lobster, and a little bitty voice for the crawfish—both with atrocious French accents—and he had the children laughing so hard one of the toddlers lost her balance and dropped on her diapered behind in the new spring grass.

A soft voice spoke over Mary's shoulder. "Pie, honey?" Mary shook her head at her mother's offer, and not just because of the sugar. She couldn't swallow so easily, all of a sudden. She felt very much separate from the crowd around her, big Catholic families, continuing the family lines and traditions.

She felt lonely.

She looked away from the laughter and the babies toward the woods. TiBoy had been right; the sky was darkening with approaching dusk and rain clouds. And Guy hadn't returned from the shadowed path to the slough. She stood, then reconsidered. He certainly didn't need her. He wouldn't stay away so easily, if he needed her. And his imminent departure would only hurt more, the more time she spent with him.

Or maybe the damage had been done, and she was only cheating herself out of the last bits of his company she'd have in a while…maybe ever. She excused herself from the table and headed for the path. Behind her she heard Ti-

Boy's oldest, complaining that she could go into the woods when he couldn't.

"It's okay," she heard TiBoy tell the child. "She can take care of herself. She's a witch."

This time, Mary could see well enough to protect her dress from the outstretched branches, vines, brambles. The air pulsed with the songs of crickets, tree toads, frogs, punctuated by the occasional squawk of a bird. Comfortable sounds. The three years she'd spent away at college, before dropping out, had held unnaturally silent nights.

She found Guy beside the slough, its brown surface still and expectant. He leaned against a tree, his booted foot propped against its mossy surface, studying his hand.

Looking at the coin.

"Hey there," she said, so as not to startle him...but he'd probably felt her approach. He always had.

He glanced up, pocketed the coin. "Hey yourself."

She didn't want to know, but some questions should be asked anyway. "The witch thing bothers you, doesn't it?"

He shrugged. "Not like it bothers Tante Eva. I don't understand it enough to be bothered."

That he didn't ask for clarification told her he wasn't anxious for it. "What are you thinking about?" she asked instead, wandering over to where a pine bough lay, felled by one of the recent storms from the height where it could have gotten sun. Its clusters of long needles felt clean and smooth to her caressing hand. Pink nubbins huddled at the branch tips, never to grow into pinecones.

"Us," said Guy, and her hand on the pine needles stilled. Did he mean he *wasn't* planning on taking that job in Assumption Parish right away? Did he mean that maybe they could get to know one another as they were now, instead of as ghosts of the friends they had been?

But then he said, "I remember how we wanted to build a tree house," and her stomach sank. Memories again.

"TiBoy and Simon warned us that the wood rotted too fast, that we wouldn't even find trees with branches low enough."

"I don't remember a tree house," she admitted.

"That's because we couldn't find any trees with branches low enough." Guy's head tilted with his grin. "And we couldn't afford new wood, and all the junk wood was rotted."

What a dandy story—you ever consider becoming a raconteur? "Well, as long as you're okay with everything." She turned back toward the path. Coming out here had been a mistake. She might as well get back while she could still see, this time.

"Wait." She heard one of last year's pinecones crackle soggily beneath his step, and then his hand covered her shoulder. "What's the matter?"

"I've had enough trips down memory lane today." She fought the urge to touch his hand, heavy and warm, so close to her neck.

"But these are the good memories," he protested.

Until you notice they're not here anymore. Since she wasn't looking at him, she saw the little brown hound dog at his feet, watching them both warily. She knew without asking that it was his.

It provided her a roundabout way to ask the question that haunted her. "You taking the dog with you when you go?" She glanced back at him, to judge his expression with his answer.

"You want her?" he asked. That he would foist the poor animal on the first person who showed interest was not the information she'd hoped for.

"No. Thank you." She shrugged off his hand.

"You ought to have a dog," he insisted, crouching. The hound sniffed, then licked his hand. Its tail whipped back and forth with pathetic pleasure. "Living alone like you do."

"I can take care of myself."

"She's a good dog. Shy, though."

"I don't keep pets." A light drizzle touched her arms, her face. Soon rain—and night—would fall in earnest.

His expression, when he glanced up from the hound, bordered on incredulity. "You love animals! Why wouldn't you want pets?"

"Because they'll just die!" *Because they'll just leave me.* The hound skittered away at her sharp tone, and Mary bent to apologetically extend her own hand so that it could creep back, smell her, and be sure she didn't mean harm. Sweet dog. "If you're going to leave, take the dog with you. You can't just get something to care about you, then leave it. You can't—"

Her voice caught. She stood, but not fast enough to escape Guy, who grasped her arm to hold her still as he came around in front of her. "What's *wrong?*"

"You." She managed not to cry. "Dumping this dog."

Confusion and honest concern played across his face. That was the problem. He didn't mean to hurt anybody. But he hurt them anyway. "I'll take the dog with me. I just thought maybe you'd be lonely."

She considered hitting him—but he was so damned earnest! And obtuse. "I've done just fine, thank you."

He didn't let her go.

"I'm getting wet," she pointed out.

He continued to search her face, as if for something he couldn't immediately find. She realized that if he found it, whatever it was, he would kiss her again.

She wasn't sure whether to hope or fear for that.

Then, in the shadows and misty rainfall over the quiet slough, something drew her attention from him. Past his shoulder, she saw a wavery smear of...light? The eerie blue-green faded, then pulsed brighter, somehow menacing in its unearthly dance. She recognized it from Guy's description, from her vision back at Cy's house—and she wondered if it recognized her.

The *couchemal!*

CHAPTER SEVEN

Something had upset her. She wouldn't even meet his gaze, staring instead toward nothingness, eyes haunted.

Guy didn't know how to soothe her, since he wasn't sure what had upset her in the first place—the *dog?* But gazing down at her in the twilight mist, holding her, so very desperate to know she was his Mary and not some Wiccan stranger, he had the strong urge to kiss her. Not necessarily to make it better, either. Just to kiss her. Silly, since he'd never kissed the old Mary.

She raised her hands to his face, her palms cool on his cheeks. He leaned closer. She tried to turn his head. He leaned even closer before realizing, from the pressure on one side of his jaw, her intention. She meant to turn his face away from hers. She *didn't* want to kiss him? He followed the guidance of her hands, releasing her shoulders to turn, half stooped, as she kept pushing.

His breath stalled in his lungs. He recognized the pulsing illumination, the bluish green cast. Even before the giggle, he recognized it.

But it giggled anyway. "Giiiiiilllllly!"

Mary's hands slid from his face and found refuge around his upper arm. She hadn't seen the *couchemal* before, he realized, torn between concern for that haunting, childish voice and an old sense of responsibility for the female beside him. She'd had to take his word for it until now—just as he'd taken her word that it would go away. That realization added a few pounds to his usual lead-in-the-stomach reaction to the drizzly setting, the unsteady light, the eeriness of it all.

Not only was this the giggling voice—the spirit?—of his dead cousin. It had come back. Even after they'd buried him.

"Come see, Gilly," called Lazy through the mist, the woods, the twilight. "Come see what I found. You gotta see." The repeated plea hurt, as well as horrified. He'd ignored it once already this week, sure that Lazy would soon be at rest.

But instead, the boy's torment seemed to have increased. Sort of. It giggled again. But Lazy used to giggle when he was nervous, too.

Guy said to Mary, "Go back to the house."

"What?"

He moved to the edge of the water, which was gooey with needles and leaves but relatively clear of brambles. He edged along that clearer space, stepping into the water once to go around a pine-tree trunk, wondering if he could get farther this way.

The light receded flirtatiously. "Pleeeease," called the little-boy voice. "You know now, Gilly. You gotta come."

The dog whimpered, somewhere behind him.

Something cold touched his arm—Mary's hand, because she'd followed him. Her touch rapidly warmed. "What are you thinking of doing?" she asked, her voice wavering.

You're a witch—figure it out. The light drew back even farther, roiling, ethereal. Falling mist seemed to curtain it.

"Go back to the house, Mary," he repeated.

"Without you?"

He looked from the light nearing the swamp, to her—rain damp, eyes wide, face pale. Did she realize that he couldn't just leave her here, in the rapidly thickening darkness? It felt like emotional blackmail. He looked away, waded a foot into the slough to look around the unending trees. She leaned with him, not letting go. Did she want him to protect her, or her him?

Surely she could keep herself safe. She was a witch, right?

But he didn't understand her being a witch.

"Pleeeeeease ...." If only Lazy had used that tone the day he died, maybe Guy would have stayed closer, watched over the boys, kept them alive. How could he ignore it now? How often did someone need something so badly, he begged for it from beyond the grave? It wasn't like he, Guy, had so much to lose.

Maybe he didn't need a boat.

The pressure of Mary's small hand on his arm only increased.

The light receded farther, dipping behind trees, seeming to submerge and then emerge from the water. The mouth of the slough spread into the bayou, more water channels than ridges of land. Brown water encircled the flared bottoms of cypress trees and the small wooden knobs of their "knees"; water caressed tangles of exposed pine roots over muddy hollows on the banks of those few ridges. He thought he saw a hint of nebulous greenish blue light vanish behind a shank of Spanish moss, into the darkness.

He'd grown up around here. He could maybe follow it.

"Please?" But that wasn't Lazare. It was Mary, her voice a liquid whisper, her hand still outstretched to touch his arm. She couldn't stop him—probably not even as a witch. He was bigger, he was stronger, and he needed to—

Then she said, "Please don't go."

And something in her tone cut him, hurt deeply. Against his will, he spun to look down at her in the darkening gloom. She stared back at him from the bank, something near agony in her golden eyes, dewed lips parted, little spikes of damp hair sticking to her cheeks. *Please don't go.* She didn't say it again, but her very expression, her very posture, repeated it.

Little witchy silver stars dangled from her ears, and there was a star pattern on her silver bracelet, and the black she wore suddenly seemed more Halloween than funeral-related. And he had a chance to go after the old Lazare ...

Instead, he stayed for the new, and unknown, Mary. Lazy's call to him—"Giiiiilllly"—faded away, as if on the wind...but there was no wind.

Guy sloshed out of the slough, jeans heavy-wet around his calves. Mary couldn't hide the relief that softened her gaze, relaxed her posture, as her first *couchemal* encounter ended.

But it hadn't ended for Lazy, or Guy. It would happen again. She'd made him choose between them, and he'd done nothing to ease Lazare's pain. Lazare, still in limbo, would come back, and come back, and come back. Guy had left it undone yet again.

Mary's hand, small and warm, tugged gently on his arm. "It's...it's gone now."

"No, it's not. You said he would be put to rest when we buried him." He must have looked as frustrated as he felt. Her hand fell from his arm, finally, and she stepped back.

"I thought he would!"

"You're supposed to know, aren't you? He's a ghost!" He gestured toward the bayou, where Lazy had disappeared. "And you're a witch. You should know about this stuff, right?"

"It's not as if we fraternize!" she snapped back.

Damn—no, dang it. No, damn it! He'd stayed to keep her safe, or that was what he'd told himself, and now he would by God keep her safe. "Come on," he said, and headed for the path, relieved to hear her and the dog following.

He'd lain awake this week, listening to his baby cousin—his dead baby cousin—wailing for his help, and doing nothing. He'd told himself that peace would come for them both with the funeral. He'd been wrong.

"You said he'd be okay when we buried him," he repeated, holding branches away from the path for her. They'd made it halfway back to the yard before it occurred to him that he'd never held stuff out of the way of the old Mary, his best friend Mary. She'd done just fine for herself.

He didn't have the heart to let a branch go and see if she could catch it before it snapped against her, old times' sake or not.

"I thought he would," insisted Mary, behind him. "According to your religion, to his religion, he should be." As if Lazare's appearance symbolized a strike against all of Catholicism. She didn't know Lazare hadn't been baptized. They made their way through the woods and the damp, him pondering that, and she added, more quietly, "I hoped he would."

By the time they reached the floodlights of the backyard the tables sat empty in the rain, as if the family had evaporated into time, rather than taken shelter inside—which, from the noise, he could tell was the case. Then again, his *current* family waited inside. The family he'd once known, with Lazare and their late mamère and Guy's best friend Mary, had indeed evaporated.

He looked at the woman beside him. She ran a hand through her short, dampened hair; it glistened in the artificial lights. *She* glistened, sheened with dew, trimmed with silver. A strange mixture of the girl he'd once loved like a sister, and a woman he wasn't sure he had it in him to know. She looked so...unreal, all of a sudden. But they'd just seen a ghost. Everything seemed unreal.

"You okay?" he asked, regretting his temper already.

She nodded. "I think I ought to go, though," she admitted. "Your family's waiting for you inside...."

Another reminder that she was no longer part of that family, any more than he'd remained part of hers. Funny how that had ended up, his family with a priest, her family with a witch. He wondered why it bothered him to think of it as a contrast.

"Drive carefully," he told her. He wanted to tell her something different, something more, but he didn't know exactly what. "Let me know if you think of something we've overlooked about the coin...."

"Will you still be around?" What should have been a casual question hung between them. Her eyes shone at him in the floodlights. A droplet of water hovered on the tip of her upturned nose.

"I...don't know." He couldn't stay here indefinitely, not with the roofing job finished. But he couldn't leave while Lazare still wandered the swamp, could he?

He couldn't leave her.

"The number at the Wellness Club is listed, if you need to get in touch with me. I'm there most days." Another uncomfortable pause.

She kissed him.

He would have kissed her back, if she hadn't been so quick. One minute her lips skimmed his, the next she'd backed away, looking embarrassed. "Take care?"

He raised a hand in a confused farewell, taking a few steps toward the side of the house to watch her reach her truck safely. "Take care of yourself."

Just in case he didn't get the chance for a goodbye.

The little hound followed Mary halfway across the front yard, then sat, confused. Guy watched Mary get into her old blue truck, watched her drive away. Then he glanced back toward the forest, with its omnipresent chirring of bugs and amphibians, its scent of dampness and mystery. Here be ghosts.

And he knew one of them.

While he stared at the woods, feeling suddenly lonely, the drizzle increased to a louder rain. It drummed the tables, and the new roof on the house behind him. It pelted at his hair, his face, his T-shirted shoulders. A flare of distant lightning strobed edges of the woods, beyond the floodlights.

His breath froze in his chest. What—?

It waited.

Darkness again. Had he actually seen someone out there in the woods, some sort of face staring back at him? The hair on the back of his neck stood up; goose bumps flared up and down his wet arms. Even as his breath returned, of necessity, his gut knotted at the half image that haunted his memory.

Thunder rolled softly by, echoing the lightning.

"Hey, bro, you coming in?"

Guy spun, startled, before he recognized his brother Ralph's voice. The priest stood in the kitchen doorway, holding open the door as an invitation into the warmth and the light. Guy looked over his shoulder, back at the woods.

A second, pulsing flare of lightning showed only trees.

He ducked inside, accepted Ralph's concerned pat on his shoulder before his brother went into the living room. Maybe he should go back with his parents to Assumption Parish tonight. He could crash for a night or so in the room that had seen him through high school, get another contracting job with old Pete, consult a priest—other than Ralph, who'd worry overmuch—about Lazare's spirit. Away from here, he might not even have to worry about the *couchemal,* right?

The lure of shedding this weight of responsibility clashed with the weight of the doubloon in his pocket, and the all-too-clear memory of his cousin's voice across the muddy waters.

From the dark living room, he heard the purr of a movie projector. What better way to top off a family reunion, he guessed, peeking in. Simon, and his and Mary's parents, were still here. TiBoy's kids lay asleep, little blanket-draped lumps across the living room rug, and the other Poitiers had perched on chairs and sofas and the floor, watching the jumpy black-and-white images on the wall.

Guy groaned inwardly when he recognized what had to be himself, not quite three years old, summer-blond, wearing only a diaper. Several older boys—his brothers and Simon—ran past, yelling. But baby Guillaume didn't change his course, and ended up beside a blanket on the grass. A bald baby there levered herself up with her arms and blinked blearily at whatever grown-up had wielded the movie camera.

"Who's that baby, Gilly?" called the voice behind the camera, sounding way too young to be his mother.

Little Gilly blinked upward, squinting in the bright sun, then grinned and flopped down next to the rug rat. "My baby," he announced, picking up one of the infant's toys and making it bounce, too close to her face. The baby didn't mind; she just laughed and fell back onto the blanket.

"Your baby?" The grown-up voice behind the camera sounded amused. "What's her name?"

"May," announced Guy's two-year-old counterpart, getting the two syllables of "Mary" mixed up into one.

Guy decided he needed a beer and ducked back into the kitchen, strangely shaken. He should hang around Stagwater a while longer, make sure he'd tied up any loose ends from his past once and for all...with Lazare and with Mary Margaret.

Lazy first, though.

Maybe she needed to start dating.

Mary decided this on the night of the full moon, when her friend Brie answered the door, looking radiant in her not-quite-necessary-yet maternity dress. Mary suddenly wanted to cry—and the feeling didn't totally surprise her. She'd said goodbye to Guy on Saturday night, and by Wednesday she'd found letting go more difficult than she'd imagined.

Lady praise, she'd never slept with him, or she'd probably be a basket case. She already found thoughts of him intruding on her work at the Wellness Club, her improvements on her rickety but beloved home, everything but her psychic abilities. But she couldn't seem to receive any clear impressions about Guy himself. Either she didn't really want to see...or he'd left already.

She missed him. Which, she'd decided, was silly. He'd been back for barely two weeks, after an eleven-year absence. If she was crying over romantic movies, singing tragic love songs to herself, and now staring at Brie's barely showing pregnancy with a sense of loss, that surely had more to do with Mary. Guy Poitiers's momentary return to her life had, at most, waked her from her complacent dream, and in doing so triggered her dissatisfaction with that dream. With her life.

If she planned on getting depressed over the idea of romance and babies, the only solution was to start meeting men. Right?

"Mary?" Brie looked concerned. "You okay?"

Mary nodded, embarrassed, and ducked into her friend's antique-filled living room. "I know I'm early. I was hoping maybe I could hang around at your place—or next door, at Sylvie's—until the ritual. Instead of driving home, just to turn around and come back. You know what my truck's like."

Lie. Or, at least, half-truth. She'd looked forward to tonight's esbat, or full moon, celebration since she'd left the family reunion four days ago. After a long day at the club, she hadn't been sure she could stand the wait for companionship any longer. The houseboat would just have felt too lonely.

Brie nodded, red hair bouncing in its scrunchy-tied ponytail. "You shouldn't bother to ask. Sylvie's already here, working on dinner. We're having company." She turned toward the hallway to the kitchen. "Hey, Syl! Mary's staying for dinner!"

"Wait a minute! I didn't mean—"

With a wave of her hand, Brie dismissed the protest, leading her into the red-tiled kitchen area. "Too late, you're already invited. It'll work out great this way. Boy-girl, boy-girl, boy-girl."

Sylvie looked up from a steaming pot, her soft expression encompassing both welcome for Mary and amusement at her sister-in-law's take-charge attitude. "My dear husband got someone to help him add a room onto the cottage. Since he and Steve—" she nodded toward Brie, as if

Mary didn't recognize her friend's husband's name by now "—are going out tonight anyway, to give us witches the run of things, Rand invited this new guy along with them. Which means dinner in between."

"And I'm a better cook than Sylvie," finished Brie, stepping in to relieve the brunette of the spoon.

Sylvie gave it up happily. "It's really no trouble for you to stay, Mary. This way, Rand's friend won't feel like the only non-family member. It's not like a triple date or anything."

Which, thought Mary, leaning back against the wall, was an odd choice of words, considering her own thoughts on dating these last few days.

"Interesting that Mary would show up just in time, though," said Brie teasingly. "No such thing as coincidences, hey, kid?"

Mary tried to stir up some enthusiasm. Maybe this new guy would be attractive, kind, interesting. Maybe she'd look at him, and her pulse would race, her spine would melt, and her breath would fall shallow. Maybe she'd feel something like what she knew Brie felt for Steve, and Sylvie for Rand. But she doubted it.

A few years ago, she would have resented the idea that she needed a man. She could do just fine without a man. But Brie and Sylvie seemed so head-over-heels happy; she'd begun to realize that the right mate could surely provide the icing on the cake of a happy life.

For a brief, unreasonable moment, she resented Guy for spoiling her pleasure in her life's little routines. Then she wondered if she'd brought his face to mind merely to put this new fellow at a disadvantage. Too bad; she was an optimist. The sun had been shining for four days straight. Spring would arrive this weekend, on the equinox festival of Ostara—light and dark would balance, and life should seem bright again.

"I bet that's Rand now." Sylvie cocked her head. "No, wait. That's a motorcycle, isn't it?"

Mary had one of her déjà vu feelings. It shivered through her stomach, making her pulse race better than she'd imagined her dinner partner could. A motorcycle?

She walked back into the living room, almost as if drawn, followed by an unsuspecting Sylvie. She peeked out of the window, and indeed saw a motorcycle pulling up in front of the duplex. It looked a lot like Guy's motorcycle.

Her stomach sank as Sylvie's slim, ponytailed husband lifted the helmet from his head. *What did you think... that your unhappiness could conjure him up for you?*

Then the hearse that Rand normally drove to advertise his haunted-house attraction pulled up behind him. The sense of déjà vu increased, even as Mary's stomach clenched—as usual—at the very idea of someone using a hearse for a casual conveyance. She hated death, and she hated hearses.

But she suddenly realized she wouldn't hate the sight of Guy Poitiers getting out of one. Which then happened.

She didn't forget the ending of *all* her dreams.

He looked good; didn't he always? He wore his usual jeans, boot tips poking out from beneath them, and a clean-with-the-creases-still-in-it long-sleeved white shirt. He'd dressed, she realized with a sudden and tender amusement, for dinner.

But the main reason he looked good was that she'd feared she'd never see him again.

"Wait a minute," murmured Sylvie behind her, as they both watched the men toss and catch their respective sets of keys, probably talking about how their vehicles drove. "Isn't he—?"

Isn't he gorgeous? Don't his eyes seem to glow? Doesn't he have the sexiest walk? Aren't his shoulders broad?

Isn't he supposed to have left town?

"No such thing as coincidence," Mary said, for lack of a better explanation. She pulled foolishly back from the window as Sylvie beckoned the men to Brie's side of the duplex.

"Something up?" asked Brigit, appearing from the kitchen hallway with a dish towel in her hands, even as the front door opened and Sylvie surged toward it.

"Hi, honey, I'm home!" Rand caught his willowy wife to him with one arm and kissed her thoroughly enough to leave no doubt of his affection, but not so long it embarrassed their guest. "This is the guy I met at the hardware store. Guy Poitiers—"

But Guy had already stepped into the living room, filling the doorway with his rangy form, and was blinking in surprised semirecognition at Sylvie.

"Um . . ." he said, his voice low with uncertainty.

"We've met," Sylvie admitted, glancing toward Mary. Guy followed her glance—and stared.

Mary stared back. Had she just been thinking that her pulse might never race again? Her spine might never feel like melting, her breath might never fall shallow in her chest? She'd been wrong. He hadn't left yet!

She raised a weak hand. "Hey there."

Guy stepped toward her—and Brie intercepted him.

"Get out of my house." The redhead's posture, tone, and flashing gray eyes all telegraphed fury. If any of Mary's circlemates could appear menacing, it would be the fiery Brigit.

"What?" Mary, Sylvie and even Rand asked the question in startled unison.

Guy frowned, more in surprised thought than in anger. "But I was invited . . ."

"Not by me or my husband. Leave. Now."

"Wait a minute," protested Rand.

But Guy said, "Fine." And, holding out his hands to show that he meant no harm, he backed out the way he'd come.

Mary looked at the empty doorway from which her long-ago friend had vanished. She spun to stare at Brigit, whose posture softened as soon as Guy left. What about Guy could upset someone as powerful as Brigit into acting like—?

Like Guy's tante Eva. Mary looked again toward the open door. Her old life versus her new life.

She chased after Guy.

CHAPTER EIGHT

"Guy, wait up!"

To Mary's relief, Guy, striding down the front walk away from her, did pause. He held his back and neck stiff, restless with impatience. That gave her a chance to catch up with him, circle him and see his face again.

He looked angry, maybe hurt. She could understand that, having gone through the same thing with his aunt.

She caught his callused hand in hers. "Don't let Brie chase you away. She's not normally like that."

"Another witch?" Guy lifted curious eyebrows, his expression summing up his take on her witch friends.

Since she wasn't allowed to say one way or the other—Brie was the only member of her circle who kept her Craft secret—Mary merely insisted, "Something else must be going on."

"I'm sorry, man," added Rand, loping down from the front porch. As he reached them, Mary let Guy's hand fall from hers. "I wouldn't have invited you if I'd thought they'd freak out."

"She didn't freak out," Mary said defensively. "Something else—"

"What's up?" As if the situation weren't chaotic enough, Steve Peabody, Brie's husband, strolled up the walk from his parked Volvo. Unlike the other two men, Steve wore a button-down shirt and a tie. "Some kind of lawn party?"

While Rand made introductions, Mary looked back at the porch. Sylvie glanced over her own shoulder toward the doorway, where Brie, hand spread over her abdomen, stared at Guy with a mixture of confusion and dislike.

Mary returned to the porch to stand nearer them. "You aren't going to earn hostess points for that one. What's wrong?"

Brie shook her head. "I wasn't trying to earn points, I was trying to protect my baby. The wards went off when he came in."

"What?" Sylvie and Mary asked together. Most people's homes exuded a perimeter of energy, preferably positive; witches deliberately strengthened theirs. Sometimes these wards could keep out evil. Usually, like a psychic alarm system, they merely "tweaked" the home's owner when something evil tried to enter.

"You think I'd pull that evil-sorceress act if I didn't have a good reason?" Brie said now, challengingly.

"He's Mary's friend," Sylvie pointed out, while they watched Steve look from his brother-in-law toward his wife. "She'd know if the guy were evil. *I'd* know if the guy were evil!" As an empath, Sylvie sensed those kinds of things.

Brie raised an embarrassed hand and rolled her fingers at Steve, not quite managing an apologetic smile. "I didn't say he was evil," she insisted. "I said that something evil—"

The coin. Pieces clicked together, and Mary drew a startled hand to her mouth. "Of course. Come on." And, grabbing Brie's wrist—willing a little extra confidence toward the pregnant woman with her touch—she led her circlemates down to the yard, where the men stood.

Guy seemed fidgety, anxious to leave—like she'd let him go that fast! Mary hadn't quite recovered from his being here in the first place. "You've got the coin on you, right?"

He squinted down at her. "Um . . . yes."

"Do me a favor and show it to them." When he hesitated, she poked him in the arm. "They're friends, okay?"

Guy glanced from one face to the next, then shrugged, dug in his pocket and withdrew the doubloon from the funeral.

It sparkled, newly polished, in the red cast of the sunset.

Rand did a wolf whistle through his teeth, and Sylvie said, "That looks like an eagle."

"Double eagle," said her brother Steve, leaning over her shoulder. "Twenty-dollar gold piece. Where'd you get it?"

Brie, after taking an instinctive step backward, nodded. "That could be it. Could someone—?" She met Guy's reluctant gaze, obviously uncomfortable herself. "Mr. Poitiers, I know you don't owe me any favors, after how I acted, but would you please humor me and let Rand bring that onto the porch?"

Guy looked to Mary before deciding, which surprised her. Then again, he was among "her people" now. She nodded. He handed the coin to Rand, who sauntered "inconspicuously" to the porch. This time, Mary watched Steve's face. When Rand reached his and Brie's door, Steve frowned for no reason—no mundane reason, at least. But cynical Steve wasn't as in tune with his house's wards as his witch wife.

"That's it, all right," confirmed Brie, with a shudder.

Guy stared at Mary, eyes intense. "What is going on?"

"You'll get used to it if you hang around this bunch," Rand assured him, grinning. As Guy and Mary reached him, he handed the coin back, then sniffed. "Do I smell something burning?"

Sylvie flew into the duplex after him.

Mary took Guy's arm, careful to avoid the coin. The cotton of his shirt felt crisp beneath her fingers. "This is going to sound kind of weird, okay?"

From the lawn, Steve made an amused sound.

Guy rolled his eyes, and when he spoke, his voice was throaty. "I can handle it."

"That coin is evil, and you should get rid of it."

"What?" He yanked his arm free of her.

She planted her hands on her hips. "You said you could handle it!"

"And he said it's worth twenty dollars."

"You can't spend twenty dollars to get rid of evil?"

"Actually," Steve interjected, "I said it *was* worth twenty dollars. Back in . . . when's it dated?"

"Eighteen forty-five." Apparently Guy had been studying his mysterious coin in the past few days. The past few days, while she was mourning his absence, he'd been in town all along. Working. Did he plan on *staying* here awhile?

"I'd imagine it's worth more now," Steve assured him. "So where'd you get it?"

Guy looked at Mary. She shrugged—it was his coin, that made it his story, right? She noticed Steve narrowing his eyes, reporter's instincts perked.

Then Rand poked his ponytailed head out the doorway. "Dinner's saved—er, served."

Guy looked meaningfully at Brie; Mary could tell he'd rather eat dirt than come back in without an apology. Well, she wouldn't be stopping by Tante Eva's dinner table herself.

Steve folded his arms, also watching his wife, who, to her credit, handled the situation nicely. "I'm sorry for being so abrupt a few minutes ago, Mr. Poitiers," Brie explained. "Any friend of either Rand's or Mary's is welcome in our home."

Guy shifted his weight, fought a smile, then stopped fighting it. "Thank you. And call me Guy."

"But I'm not real fond of suspicious objects in my home. Once burned, twice shy. So unless you leave that coin out here—in one of the cars should do—you won't make it across the threshold." Brie smiled. "Guy."

His mouth opened, more in surprise than from the intention to say anything. Mary bit back a giggle at the image of pretty, pregnant Brigit facing down a big, broad-shouldered Cajun.

Fond as she was of Guy, Mary knew who would win that one.

"Here's the key to the Volvo," offered Steve, with apparently the same thought, as he moved past them to finally greet his wife. Mary took the keys from his extended hand while he and Brie kissed, and she walked Guy back to the gray car.

Guy stood surprisingly quiet as she opened the passenger door to allow him to put the coin in the glove compartment. Only as they started up the walk—now the only ones left outside—did he catch her shoulder so that she stopped and looked up at him.

"You've got some truly strange friends, Mary Margaret," he told her, raising his eyebrows. "That's a fact."

"You're one of them," she assured him with a grin, and patted his hard, white-shirted arm.

She *was* glad he hadn't left yet.

Over dinner, Guy finally gave Steve—the clean-cut one, married to the redhead, right?—an answer to his question. "I got the coin at the cemetery."

"You got the evil coin at the cemetery," echoed Rand, and whistled the "Twilight Zone" theme. Guy liked Rand, who'd proven easy to work with, even fun. They'd met at the hardware store, where Rand had been trying to get a recommendation for a contractor, the day after the funeral and family reunion. Since all he currently needed was a foundation poured, a fairly short-term job with which Guy had a lot of experience, Guy had taken him up on it. "I can't wait to hear— Ow!"

Sylvie, who'd obviously kicked Rand under the table, smiled.

Amused, Guy grinned down at Mary, beside him. He could do worse than be counted among her friends. They were a pleasant group, smart and easygoing—except where "evil" coins were concerned. Comfortable in their company, Mary returned his smile with a sweet one of her own. She looked glad just to see him, to sit by him. That felt surprisingly good.

After four nights waiting for Lazare's summons to repeat, four nights waiting with a borrowed canoe for the reappearance of the *couchemal,* Guy could use some good feelings. Especially since he'd started seeing things other than *couchemals*. He'd awakened suddenly last night— awakened scared. When he looked out the window, he could have sworn he'd seen someone in the woods, staring up at him, like on the night of the reunion.

Then it had been gone. Again. He tried not to shiver.

Mary looked abruptly back to her spaghetti—no meat sauce—and blushed. Guy realized that the others were watching them both. Matchmaking, maybe. They had no idea the disservice they might be doing their friend, what with his latest plans.

The coin, mouthed Rand through his amusement, like a stage director cuing someone with his line.

Oh, yeah. The coin. "After the funeral, Mary Margaret and I were talking—" he didn't miss the glances exchanged at his use of her full name "—and this guy walks up to me, asks if I'm related to Lazare, and hands me a coin. He said...um..." He hesitated, remembering.

"That he'd been going to leave it on the grave, but he had to be sure," Mary finished for him. "He didn't say of what."

Yeah, that was it. "And he said that it was my problem now. Whatever that meant." He shrugged.

Brigit Peabody raised a prophetic eyebrow. "It meant that he knew the sucker was evil, is what it meant."

"That doesn't make sense. Not just the evil part," Steve added quickly, to his wife. "But even if he thought it was evil, why would he want to leave it on the grave of a dead boy? Or give it to the boy's cousin? Is it a superstition?"

"Maybe...." That was Mary, beside him, her voice so soft that it interrupted the others' conversation, and their eating.

She shook her head, as if not yet ready to speak her thoughts. But her haunted eyes worried Guy.

"You'd never seen this person before?" asked Rand.

"Nope. He was about my age, blond." Guy nodded, pointed at Rand to punctuate his memory. "Broken arm."

Now Steve, who'd twirled some pasta onto his fork, paused. "Arm in a cast?"

Guy nodded; he noticed Mary did the same, even as she battled through whatever idea she clearly disliked forming.

"I was at the funeral to take some pictures for the paper. As I was leaving, I saw a man with a broken arm. He drove a trashy red Mustang with bad brakes."

Mary looked at Steve. "You took pictures at the funeral? I didn't see you there."

"Thanks. I try not to be obvious at those things." Steve scooted his chair back from the table. "Hey, Red, have we still got the newspapers from the last few weeks?"

"In my workshop," answered Brigit. Her husband excused himself and went out a back door from the kitchen.

Guy glanced down at Mary again. The comfort level he'd sensed off her had definitely dropped; she hadn't touched her spaghetti for several minutes now. "What's wrong?"

She shook her head, little silver earrings lapping against her neck from beneath her short, honeyed hair. "Nothing."

Like he would buy that; he'd known her since she'd worn diapers. He caught her hand beneath the table, like at the reunion on Saturday, and felt better about it this time. "Come on, *chère*. Spill it."

She glanced up at him, met his eyes uncertainly. "The reason that man might put the coin on the grave, or give it to you. I think—" She shuddered, and he realized that her eyes had focused on nothingness. It gave him the creeps.

So did Sylvie coming around the table, putting her slim hands on Mary's shoulders. "It's okay. What do you see?"

Mary shook her head, apparently shaking off whatever vision she'd flirted with. "I don't have to see. I know. The coin belonged to Lazare. That's why the man gave it to you, Guy. The double eagle belonged to Lazare."

But where would an eight-year-old boy get an antique coin?

Then Steve returned from the workshop, newspaper in hand. "Is this who you saw at the cemetery?"

The photograph actually showed three men, all about Guy's age, good ol' boys, from the look of them. But the one in the middle, even without a cast— "Him."

"Bobby Lee Picou," announced Steve. "He was in a drunk-driving accident last week, off highway 43."

Guy hardly listened, because Mary had reached out and pulled the paper back down to better see it. She raised her wide golden eyes to Guy's at the sight of the headline.

He wasn't ready to meet her gaze, though, for staring at the headline. It read Body Found In Swamp.

Bringing corpses into the conversation ended dinner with surprising speed.

"You're saying that those three men found Lazare," Mary clarified reluctantly, after they'd relocated into the den.

"Several weeks ago, a Mississippi man drove his car into the Pearl River," Steve explained from the relocated kitchen chair he'd straddled. "A bunch of his townsfolk came over to help search. These three found older remains. Apparently..." He eyed Guy, who sprawled between Mary and Rand on the camelback couch. Guy nodded at him to continue. "The body must have been trapped in a tree by high water, which kept the bigger predators away. After all the rain this winter..."

"It washed out?" If Guy felt any of the queasiness Mary did, his deep, steady voice didn't give him away.

She tried to follow his example. "So if Lazy had a gold coin on him when he died, they might have taken it?"

Guy leaned forward, tensing. Sylvie, perched on the edge of the sofa beside Rand, met Mary's gaze with solemn concern.

"His pockets wouldn't last that long," Rand cautioned. "Only something practically indestructible, like nylon or plastic—or fruitcake."

"His wallet," guessed Guy, eyes narrowing. "One of those plastic things kids make. He wore it on an army belt."

"Nylon," deduced Sylvie.

"Those sons of—" Guy's hands became fists as he stood.

"Speculation," cautioned Steve. "You said yourself, where would your cousin get a gold doubloon? You don't know those men did anything."

Guy turned to him. "But I know someone who could tell me."

"Picou?" Rand shook his head. "Why would he admit anything?" Guy scowled. Rand shrugged. "Then again..."

"Let me see your car key." Guy dropped his shoulders in exasperation when Steve stared at him. "Not to drive, to get my coin. I'm skipping the movie, if y'all don't mind."

"I've got to tell you something first." Steve stood, followed Guy to the front door. When Mary stood, too, Steve held up a cautioning hand in a bid for privacy, then followed Guy out into the night.

She moved to the window, not liking this at all. He would do something crazy, get into trouble. Leave.

"Um..." said Sylvie, and Mary glanced back. Her friend's eyes held more concern than seemed merited. "I think I know what my brother's telling Guy, and I'd bet he's not saying it in front of us so that we won't jump to any spooky conclusions."

A sense of foreboding trickled, cold, through her. "What?"

Even Rand looked concerned as Sylvie lit on the spot Guy had occupied. "Those other two guys in the picture?" Sylvie hesitated, as if taking Mary's emotional pulse. "One of them disappeared."

"Wait a minute," protested Rand, leaning his chin on her shoulder. "You don't mean hocus-pocus, poof, spontaneous-human-combustion disappeared, do you?"

Sylvie shook her head—as much, Mary suspected, to escape her husband's breath tickling her feathery hair as to deny his suggestion. "As in he stopped going to work, just took off. The authorities figure he was upset over his friend's accidental drowning. That's the other man in the picture, Mary. He's dead. And if the coin is evil, they had the coin..."

"Lords above," murmured Brie from the kitchen hall-way.

For a moment, Mary couldn't breathe. Could the coin connect with this—could it be *responsible?* She heard a motorcycle engine gunned, felt her heart jump with the noise, and ran to and out the door. Sure enough, Guy straddled his bike, denim jacket pulled over his white shirt, ready to leave again—no goodbye. Steve was turning away, giving up on dissuading him. He touched a supportive hand to the back of Mary's shoulder as she ran past.

Seeing her, Guy cut his engine, his choke. "What?"

"What are you going to do?"

He set his shoulders. "Whatever I have to."

"So take me with you." She hadn't expected to say that. Cypress would be here any minute to celebrate the full moon that even now rose, a huge golden blur behind a veil of clouds. But she could celebrate the esbat alone.

Guy shook his head, adamant. "No."

"Why not?"

He widened his eyes. "Because I might end up beating the..." Then he ducked his head, breaking the intensity of the statement. "The stuffing out of this jerk. I was taught not to do that in front of a lady, okay? Stay here with your friends."

"Steve told you about those others, right?"

"One got drunk and drowned, the other took off. Don't make it spookier than it is." Guy held her gaze for a long moment, then looked away. "Mary Margaret, I have to go now."

She took a deep breath. "Then when are you coming back?"

He didn't say anything. She could suddenly hear the crickets, from the scrub-filled lots across the street, and some kind of night bird screeching. Her breath slowed in her chest. He wasn't coming back? Of course not. This was Guy.

"We finished pouring the foundation today," he explained, almost gently. "Lazare hasn't shown. I figured I'd head west tonight, after the movie, maybe talk to my brother about this."

She noticed the bike's full saddlebags, the duffel strapped atop them. And then? "What about the dog?"

"She's out at Rand's cottage for now. His assistant's going to watch after her until I decide where I'm settling next."

She didn't like this, not at all. Not because she'd dreamed it. Not because of any premonitions. Just because it hurt. He was leaving, again, and he wouldn't even take her with him.

As if she'd go. She had a life without him, damn it. She ought to march back into Brie's house and show him how much she cared if he ran off again. Instead, she said, almost whispered, "You weren't even going to say goodbye."

He raised his gaze to hers, and failed in his attempt at nonchalance. Putting his weight on the foot nearer her, he leaned off the motorcycle and tentatively gathered her into his arms. She let his embrace swallow her into his warmth and his scent. She wouldn't cry. Not again. Not for him.

"I'd already said goodbye, *chère*." he murmured into her shoulder. "I just didn't want to do it again. I may not even be gone that long, eh?"

Like a blow, the memory shuddered through her. *Fifteen-year-old Guy, chucking pinecones out into the slough, not fully looking at her. "I may not even be gone that long, eh?"*

And he'd been gone for eleven years.

When he now added, "I'll call," it only mimicked his previous promise to write. All this lacked was a pinkie swear. She pulled out of his arms, backed away. The security she found there was illusory; she wouldn't give her energy to an illusion.

But if he meant to carry an evil coin with him, she could do something. Pulling off her necklace, the one with the charm holder, she unfastened a small clamshell she'd found the last time her family drove to the Gulf of Mexico. Nature had worn away a small hole at the top, perfect for hanging. She'd painted the edges silver, with a silver rune of protection inside it.

She pressed it into his hand. "Take this, to keep safe."

Guy hesitated, looking from the shell in his palm to her.

She rolled her eyes. "I don't do bad magic! Put it with your rosary, if you're worried."

"I don't have a rosary, and that wasn't what worried me. Thanks." He slipped it into his jacket pocket, started the bike again, pulled the choke. "Take care of yourself?"

I guess I'll have to, won't I? She watched him until he pushed the choke off, kicked his stand up, and drove away. Again. A faint rumbling, a faint flickering of light behind her caught her attention, and she glanced up to see that the moon had disappeared behind heavier clouds. More rain soon.

She looked back down the street, but Guy's motorcycle had already vanished.

More rain.

He found the jerk easily enough. Phone book. Name on mailbox. And Bobby Lee Picou even answered the doorbell. "What the hell are you doin' here?"

Guy stared at him. What did Picou think, that he'd come to play poker? Have a few beers? Even if this guy hadn't done what Guy suspected, the fool had given him a gold doubloon. In a cemetery. Was it that unlikely that Guy would look him up?

He didn't like staring at Picou, because they looked alike. Not movie-of-the-week, family-resemblance similarities, but they were the same type. Tall, male, mid-twenties. Jeans. Boots.

Guy didn't want to be grouped with this son of a . . . gun.

But Picou looked nervous, too, glancing across the front lawn toward the dark street and the motorcycle, as if something lurked over Guy's shoulder. That gave him the creeps, much worse than Mary's haunted eyes had. "I want to know about the coin."

Picou glanced into the dark again. "Jeez—you might as well come in. But you ain't stayin' long, got it?"

At the unexpected hospitality, Guy listened for the sound of anyone else in the house, and mentally double-checked the street for other cars—there hadn't been any. Just the trashy Mustang Steve had described. The house should be safe. All he could hear was the sound of wind against the house. He'd felt it all the way here. Storm coming.

"Folks' place?" he asked, entering a wood-floored foyer.

"Yeah." Bobby Lee shut the door with his good shoulder, then bolted it. Again Guy tensed, aware that this guy might not be above an ambush to get out of trouble. "What's it to you?"

"It's nice, that's all." Nicer than either of them was likely to have at their age. Then again, Steve Peabody wasn't much older than them, was he? And Rand owned a cottage and a big haunted house. Maybe it had something to do with being married.

Guy noticed pictures of Bobby Lee in the hallway, and of obvious relatives, sisters, parents. Graduation and wedding pictures. He didn't want to think that this guy had a family, too, a mother to fret about his broken arm, a father to shout about the DWI. He didn't want to think of him as a person, any more than he wanted to be like him. But, hell. Guy couldn't have roughed him up, anyway, not with the broken arm. He hadn't thrown the first punch since high school; he wasn't sure he still could.

The curse of being a nice guy. He wouldn't rob corpses, either. But, he decided as he reached into his jeans pocket, he wasn't quite ready for sainthood. "Think fast," he said, and threw the doubloon. An easy, underhand toss into a shiny arc. Anyone could catch it one-handed.

Bobby Lee Picou leaped backwards as if the hallway had started raining snakes. "Don't!"

The coin landed hard on the wooden floor, bounced, then rolled to the baseboard and lay still. *That coin is evil, and you should get rid of it.* Mary's words echoed back at Guy. It looked like Picou had the same bias as the witches.

"What the hell'd you bring that for?"

"To get some answers." Guy stepped to the coin, caught it under the sole of his boot, and skidded it toward Bobby Lee.

Again the man dodged, backing toward the archway into the kitchen. Guy could see out the window that the storm had hit.

"Where'd you get it?" Guy repeated the move. The coin skidded onto linoleum, after Bobby Lee. "Why'd you give it to me?"

"Stop it!" Bobby Lee's forehead shone with sweat as he waited, muscles bunching in readiness, for Guy to come at him again. "Jeez!" His voice cracked.

"You gonna tell me?" This time, Guy picked up the coin.

Picou sagged against the counter at the sink. Relief made him bold. "I don't have to tell you nothin' 'bout nothin'!"

"You wanna *swallow* this?" Guy hefted the coin, and took some guilty satisfaction at how Picou blanched. "I can do it."

Still Bobby Lee hesitated.

"Look, Picou. I already know you stole this off my cousin's body. I'd have *fun* stuffing it down your skinny throat!"

Mary had been right. God in heaven, she'd been right. Bobby Lee nearly fell, and had to catch his balance. "You know?"

Guy tossed the coin, so that it caught the fluorescent light in the kitchen in bright flashes, and caught it in a fist. This man would pay, and pay big.

"You don't have no tape recorder or nothin', do you?" Bobby Lee glanced toward the dark window, then pretended he hadn't.

It waited.

"Talk!" snarled Guy.

"Okay! We...we were out in Earl's skiff. We pulled over to a ridge to grab a bite, take a leak. Then Earl saw this skull. We thought he was snakebit, the way he yelled. It was pretty gross, really. Not all the bones looked to be there—"

"The coin?" warned Guy through gritted teeth, not about to listen to details about his cousin's corpse.

"Yeah, well, we didn't know for sure the wallet went with the bones, you know? It was a couple of feet over. Filthy, too."

It waited. Need.

Guy stared, wishing the man weren't already injured and wondering if he could justifiably overlook that fact after all.

"So we kept the coins!" Now Bobby Lee turned defensive. "Fine! I gave mine back, didn't I?"

Coins? "There were more?"

"Three. Like we was each meant to get one, you know?"

"So where are the others?"

"They disappeared with Clem and Earl, okay?"

Evil? But even if he believed Mary, even if his skin crawled when he looked down at the doubloon in his hand, Guy couldn't follow her advice and get rid of it. It had belonged to Lazare.

Lazare had said Guy "knew now"—after he had the coin. Lazare said Guy had to come.

He shoved the coin back into his pocket. "You're a real..." Dozens of labels flitted through his mind, but it was still Lent. "You're real pitiful," he finished. "You know that? What if those coins had been evidence of how the kid died, huh?"

"Look, man, you think I'm not already sorry we took the damned things? My buddies aren't gone, man, they're dead! Both of 'em! The cops think I made it up about Earl, but I saw it. This hand, all bones and tendons, muddy, and with moss and stuff on it. That's what got him. And then this fog of people cryin'—"

The wind blew a patter of rain against the kitchen window, and someone knocked slowly, deliberately, at the back door.

Thud. Thud. Thud.

Picou whimpered, blanching. "He's back. The Reaper's back, man. Get the hell away from me with that thing."

Guy looked toward the door, then back at Bobby Lee, his mouth falling open. "You think it's *Death?*"

"Get the hell outa here, or I'll get my gun!"

Thud. Thud. Thud. Like someone was using something wet—or a dead animal—to knock with.

It waited. Hunger.

Guy said, with careful patience, "Let's turn on the back porch light and take a look. If you've got a gun—"

"Get *out!* Now!"

Guy wished he could see what was outside. It felt...wrong. Bad. *Evil?* But by this point, so did Bobby Lee Picou.

Guy left the front way, through the rain, into the pool of streetlight where he'd left his bike. He heard Picou shut and bolt the door behind him—no shelter there.

It shuffled forward.

Guy reached the bike, put his helmet on. It both muffled and magnified the sound of the rain. He put on his gloves. He straddled the bike, inserted the ignition key. Pulled the choke up. Started the bike. It trembled beneath him.

Need. It shuffled forward.

The wait to push the choke off had never taken so long. He felt like a target. The Reaper? That was crazy...wasn't it?

He fingered the shell amulet Mary had given him, in his pocket.

It paused, repelled. No!

Guy shook his head, set the bike straight, kicked out the center stand and eased away from the curb. This wasn't something to bring to Ralph. This was something to bring to Mary.

He just wished to God he wasn't bringing danger with it.

Inside the house, Bobby Lee Picou listened to the sound of the motorcycle going away. Then...silence. The rain was slowing, too. If he'd been a praying man, he would've fallen to his knees in thanks. Instead, he peeked out several windows.

Nothing. Wet lawns, empty street. It had worked. He'd sicced the old Grim Reaper on someone else. Went to show he'd been smarter than Clem and Earl all along.

He opened the front door, stepped into the faint sprinkling of rain, just because he could. Just because he was free of that thing. Just because—

It struck.

Yesss...

CHAPTER NINE

Mary knew there was no such thing as a bad tarot reading, that the future remained fluid. Even the most disturbing spreads provided a warning that allowed one to change that future.

But this was as close to a bad reading as she'd ever come. On the card she held, a skeleton, scythe in hand, danced happily across a field of corpses: Death.

She realized, of course, that the Death card rarely indicated actual death. Usually it simply bespoke transformation, the end of one cycle and the start of a new one—like graduation, or getting a new job. But in this reading, it didn't mean graduation. In this reading, Death meant death.

Guy's death. She knew it. Psychically. Instinctively.

She almost swept the cards off the table, almost rejected the reading—but, of course, then she wouldn't understand its message. Death would come only if she couldn't change the flow of events. Once she unlocked the secret of the warning . . .

She shifted from kneeling on the floor before her coffee table to a lotus position, and practiced her breathing to better ground herself. She remembered the water flowing beneath her, nature surrounding her, full moon above. Protection. Safety. Wisdom?

Was all the hassle of being Wiccan—her brother's jokes, her parents' worries, Guy's discomfort—worthwhile, if she couldn't find a little wisdom in it?

She looked back at the spread, and tried not to feel intimidated by the number of Major Arcana cards that filled it. The more Major Arcana cards, the more solidly set the

future. This spread held five: The Lovers—could she deny
who they symbolized? The Fool again, reversed, setting out
on his dangerous journey. The Devil, a self-bondage to material wealth. The Hermit, reversed, standing for a refusal
to accept advice or assistance. And, of course, Death.

Five cards, out of a ten-card spread. Okay, no such thing
as a bad reading—but neither was this good. She continued
her breathing, steady as the lapping of water against her
boat, and tried to let the pictures piece together their story.
Guy would set out on a foolish trip—please, not the one
he'd left on tonight! He would leave, and because of his refusal to accept help, maybe from her—Queen of Cups—he
would meet his death.

She couldn't tell if their being the Lovers would help or
hinder him. The material bondage indicated by the Devil
confused her, too; one gold piece hardly seemed worth such
a strong caveat.

She vaguely recognized the sound of an approaching
motor; assumed a boat with an outboard motor was coming near. Someone heading through the bayou for some
night fishing would probably ignore her No Wake sign,
would probably set her home bobbing as it sped past. But
instead of approaching, the motor cut. Only then did its lo-
cation, the road, match her premonition: Guy?

She might as well have been buzzed by a speedboat, the
way her world swelled and dipped beneath her at the
thought. He'd come back? Better for her heart, of course,
if he stayed away, instead of upsetting her world all over
again. But she looked at the image of Death dancing across
his grisly harvest, and knew differently. If Guy came back,
she still had a chance to change the future laid before her.
She still had the chance to keep him from setting out on a
fool's mission, from meeting death.

Far better that he live—whether he broke her heart or not.

Her hands skimmed over the cards, collecting them before he got here, wrapping them in watery silk. She needed
to warn Guy somehow, but not by dropping the worse cards

in his lap. Her ethics made her wary about creating self-fulfilling prophecies by blurting out frightening possibilities.

If he *was* to die, she couldn't live with the knowledge that it might have been at her suggestion.

As she put the silk-wrapped cards in their box, she wondered if she could live anyway. Dangerous, foolish thoughts.

Thunk, thunk, thunk. She jumped, as if unprepared for the summons, then unfolded her legs beneath her jumper's skirt and stood. Logically she knew she should peek out a window—should have locked the door in the first place. But instincts defied logic. She dived across the room, threw the door open. Then she threw herself at the broad-shouldered, wind-and-rain-blown man who stood on her deck.

Belatedly Guy's arms closed around her, damp denim surrounding her with his strength. Her cheek pressed to his chest, and she could hear the accelerated beat of his heart even as one of his big hands buried itself in her hair, even as he laid his own cheek atop her head.

You can't have him, she thought angrily at the skeletal image that remained in her mind. *I won't let you, not when I—*

What? Oh, Lady bless, what? How deep did her affections for this man run? And how could she possibly trust them, or trust him with them? Especially if— No. *You can't have him.*

"Um...Mary?" Guy's voice seemed to rumble through her. "Can I come in?"

"What?" She blinked up at him. "Oh! Uh-huh." Just as slowly, she eased her hold on him, stepped inside. Now she was damp, too. She didn't mind. He'd come back.

He walked into what served as her living room, filling it like last time, and she saw just how wet he was. "You've got to get out of those clothes!" Not that she had anything for him to wear, except maybe a blanket. The idea tingled through her, shocked her. Surely she didn't find imminent death arousing?

Then again, it had worked for soldiers across centuries. What better way to denounce death than an affirmation of life? She felt almost disappointed when Guy hefted his duffel bag.

"I brought a change with me. Can I use your bedroom?" A shiver warbled through his sentence, testament to how the chill crept in as he let down his guard.

"My pleasure," murmured Mary, and he vanished through the doorway in question.

She stared at the bedroom door for some time, trying to wrench her mind away from images of him stripping beside her bed and toward how she would warn him about the danger he faced.

She did not succeed.

He walked, barefoot, back out of the bedroom, just starting to button a blue work shirt. Oh, my, but he had a beautiful chest, hard and tanned, with swirls of golden brown hair shadowing the valley between his pecs before tracing a line into the waistband of his jeans. And he was *covering* it?

Mary suddenly felt very shallow, and practically ran to the galley to escape that feeling. "I'll put on some tea."

"Got any coffee?" he asked, following her to the counter that divided the galley from the living room.

"Nope. Sorry. Herbal tea, juice, or plain water." She glanced at him, and he shrugged his broad shoulders, treating her to a tired version of his charm-the-pants-off-you smile.

"Tea sounds great."

Since that smile did little to dispel his attraction, she turned back to pouring bottled water into her teakettle, then setting that on her hot plate.

"I thought you were mad at me, when I left." Guy's husky voice hardly helped her escape this sensual spiral, either.

"I wasn't thrilled about your leaving," she admitted, lifting two mugs off their hooks. "But I'm glad to see you again."

"I wanted to tell you what I found out."

"The Picayune men found the coin with Lazare's body, right?" After setting the tea bags, she had to turn back to him. He hadn't tucked his shirt in yet. That seemed such a casual, sexy thing, suddenly. "And it's cursed."

His lips parted, surprised. "Okay, yes. You were right. But there's more." Then he leaned across her counter, his folded arms resting not far from her. "There were three coins, not just the one. Each man took one, and now one's dead and one's missing. Bobby Lee Picou thinks the Grim Reaper got them."

She stared, remembering the tarot card. "Death?"

"One and the same. Someone knocked on his back door while I was there, and Bobby Lee freaked. He wouldn't even let me take a look before he chased me out the front way." He paused, glanced uncomfortably at his crossed arms.

"You felt it, too," she realized. "Something..." She could almost picture it: *A figure of darkness moving slowly, as if from age, reaching bony claws toward the back of someone's neck.* Guy? No... "Was Bobby Lee wearing a green T-shirt??"

"Picou? Yeah, he was."

She closed her eyes; didn't want to know. It had already happened, she couldn't change it, so she didn't want to see—

Guy's arms surrounded her, warm and protective; he'd circled the counter, and now his concerned embrace helped free her thoughts from that image. "Are you all right?"

She nodded, not wanting to move, afraid he would let go of her again. "I am now. I'm—" She did move, enough to look up at him. Bits of bronze glinted in his hair, mussed from the motorcycle helmet, or maybe from pulling a shirt over his head. His blue eyes awaited the rest of her sentence. "I am so glad you came back, Guy. Truly glad."

He looked quickly away, and her timer rang. He let her go; bewildered, Mary rescued the teakettle, turned off the hot plate, poured the tea. Her hand started to shake when she lifted his mug; his own hand closed around it, steadying hers.

"Mary...." His voice cracked. He swallowed, made his gaze meet hers. "I came back to ask a favor. I need your help."

Oh. Some of the pleased excitement she'd been feeling drained from her like suds from a sink. He had come back for pragmatic, not passionate, reasons. But at least he'd come back.

She let him have his tea, and took her own before detouring around him and into the living room. She sat very carefully on the couch, placing her mug on the coffee table. "My help?" She hoped she achieved a casual, friendly tone. "What kind of help?"

"I need you to help me find where the coins came from."

"Didn't they come from Lazare?" But of course— Lazare must have found them somewhere first. "You mean, where Lazy got them? Over *eleven years* ago?"

Guy joined her on the couch. "I remembered something on my way to Picayune tonight. Lazare ran away earlier that summer. Remember? Tante Eva and Nonk Alphonse had been trying to reconcile, and Lazy was living with them, but he ran away..."

She didn't want to remember; couldn't help remembering. "The police came looking for him...."

"And three days later he showed up safe and sound, and he and Tante Eva moved in with us again. He'd hidden in the swamp, remember? And afterward he got real obnoxious..."

I've got a secret, I've got a secret. She could picture the young face, black hair tousled, shining eyes creating a mask behind which his real emotions lay. Practically a child herself, Mary hadn't understood. Now she realized, with the same certainty with which she received most of her psychic impressions, that Lazy had run away from an abusive father. No wonder Tante Eva remained such a frail, frightened thing to this day, married to a man she despised, unable for religious reasons to divorce him.

Nonk Alphonse hadn't even attended the funeral.

But Mary's mind had wandered, perhaps deliberately, from the issue at hand. "You think he found the coins in the swamp."

"That has to be what he's tried to show me, but following him—it—won't work. I need to know where, first. You've always been able to find things, you know you have. Help me find out where Lazare got those coins, and if there's more of them."

He looked so earnest, needing her like this. At least, needing her psychic abilities. He didn't want her as a woman, or even as a friend; he wanted her as a fortune teller.

She looked down at her hands, lest she show him how much that hurt, feeling petty for it. "What would that accomplish?"

Guy laid a warm, heavy hand on her shoulder. "Men might be dying over these coins, *chère*. Do you think it started with two men from Mississippi?"

He held her shoulder until she had to look back up at him, slow and horrible comprehension seeping into her very bones.

Guy said, "Lazy's death may not have been an accident."

He watched the emotions play across Mary's expressive face at that idea. He'd had to pull his motorcycle over to the side of the road—in the rain, yet—when the realization hit him. Only his sense that the doubloon made him a target for something, somewhere, had kept him from standing there indefinitely.

Assuming, of course, that Bobby Lee's fears and Mary's predictions held any grains of truth. Guy didn't plan on risking it. He glanced toward the window, which reflected the room back at him. The sense that something could come out of the woods at him, anytime, wouldn't let him stay long anywhere.

Mary tried to say something, swallowed, and then managed, "Joey." And Guy felt like an ass—a complete jerk. How could he have forgotten her brother?

"Maybe it didn't kill him, *chère*. I don't know. Maybe whatever it is pulled the tree over when they were playing on it, and Joey drowned by accident. But I think the Reaper, whatever it is, did kill Lazy. Aren't ghosts sometimes murder victims?"

She seemed to understand. "The *couchemal*."

"That's why I've got to find out where the money came from. If I can find that, I should be able to find whatever would kill for it. And on my terms, not its."

"No," she said.

Guy had started to slide his hand across her warm back to her other shoulder, arranging his arm around her for support, but he paused. "No?"

He didn't like the conviction in the golden gaze she turned toward him. "For one thing, it's dangerous."

"If you're right about this evil business, owning the darned coin could be dangerous."

"So get rid of it!"

"And don't worry if Lazy was murdered? Let the murderer get away with it?" He couldn't believe she'd suggest such a thing.

"Nobody gets away with anything, in the end." She said it quietly, firmly. "I can call it karma, and you can call it divine retribution, but either way, if there's something evil out there, it will come to justice."

"God helps those who help themselves," Guy pointed out, and downed his tea. He wished it was something stronger.

"What about turning the other cheek? He who is without sin casting the first stone?" A surprisingly desperate note began to creep into Mary's voice. "Don't sink to its level, Guy."

"What about keeping it from happening to anyone else?"

That stopped her; she even had the grace to flush. But she hadn't given up. "We don't even know what we're dealing with. People live out in the swamp, some a bit crazy. If you go gunning for some assumed killer, what's to keep you from accidentally killing an innocent hermit?"

"Do you think I'll start blasting away at the first thing that moves?" He hadn't realized just how low her opinion of him had dropped. "Look, I can tell you aren't going to help me on this. That's your call." He stood up, went into the bedroom and collected his duffel, boots, jacket. "Sorry I wasted your time."

"Where are you going?"

"Home. Thanks for the drink." He'd pulled on socks and his boots while she stared, then crossed to the door before Mary caught up to him and grasped his arm.

"Wait!"

Okay, so he waited. When she didn't say anything, he looked back down at her. Fear widened her golden eyes, half-lost beneath a fall of honeyed bangs. She looked so small, so helpless . . .

Yeah, right. He opened the door, frowned when some windblown rain spattered into his face. Tante Eva had gone back to Assumption Parish with his parents last Sunday, the day after the funeral, but he'd been staying in the house. He didn't look forward to being there alone on a night like tonight.

It waited.

"Please don't go," pleaded Mary, still holding his arm.

He sighed. "Go where? Home? Or into the swamp to find out if Lazare was murdered?"

"Yes," she whispered. "Both. I don't want to lose you."

Oh, God. Oh, no. Her concern this evening, her embrace, should have clued him in. Her comment while she fixed the tea, about being glad he'd come back, *had* clued him in—but he'd diverted both the conversation and his own fears away from it. He couldn't have people counting on him. He'd tried so hard not to let that happen. Why had it happened with her?

He shrugged off her hold and said the harshest thing he could think of. "I'm not yours to lose." At her stunned expression, he thought, *I'm sorry.*

But if he said that, she'd know he cared, too. That would make her feel loads better about him going into the swamp, eh?

He crossed her sagging deck—dang, but she needed a better houseboat!—and started down the board "gangplank" that spanned to the bank. She jumped the distance and dodged ahead of him.

"Don't go anyway! You can't go, Guy. Believe me? Please?"

It shuffled forward.

The back of his neck prickled, and not just because she sounded witchy. "Mary—"

"Please?"

He realized with a horrible, sinking feeling that the dampness on her face wasn't just the rain. He reached for her; she glared him into stillness, and swiped the back of her hand across her eyes. "You won't do Lazy any good if you go out and die tonight, damn it!"

"All right!"

"You won't do anyone any good! You'll just go off, and never come back, and I—"

"I said all right!" he shouted. Oh, God; her shoulders sank in toward one another, her head dropped. Now she was crying in earnest. He didn't know why she'd even want to protect a fool like him, but she must want him really badly.

This time, when he reached out, she let him loop his arm behind her, let him lead her back to the houseboat, back into the warmth of her living room. He shut and locked the door behind them, shuddering off the sense of being watched. On second thought, he let go of Mary to close the curtains, too.

Frustration. Hindered. It waited.

Mary was shivering, too, far more than seemed warranted by their moment in the spring rain. Guy steered her to the sofa, then sat beside her to drag a comforter from the seat's back and drape it around her shoulders. He waited a few minutes, until he thought she'd calmed down, then said, "Um . . . Mary? What was that about me dying tonight?"

She glared up at him, soggy and still upset. "You have to promise to stay. Here. Inside. All night. Do you promise?"

"If you think something's going to come after me, I don't think I should. If it can knock, it can probably get in anyway."

"Not here it can't." He believed her; witch stuff again. "I bet it's out there, though. Promise me."

"Mary . . ."

"Promise me!" How could someone with red eyes and a runny nose actually look attractive? Maybe it was the stubborn concern in those red eyes; maybe it was the fact that her nose was running because of him, whether he deserved it or not.

"I promise." He sighed. "Okay? Here, have some—" But as he picked up her mug, she turned her face away into the couch. He heard a distinct, muffled sob. "What's wrong now?"

She shook her head. He put the mug down and pulled her, comforter and all, into his lap. "I said I'm staying, didn't I? I promise, cross my heart and hope to— Anyway, I'm here."

"I'm sorry." She sniffled into his chest. He reached toward her hair, hesitated, then laid his hand against it.

He began petting it. "Why are you sorry, *chère?*"

"For crying. It's . . . manipulative. I hate manip—" She sniffed. "Manipulation."

Guy felt a grin stretch his mouth. He hadn't been that great a catch even before his life turned into a horror flick. Now he had conversations with his dead cousin, carried a cursed coin, and was planning a nice trip into the swamp to look for a possibly inhuman killer. Bad time to get romantic.

Especially with a girl—a woman—he truly cared about.

Mary had found a handkerchief in her pocket—people still carried handkerchiefs?—and wiped at her eyes and nose. Only then did she glance back toward him, her face very near his.

The mop-up did wonders for her appearance.

He realized he was still petting her hair. He couldn't seem to stop. It felt so soft, like rainwater between his fingers. She smelled like rainwater, too.

"About the dying thing," she said slowly, as if having to think very hard to form the words. "You'll be safe here, so forget what I said about that. I've got very strong wards."

He didn't know what wards were. If they kept him from dying, more power to them. Mary was what held his attention. The comforter bundled most of her out of his view, but he could feel her weight and warmth on his lap, could feel her legs atop his, one of her feet brushing his jeaned calf.

She'd asked him to spend the night. Made him promise, in fact, to spend the entire night. Was it warm in here?

Not as in "spend the night," you fool.

He continued to pet her hair. Of course she hadn't meant it like that; a big difference gaped between a welcome hug at the doorway and "spending the night." She'd meant for him to sleep on the couch, probably, while she slept in her bed.

One room away.

He was starting to get really wonderfully uncomfortable, with her on his lap like this. He'd held her in his lap before, years ago; they had pictures of it from when she was a baby. He could remember holding her when Sneezy Bunny died, too, and the time she broke her wrist. But not like this. Then, it had hardly mattered that she was a girl and he a boy; just that she was younger, and his. Now the boy-girl thing mattered a lot.

A whole lot.

The comforter slid to her lap, and his, a crumpling of soft colored crochet. "I'm . . . not cold, anymore," Mary whispered.

He ought to get her off his lap. Things could quickly get out of control, otherwise.

He kissed her instead.

She'd wanted the kiss; he could tell by the way she opened her mouth to his, the way she leaned slowly against his chest. Dangerous, her wanting it, too. He wove his fingers more securely into her hair, turned slightly, tasted her more thoroughly. Yes, oh yes. He realized he had a free hand, and slid it down her spine, enjoying how she curved toward him.

Mary shifted her weight on his lap. He felt her pause when he shuddered at the shock waves of sensation that shot through him, then slid her questing hands around him, clutching at his jacket as if she feared he would try to physically remove her.

Fat chance. He wasn't sure he could keep her on his lap much longer, though—not like this. Not with clothes on. He managed, after several attempts, to drag his boots off with his feet. Then he drew his legs onto the couch, rolling slightly so that she eased off him and onto the cushions, so that he could swing a jeaned leg over her, capturing her gently beneath him.

She blinked up at him, wary, desperate. He shrugged out of his jacket and leaned closer to try to kiss the wariness, at least, away.

She shifted beneath him, slipping her hands beneath his shirt to skim her palms over his bare ribs, his chest. Almost as if he weren't even wearing a shirt. Good idea, he thought, and released her just long enough to get the shirt off, too.

Too soon? Too fast? He wouldn't have known from the way Mary encircled him with her arms, drew herself closer to him, kissed him again.

Things began to speed up. He drew her even closer against him, so that her hip met his arousal. Yes. She moved against him, watching his face as she did, shifting her weight to match, he thought, his expression.

Still too much clothing between them. He grabbed awkwardly at material, got hold of her jumper and drew it up, over, let it fall beside the couch. Her white blouse had hiked up with the jumper's removal, showing an expanse of her ribs and tummy over plain white briefs. They looked amazingly sexy on her.

She locked her arms around him again, her lips seeking his. He contented himself for a while with just kissing her, with them rocking together while the houseboat rocked more imperceptibly beneath them. No conversation; they'd have had to stop kissing for that. He explored the silky backs of her thighs and her firm, cotton-clad rear end, tickled her behind the knees. She skimmed her small hands over his chest and shoulders and arms the way she might have stroked velvet or fur, for the sheer tactile pleasure.

They shifted positions slightly, so that now he lay beneath her on the couch while they shared slow, delicious kisses to match their slow, sensual movements against one another. One of her feet slid its instep up and down the denim along the side of his calf. She had to recognize his erection; instead of either sliding modestly away or attacking his jeans to get at him, she simply took it in stride.

Mary Margaret? Yeah, Mary Margaret. This didn't seem at all wrong... in fact, he couldn't remember mere petting ever feeling so deep-down right. So honest.

At one point, as she nibbled at his lower lip, eyes shining down at his, she caught the hand he'd slid to the side of her thigh and drew it back up to the edge of her panties. "I like that," she murmured huskily against his lips. He thought she blushed. If so, she hid it by kissing down his jaw, down his neck, across his collarbone, while his fingers did more of what she liked. He liked it, too.

At another point, when she settled her weight too heavily onto just the wrong part of him, a muffled "Uh-uh, *chère*" had her shifting again, nibbling his ear in apology.

Who'd have thought their ability to play so well together as kids—

Guy decided not to think about them as kids, and started unbuttoning her shirt. She obligingly propped herself up, away from his bare chest, never breaking her slow, erotic rhythm atop him.

His jeans might need to be surgically removed, at this rate. She wore no bra to hide her beautiful breasts, and made approving noises as he worshiped them, whether he used his hands or his mouth, the edge of her blouse brushing his cheek.

She got experimental and reached behind and beneath her, tracing the inseam of his jeans with her fingernails. He nearly bucked off the sofa. When his eyes, which had shut at the momentary overload of sensation, drifted back open, she smiled mischievously at him.

She tried it again. Same result.

He narrowed his eyes back at her and slipped fingers beneath the elastic edge of her panties. All mischief drained from her elfin face, replaced by an awe that was almost funny to see.

Things were about to get really, really good.

That was when, in an uncharacteristic flash of forethought, he remembered that his only condoms were in his shaving kit, out in one of his bike's saddlebags.

CHAPTER TEN

"You can't go out there," insisted Mary.

They'd retreated to separate corners of the sofa, but their breathing still rasped audibly. Her pulse pounded through her like white-water rapids. Her skin still tingled from wonderful, delicious contact against his.

Guy's blue eyes looked overly bright; his movements seemed distracted. "You don't know," he managed to say, his words oddly thick, "that there's even anything out there."

Men! "You're willing to risk your life to find out?"

"The bike's not a hundred feet away, in the middle of nowhere. I'll sprint. What could happen in a hundred feet?"

"You'd be amazed at what might attack a person along that path." When he wouldn't look at her, because his eyes kept dropping to her bosom, she pulled the edges of her blouse together. Actually, though, she felt amazingly natural sitting half-dressed with him. Comfortable—except for the throbbing frustration of not touching him, of his not touching her.

Just as well, maybe. Hadn't she been glad, just this evening, that she *hadn't* slept with him before? Her every move seemed determined to compound her future misery if he left again.

When he left again. But she wouldn't think about that.

Guy swallowed, shifted. "Even if you're on the pill—"

She tried not to laugh, didn't think he'd take it well. "I don't even drink caffeine," she reminded him. "And don't even *consider* the rhythm method, altar boy."

"I wasn't considering either one." He thought for a moment. "Look, the bike isn't that far—"

"No!" She didn't like that he glared at her. If only he didn't have to risk death to get protection, she'd love to make love to him. She had wanted this wholeheartedly—while she still had a whole heart. But he could too easily break it.

"I thought men generally carried those things in their wallets." She sighed, her body slowly realizing the disappointment in store for it.

"They deteriorate that way." Guy shifted positions again, planting his feet on the floor to rest his elbows on his knees. "Hell, the ones on the bike may not be so good, either. I haven't needed one for over a year." He said this last part defensively, like she'd thought him some kind of slut puppy.

Which reminded her of something else she should probably let him know, if they meant to ever try this again; she couldn't bear to think they wouldn't. "I've got you beat," she said teasingly, drawing her knees up to her chest and wrapping her arms around them.

"Yeah?" He looked at her. "How long?"

Go on; it's just Guy. "At least twenty-four years?"

His mouth actually fell open. "You mean *never* . . . ?"

She shrugged feigned nonchalance. "This lifetime, anyway."

Guy continued to stare. Then he swallowed. "Why not?"

She winced at his unintended claim to normalcy; she hadn't asked why he *had,* now had she? "Never got around to it."

He glanced away, then surreptitiously propped his bare foot on the edge of the coffee table, effectively hiding his lap from her with a raised leg, before looking back. Even then, he didn't seem to want to meet her gaze. "Were you...saving yourself?"

"It's not a morality thing for me, I have nothing against making love. Or people who make love." She wished he would look at her. "I'm careful, that's all. Not abnormal, or incomplete, or..." She unfolded out of her corner of the sofa and scooted over to his. Touched his cheek to draw his face back to hers. Met the uncertainty in his blue eyes. Then she kissed him.

After a moment's hesitation, he kissed her back. His embrace caught her weight as together they deepened the kiss, nearly loosing the almost dormant passion they'd barely dammed up the first time. Guy seemed to recognize the danger at the same time she did, and they pulled apart in unison.

He quickly stood, and paced to the wall by the door. His naked chest rose and fell with his ragged breathing. Mary had to close her hands into fists, to convince them that they couldn't have him. Had there been a point—? Oh, yeah.

"I'm not repressed," she insisted, and he shook his head dumbly. "I'm just cautious." So many kids in high school had thought nothing could happen to them, thought they were immortal. But she had learned, too early and too hard, that nobody was immune to bad things happening. Nobody was immortal.

"Besides, I never felt close enough to anyone I dated," she admitted. "Why hurry things until the right—"

He *looked* at her, eyes wide. She'd meant to say "the right time," but he apparently thought she'd meant "the right man." If she had one, Guy obviously didn't want to be it. The rejection hurt even worse than she'd feared.

He turned back to her abruptly. "Um, Mary, I've got to get out of here." He actually grabbed up his shirt, jacket, duffel.

She shook her head.

"Look, I've got this—" He reached into his jacket pocket with his free hand, to pull out something . . . then stared at it. He poured several white, jagged pieces onto her coffee table. The shell amulet had broken.

Maybe because he'd already used it? She remembered the tarot reading, the danger she'd sensed, and now her pulse sped for reasons other than passion. "No. You can't leave."

His reaching hand encompassed their intimacy and frustration—and something more personal for him, something she could only guess at. Guilt? "No offense, *chère*, but this is becoming hell-like."

"You promised."

He closed his eyes; it was almost a wince. She supposed they could at least relieve the frustration; there were alternatives she wouldn't mind exploring. She felt comfortable with bodies—she was a massage therapist! But he didn't want her, so she didn't suggest it. Good thing they'd quit. Really.

Especially if he meant to all but commit suicide over a gold doubloon.

Guy had never spent a longer night than on Mary Deveraux's sofa. Hour after hour of darkness passed as he listened to the rain on the roof. Several times he heard Mary sigh in the bedroom, probably rolling over in her sleep.

Maybe thinking about their short-lived passion? He knew *he* was . . . but as much as their petting, he remembered the bomb she'd dropped. She hadn't *acted* like a virgin. Then again, what did virgins act like? There wasn't a secret handshake or anything to identify them, right?

She'd acted like Mary. That was how he thought about her—witch or not, virgin or not, she was just Mary. The same Mary he'd hung around with as a kid. The same Mary he'd already become dangerously fond of since returning to Stagwater.

When they were kids, he'd felt vaguely responsible for her, being both older and the boy. He'd felt responsible for Lazare, too, and look where that had gotten them. He didn't want to feel responsible for anyone anymore. That she had almost let him become not just her lover, but her first, scared him. How much he found he wanted it, deserving or not, scared him a lot more.

Mary mumbled something unintelligibly low, and her bedsprings creaked.

Fais do-do, Guillaume. Go to sleep. But too much had happened to allow that. The coin. Bobby Lee Picou. The Reaper.

He heard the rain lessen, and frowned at a new sound outside; a shuffling. He sat up on the couch, the blanket Mary had left with him falling to his waist. He could make out the square of the window in the faint illumination of her roof-mounted anchor light reflecting off the water. Nothing moved in front of it. But the faint sound continued, almost as if something were pacing slowly, awkwardly, along the bank. Guy pushed the blanket off and stood, went to the window, even as the shuffling receded. He reached for the shade, began to pull it—

An almost tangible misery punched him in the solar plexus—a wailing, a moaning, a sense of grueling loss. The shade fell from numb fingers as he backed instinctively away. Despair. Whoever made that sound despaired. Too late, always too late.

And then, nothing. Except a soft, frightened voice from the bedroom. "Guy?"

Four steps carried him to her doorway; she'd sat up in bed, her elfin face pale, her hair mussed. Had the evening turned out differently, he might well be in bed beside her, smoothing back her hair, reassuring her, drawing her body back against his. Tempting, so tempting, to cross the threshold into her bedroom, sit on the edge of the bed, gather her into his arms and tell her everything would be okay.

Too tempting. And besides, he would probably be lying.

"Whatever it was, it's gone," he assured her instead, backing away from her doorway, from the problems that lay beyond if he let himself get too close to the woman within. She lay back down, taking him at his word, but she didn't close her eyes. He could drown in her eyes. He shouldn't. "Go back to sleep."

One of them might as well.

The night songs of the woods and the bayou resumed as he lay down on the sofa again. Their lullaby didn't work. He continued to stare into the semidarkness, waiting for dawn to release him from Mary's enforced "protection." He thought about his roofing job on his parents' old house, then about Rand Garner's plans for expanding his cottage. Water gurgled somewhere beneath him, and he began to plan how someone could build a better houseboat for Mary. Use heavy-industrial plastic barrels for floatation, instead of metal ones that rusted. Maybe manage an A-frame, with her bedroom on the second story...

Eventually the darkness outside the window turned pale gray, and the local birds began to make their own racket. Guy forced himself to his feet, staggered to her tiny bathroom and splashed cold water on his face until he felt lucid. A whole night without sleep—and that hadn't been the worst of his frustrations.

Give it up, Poitiers. He had too much to do today already. Stock up for maybe a week in the swamp. Get his dog back from Rand's assistant. Borrow the canoe for longer, and maybe a shotgun, too. After all, even if he left by tonight, he'd probably have to survive several more nights in the swamp before he found the source of the coin. *If* he found the source.

He peeked through Mary's open doorway, and a softness eased into his chest as he caught sight of her, still asleep, hugging her pillow as if maybe, just maybe, she'd wished it was him.

He'd maybe be safe here, tonight... except that he might not get any more sleep than he just had. And not in lieu of more erotic activities, either. Mary's affection gave him one more thing to lose, one more reason not to track the coin— and he couldn't allow himself that luxury. If he didn't help Lazare's soul, what would be left of his own?

He made himself turn away, quietly put on his shirt, boots, and jacket, hoist his duffel and slip outside onto her deck, into the stillness of early morning. Somewhere nearby, a woodpecker drummed a hollow tattoo. Birds cawed, sang, chirped. He heard something splash in the water of the bayou, near the houseboat.

He'd kept his promise to Mary, he reminded himself, taking the path to the dead-end road. He'd stayed all night, even after she wouldn't help him trace the coin. So why did he feel guilty?

When he reached his bike, he didn't just feel guilty.

Mud coated it, wheel to wheel, rearview mirror and helmet.

He felt suddenly vulnerable—and very lucky. He wasn't psychic, but he suspected that even if he had gone for condoms last night, he and Mary wouldn't have consummated their attraction.

She had been right again. He wouldn't have made it back.

Mary knew as soon as her eyes opened that he was gone. A cynic, like Brie's husband, Steve, might say she could tell because she couldn't hear Guy moving or breathing, but it was more than that. She could feel the emptiness in her home.

She almost cried again.

She made herself get up anyway; reminded herself that Guy was his own person and that she had no hold on him. She'd tried to advise him in this, she'd warned him against seeking out the source of this evil, but he wouldn't listen. She'd done what she could by keeping him safe last night. The rest was up to him. Right?

She got to work late. She felt out of sorts. She did three massages, and had to give herself silent pep talks to keep from resenting her clients for not being Guy. Not good. Who knew what kind of energy she might leak into these people, if she didn't get a grip? Healing energy wasn't the only power that could be transferred through the laying on of hands, after all.

She wondered if maybe she should have agreed to do the trance for him, agreed to try to pinpoint the coin. She certainly hadn't dissuaded him, with her refusal.

She also wondered if maybe she should have let him go out to his bike last night, and how she'd feel today if he'd done so safely—or if she kept protection—and they hadn't stopped.

Probably a heck of a lot better than she did right now, except that he would still be gone.

She decided that at a time like this a woman really needed her friends. Then she remembered how very happy and in love Brigit and Sylvie each were. Her older sister had also found wedded bliss, and her younger sister was engaged. None of them would likely be able to soothe her bruised heart.

In desperation, she telephoned Cypress Bernard.

"Now, I'm no psychic," Cy admitted as the waiter left with their orders and their menus. Mary didn't bother to argue that everyone—even an earthy, grounded person—was psychic. They'd been over this before. "But I've got a baaad feeling about this."

Mary had related most of what she knew on their drive to the Indian restaurant in Slidell. Now she wondered if spicy had been the way to go. "You think Guy's in danger too?"

"Guy Poitiers can go ahead and take care of Guy Poitiers, honey. It's you I'm worried about." Cy shrugged out of her suit coat, then rested her tawny forearms on the azure tablecloth. Sitar music twanged in the background; the rich scent of curry mixed with other spices around them. "I talked to Brie."

Odd change of subject. "Is she okay? The baby?"

"Mama and baby are doing just fine, but when I told her I was taking you to lunch, she passed on a tidbit from that newspaper editor of hers. Bobby Lee Picou's parents have reported their son missing, just like his friend went missing. Except the friend—Earl someone—isn't missing anymore. A fisherman found him dead, drowned in some runoff."

Mary remembered the brief, frightening vision she'd received in her kitchen last night. *Something had shuffled closer....* But that had already happened. She couldn't have done anything, could she? "Bobby Lee's dead, too," she admitted. "I saw."

And Guy was next.

Cy took a sip of water, cleared her throat. She looked tired. "You know, most mundanes would hear that your stud muffin went to see Picou last night, in a not-so-nice mood, and might put two and two together to make five." She shook her head, soothing, as Mary's eyes widened. Was Guy a suspect? "Brie said to tell you, nobody else will hear it from her or Steve—that boy's coming 'round. And you already knew Rand was okay."

Mary sank back against the booth's vinyl back, relieved that Guy didn't have to face both legal and otherworldly danger, and that her friends trusted him, or at least her character assessment of him, enough not to suspect him themselves. "I don't know what to do."

Cy cocked her head, quirked an eyebrow. "Don't you?"

"Okay, yes. I know that I want to help him, that I have to help him. Joey died, too, you know."

"Mm-hmm... Sylvie and Brie might not know it, but yes, I do know. I went to the funeral then, too." Cy's mention of the funeral hardly bothered Mary at all.

Joey wasn't the main reason she wanted to help.

"We're witches, too," Mary pointed out. "Back when Sylvie realized there was a werewolf on the prowl, we helped her, because we might have been the only ones who could."

"Also true. And you know we'll help you and Guy Poitiers. If you want us to do a binding spell, to try to limit this Reaper thing's powers, we'll do it. If you want us to do a protection spell for Guy, we'll do it—with his permission, of course. If you want us to channel energy to you while you go into a trance and try to see where that coin came from, we'll be with you. The full moon's energies are with us through Saturday's equinox."

"I think..." Mary paused, looking at her hands; she hadn't swayed herself yet. How could she convince her friend? "I think I should go with him."

"Girl, you must be crazy in love."

Mary shook her head without thinking. "I find things best when I'm the one looking for them, like that game where someone says you're cold or you're warm or now you're really hot—my instincts do the same thing." She ventured a glance at Cypress, who waited, arms folded, to be convinced. "The cards didn't show me in any danger."

"For now. The future can change for the worse as easily as for the better." Cy really did look tired, drawn; Mary studied her with a healer's eye.

"Are you all right? You seem kind of down. Drained, even."

"And you," countered her friend, "are just trying to change the subject. Things have been busy since the buy-out, and we're all working really hard, but I will be fine. It's you we're talking about."

"But we're not just talking about me, are we?" Mary fidgeted with her spoon, stared at her upside-down reflection. "We're talking about me and Guy."

"If you're talking about you and Guy going into that swamp, you aren't getting my approval." Cypress sighed, and reluctantly relaxed her posture. "But you know you've got my support."

"I haven't decided yet," Mary admitted. She did want to help him, very much. But to go into the middle of watery nowhere, hunted by a creature that drowned its victims, wasn't sane—was it? "I really haven't."

"Let me know when you do decide," instructed Cypress, digging into her purse. "And you be careful, you hear?"

Mary attempted a brave smile. "Nothing's going to get us." She wouldn't let it. *Guy* wouldn't let it.

Cypress leaned across the table, pressed several foil packets into Mary's hand, and winked at her. "That, too."

By time she left work, Mary still didn't know what to do. So she let her subconscious take over, while she drove, and ended up at the boat landing, on the river. When she slid to the clamshell-covered ground, her driver's door didn't creak the way it usually did. Guy must have oiled it. The truck ran better, too.

She shut the door and took a deep breath, letting the scent of water and mud and new foliage fill her lungs for a minute, before she walked down the rutted, muddy road to the boat launch.

River water the color of creamed coffee lapped higher than normal against the concrete incline, from which boats on trailers could be set afloat. The slanted light of the approaching sunset sparkled off the surface, though, muddy or not. It cut through raggedy drapings of gray Spanish moss, and fell in pretty patterns through the leaves of trees and vines to speckle the ground and the river. And the bayou, she thought, looking at the trees that marked the other side of the river, the insubstantial bank. And the swamp.

A blue heron flew by, neck slightly bowed, and a holy feeling filled her, as if the arms of Mother Nature surrounded everything in sight. She shouldn't be afraid. Nature had an order. You were born, you lived, you died, and you were reborn—in one form or another, anyway. Rain fell to the earth, became rivers or lakes, then evaporated upward to become rain again.

But it still scared her. Death still scared her. She feared meeting it face-to-face—and not just in the form of the skeletal assassin of Bobby Lee Picou's fantasies.

She didn't want to lose the people she loved. And she didn't want to watch Guy Poitiers die.

But her only other choice might be to not watch.

She took another deep breath, watching the play of light on the water, letting the reflections blur and reform into images, like a movie screen in her mind. She tried to see Guy....

Here, just as she'd suspected. He wrestled an aluminum canoe toward the landing. He looked weary, and determined.

She blinked, returned to the present, reoriented herself to her surroundings. It hadn't happened yet. Tomorrow morning, she thought. That was what she wanted to know. She let her mind's eye skim over other questions.... Where was he now? Close, but not at his family's home. Hers? Her heart leaped, but wishful thinking had overwhelmed precognition in that. Not hers. Safe?

Yes. Wherever he was, he seemed to have found a way to be safe. And he would be here tomorrow morning. She'd seen it.

But she was putting off the hardest part. The coin. She took another deep breath, became one with all things and all times. Her dislike of looking into the past rippled through her...instead of fighting it, she pushed through it. It felt like a river flowing upstream for her, though; like the sun setting in the east. Widdershins, witches called such counterclockwise movement. But, like everything, it had its place in the Lady's world. The coin...

And then she felt it, a dark tug deep within her—*you're warm.* Yes, it had come from here, from the river, the bayous, the swamp. It had come from *there.* She turned slightly, to match her internal compass, then opened her eyes and looked at the already deepening shadows of the sunset swamp.

It came from in there... and she could find it.

She just didn't know if she should.

The heavy wooden door swung silently open, and Guy stepped into Ste. Jeanne d'Arc Catholic Church. He'd half expected to find it locked. He guessed God took care of these things.

The door shut behind him and echoed.

The smell of old incense tickled at his nose, along with the richness of wax, the lemon tang of furniture polish. Sunset cast streaks of color through the stained-glass windows on the west side of the church, across gleaming pews, across the sparkling bank of votives where Tante Eva had lit her candle for Lazare. Above the altar hung a representation of the risen Christ, arms lifted as if extending blessings upon the world. A holy place.

Maybe he shouldn't be here.

He didn't know where else to go.

He stepped farther inside, dipped his right hand in the holy-water font and genuflected, crossing himself with long-practiced, if long-denied, ease. His footsteps echoed back at him from the high ceilings as he headed up the aisle, then slid into a pew and knelt. His family used to take this pew; the Deveraux family had sat just in front of them. He'd once tied Mary's braids together here, during the profession of faith. Not a week ago, they'd stood here together for Lazare's funeral. Part of the natural order, he remembered. Baptisms, first communions, confirmations, marriages and funerals. Once he'd started high school, and his hormones had kicked in, he used to play with the idea of marrying some local girl here at Ste. Jeanne. Maybe even Mary Margaret, though at the time he would rather have eaten a bug than admit it. That had been before he lapsed— "strayed," Ralph liked to say, because that implied he might return at any time. That had been before Mary became a witch. That was before the *couchemal*, and the disappearances in Picayune, and Bobby Lee Picou's Reaper.

Today he found the possibility of his funeral far likelier than his wedding.

He raised his face toward the figure of Christ almost in a challenge. Suicide was a mortal sin, but he didn't mean this to be suicidal. Sure, two men from Picayune had vanished and were probably dead. And, yes, he had almost smelled the death that had lurked around his motorcycle, this morning. But he wasn't going into this hoping to die.

He just wouldn't let the fear of death stop him from doing what he had to do.

It wasn't like he had much of a future, anyway; he hadn't worked toward one. Unless he could square things with the past, he wouldn't be able to *make* a future, either. His inability to save Lazare and Joey eleven years ago, his inability to somehow answer Lazare's echoing pleas now, would just eat away at him. He'd make life miserable for anyone around him, too.

Anyone specific?

He slid out of the pew and moved to the cast-iron rack of votive candles, dug into his pocket for a bill and slipped it in the collection box. Only after he'd knelt and bowed his head for a moment did he realize he wasn't exactly sure what he wanted to pray for. Lazare, of course. Himself. Even Mary. That everything would turn out as it should, even if he wasn't sure what that might mean.

That he would be able to handle whatever happened.

The angle of colored light across him warned of the approaching sunset; he had to get to the safety of Rand Garner's cottage, securely warded by Garner's witch wife, before darkness fell. Guy struck a match, lit a votive candle. Still stumped for the right prayer, exactly, he turned to an old and easy phrase he'd known since childhood: "Thy will be done."

Then he crossed himself—in the name of the Father, the Son, and the Holy Spirit—and rose, moved across the marble floor toward the exit from this sanctuary, toward the approaching night. He felt better. Not more confident, really. Just better.

Maybe he should try attending a service again.

Assuming he lived.

CHAPTER ELEVEN

She found him exactly where she'd envisioned him, awkwardly hauling an aluminum canoe from the top of an unfamiliar Jeep, toward the dawn-lit water. Hearing her truck, he lowered the boat to the ground and watched her park.

She set the parking brake, cut the engine and took a deep breath. She should've gotten over her fear of rejection some time ago. Yet, as she returned the gaze of the tall man at the landing, his hair burnished gold in the streaks of rising sunlight that cut over the heavy treeline, Mary feared just that.

Even if he were the one who'd asked for help.

Nothing to it but to do it. She opened her door and slid out, pleased to see Guy's little dog scamper toward her, its tail whipping back and forth. It greeted her with the warbling bark peculiar to hounds, then darted back toward its master.

Mary raised her hand in greeting.

Guy returned the gesture. He wore jeans—as usual—and a faded purple LSU sweatshirt with the sleeves butchered off near the shoulder. He looked good. What a surprise.

She fixed a smile on her face, willing some confidence around herself, and headed down the rutted mud-and-shells drive to where he waited. "I changed my mind," she announced. "It's a person's prerogative, right?"

"How'd you find me?" he asked, after gazing at her, lids heavy, just long enough to make her insides flutter.

She wiggled her nose at him, like the classic television witch. He grinned—she suspected in spite of himself. "Let me help you carry that." She grasped one end of the canoe. With a shrug, Guy hoisted his end—closer to the middle than hers, so that he took more of the weight—and together they carried the boat to the brown water's edge.

"You'll head me in the right direction, then?" Guy asked as he slid the canoe into the water, catching its lead rope to secure on a handy pole. "I thought you felt it was too dangerous."

"I still do," she admitted, following him as he headed back toward the truck he'd driven.

"Not to mention," added Guy, "that the Reaper would pay for his sins without my help." His voice sounded just a little smart-alecky, as if he were mimicking her.

"I didn't say that, exactly. And I'm still not out for vengeance. But revenge isn't the same as stopping it."

"Could be," he warned. They reached the Jeep—borrowed, she suspected, with one of her flashes of insight—and he extracted two large trash bags, handing each to her. A tent, she decided, from the weight and feel of the first one, and something squooshy—a sleeping bag. He'd wrapped both against the possibility of capsizing. Then he lifted out a cooler and a rifle case.

She stared at the rifle case for a moment, then looked back up at him. He met her gaze evenly. She didn't oppose guns, exactly, but unlike some of her friends, she wasn't comfortable with them, either. She didn't like being around them. Especially not right after someone had been talking about vengeance.

The angle of his head, the directness of his eyes, warned her not even to start this argument. She decided she'd better prioritize her fights—save the big guns, so to speak, for the more immediate issues. Instead of commenting on the rifle, she turned and carried his sleeping bag and tent toward the canoe.

He followed, his long stride keeping up with her easily, while the dog scampered from the water's edge to them and back several times. "So... which direction should I take?"

Once she'd deposited her loads into the canoe, she pointed in the general direction she'd felt the tug before. "Thata-way."

He snorted, loading his supplies. "A bit vague, eh?"

"That's why I'm coming with you."

She almost laughed at his expression. Almost. She'd made it halfway back to her truck before he caught up with her, so he must have stood there, poleaxed, for at least a min-ute. *"What?"*

"Coming with you." Opening her passenger door, she retrieved her own sleeping bag and passed it back to him, then grabbed two duffel bags. She used her hip to shut the door. "Do you have any more sacks? I didn't think about waterproofing."

"I don't remember inviting you along, Mary Margaret."

"You asked for my help," she reminded him.

"I didn't mean, you come with me. I meant, you tell me where to go and I'll go there."

She grinned. She could tell him where to go, all right. But southern ladies—even, or especially, witches, were more re-fined. "It's more complicated than that. At this point, I only have a general impression. But as we get closer, my sense of the coin's source should grow stronger. You can't have my magic—" she added her duffels to the small pile in the middle of the canoe "—without having me."

"Well, I don't need the responsibility of 'having you,'" he told her testily. "I'll find the place on my own. Now, ei-ther you take your bags back, or I'll leave with them."

"I get to come, too," she warned him.

"I'm the one with the boat."

"I can borrow a skiff and find you before the day's out. Same way I can find where that coin came from."

He folded his arms; why did this scene feel vaguely fa-miliar to her? "I," he pointed out, "can go faster."

"But I—" she planted her hands on her cutoff-clad hips "—will have some idea of where I'm going."

Staring contest. Judging from the squawks and caws, trills and warbles, the rising sun had woken every bird within miles. The air held a faint chill. Adventure . . . or danger?

"Joey died, too," she reminded him—and won.

"You always were a pest," Guy muttered, striding back toward the vehicles. "I'll get you those extra trash bags."

She found herself admiring his retreating jeans pockets, and quickly turned her attention to the dog. At least Guy knew when he was licked.

So to speak.

From the moment Guy pushed the canoe into the river, wobbling it as he stepped in and took the aft seat, Mary decided she would enjoy at least part of this trip. The suspended, buoyant sensation felt both familiar—she lived on the water, after all—and liberating, since this time she had no houseful of belongings around her. This time it was just her, Guy, the dog, and a mound of plastic-wrapped supplies between them.

Just them, and the swamp.

But then, they must have canoed together as children, right? She didn't bother tracking down the specific memory, but they got the hang of working together almost immediately, and hardly zigzagged at all.

For the first half hour or so, as the sun rose higher, they stayed on the main river. Oak, river birch and black willow trees crowded together, greedy for sunlight, on the banks. The occasional piece of clothing tied to a tree marked trotlines, and more than once a distant buzz alerted them to an approaching motorboat. Most slowed down to pass them. Once a skiff bounced by at high speed, its fore end high out of the water, and Guy had to steer the canoe quickly into the wake to better handle the jostling waves. Even in silent water, sudsy spots on the surface indicated the recent passing of faster boats.

Mary wondered why Guy hadn't borrowed one of those. But then they passed under a highway, through the muffled echoes of cars overhead. It was like passing through a huge gate framed by concrete supports, a gate into...where? That was when she felt the tug, felt their uncertain destination change.

"We need to go left," she called back, careful not to lean.

Being in back made steering his job. "Port it is," he answered, and slanted them in that direction. They'd passed several channels and sloughs opening off the main river. He took the next one that presented itself.

That was when their surroundings slowly changed. The sunseeking trees gave way to more pines, many leaning or exposing tangled roots where they overhung the bank. Cypress trees clustered in the water where no banks existed. When the bayou narrowed, sunlight became a more sporadic companion, returning only when the channel widened again. The yellow and purple of wild jasmine and wisteria sometimes joined ivy and Spanish moss in swarming over the plentiful trees; occasionally an early red trumpet flower flashed orange through the woods' shadow. Duckweed, the tiny floating plant that would by summer carpet whole bayous, clustered, despite the early season, in green puddles around floating bits of driftwood or in still pools away from the main channel. Other boats existed only as a distant buzz; at one point, a distant putting motor echoed its bass tattoo like Indian or voudun drums—either of which could have thrummed through this swamp at some point in its past.

Then even those were silenced, leaving Mary and Guy with the hushed sound of birds and wildlife, the dip of their paddles and the spattering of water as they lifted those paddles from the water for another stroke. *As if we were traveling back in time,* Mary thought with a shudder. The last place she wanted to go.

Perhaps Guy felt the same. When he finally ventured conversation, he chose the past. "Do you ever think about it?"

Dip. Pull. Lift. Spatter. "What?"

"The day it happened."

The day...? Oh. *That* day. "Nope."

"Never?"

"Positive thoughts attract a positive reality," she told him. "Negative thoughts don't. I don't want to remember it."

His silence indicated that he was considering that. "It still happened, whether you remember it or not."

"You enjoy remembering it?"

"Only one part," he admitted, as if posing a riddle. She almost wondered at what he could possibly have enjoyed about that awful day. Then she caught herself, and scowled.

Too bad he couldn't see it.

"I keep wishing," said Guy, more seriously, "that there was something I could have done. You know? If I hadn't left them alone, or if I'd gotten back faster, or even heard one of them yell."

Dip. Pull. Lift. Spatter. "It's not your fault."

"I know that."

"We couldn't—" No. Change that. "*You* couldn't have known something would happen." Maybe *she* could have. But she hadn't.

Dip. Pull. Lift. Spatter.

"Hey." Cold water droplets rained across her sun-warmed shoulders, and she cringed, more from surprise than from displeasure. The dog—Guy had named her Drifter—barked in delight at the play, and Mary wobbled the canoe, twisting around to stare at Guy.

He didn't quite smile at her—didn't look to be in a smiling mood. But his eyes crinkled encouragement. "It's not your fault," he echoed.

She felt herself softening beneath his gaze, and turned back to the canoe's prow.

"I didn't mean that I *should have* helped," Guy explained from behind her. "Just that I wish I *could have*. I'd give years off my life to have been able to do something.

Something, so they could have grown up, gone to high school, played baseball, discovered girls . . ."

Each word, each image, struck at her. "Please don't."

Dip. Pull. Lift. Spatter. They had to detour around some encroaching cypress, and Mary ducked her head to avoid the shroud of gray Spanish moss draping from its branches, over the water. The side of the canoe scraped against one of the numerous "knees," above-water roots that surrounded the trees.

She tried to soften her reaction. "I don't like to think about it. I don't want to. Don't you understand?"

Dip. Pull. Lift. Spatter. "I just thought maybe you should know why we're doing this." Guy's voice sounded gruff— and very young. *I'm sorry.* But she didn't dare say it. If she apologized, he might think he could continue regaling her with the past. And she couldn't stand that.

Still, the idea worked at her like an incoming tide as the morning wore on. She directed them down several forks, some so narrow only a canoe or pirogue could make it through. Gliding even deeper into the swamp, aware that she should most confront the very things she feared, she had to wonder if one bogeyman at a time wasn't enough.

Apparently not. Long-neglected images of her youth, as if sensing the timelessness of this place, battered the mental barriers she'd set. Perhaps good memories—despite reminding her of what she'd lost—wouldn't hurt so terribly.

Once, when their combined families went to the Audubon Park Zoo, Lazare and Joey had gotten lost—Lazare's doing, of course. The older kids had split up into search parties, and Mary and Guy had gotten lost themselves. They'd pretended they were trekking the wilds of Africa, and between them had scrounged up enough money for a candy bar before TiBoy and Anne came across them.

More than once, Mary's dad and Guy's had driven both clans to Mississippi's Gulf Coast. She couldn't temporally separate the memories of splashing through salty, shallow green waves, digging in the sand to make castles or find buried treasure, trying to avoid jellyfish while collecting shells and hermit crabs. Usually both carloads of mixed children would get root-beer floats on the way home. She could remember the sweetness, and how sometimes, if she was in the same car as Joey and Lazare, the two little boys would fall asleep on top of one another like sandy puppies, before ever finishing their drinks. Guy had usually finished his float, and theirs, and sometimes hers. Though she had only sometimes ridden home with Joey and Lazy, she had almost always ridden home with Guy, sitting on gritty, damp towels and playing silly car games to keep from getting bored.

Mary began to notice a pattern here.

She'd lain upstairs in bed, sick with the mumps, and listened to her mother tell Guy that no, Mary couldn't come play. Later, her mother had brought up some wildflowers Guy had picked, to help Mary get better. She couldn't have been more than six.

Memories of church included Guy. Memories of afterschool adventures included Guy. Guy had explained to her why her bunny had died. Guy had taught her to swim. They'd spied on TiBoy and Anne, when their siblings briefly dated, and giggled themselves silly when the teenagers kissed. And then, several years later, when Guy's voice had started to change and he'd gone from skinny to lanky... Yes. She could remember him towing her along the bank of the bayou, rolling his eyes at Joey and Lazare, who were chanting in the background: "Gilly and Mary, sitting in a tree..."

They hadn't actually kissed, though, had they? They'd thought about it, and almost had, but then TiBoy had pulled up—

Mary stopped paddling for a moment, her mind reeling from the memory. Lazare and Joey had died that day. She and Guy had slipped away to talk about her starting high school, and he'd invited her to the first dance, and they'd almost kissed, but then the tragedy had wrenched all that away—

"Need a break?" asked Guy. His voice made her jump, because the sorrow of his absence had filled her once again, so thick she could drown in it. No wonder she'd stopped remembering; doing so, she'd avoided not only the pain of Joey's death, but also the pain of having lost her other half.

Guy.

Little good the realization did her now. He'd gone away, they'd never had their dance, and now he'd become someone else. Someone she could no longer count on to always be there. She might never count on someone for that again.

"Mary?" he prompted, helping draw her back from the past as surely as he'd tossed her into it.

"Uh-huh." She looked around her again. Spiky palmetto, elephant ears and arrowhead plants overgrew the banks. So did climbing blackberry briars, prickly despite their white flowers, and saw-edged cut-grass. And she wore shorts

"Farther up, I think," suggested Guy, as if reading her mind. This time, she merely nodded, not trusting her voice.

Time had become a very ethereal concept, in the swamp.

She would *not*, Guy thought, have been able to catch up with him in a skiff. For one thing, he could tell Mary was more tired than him. It was barely time for lunch, and he already felt incredibly stiff and tired. For another thing, they'd at least once maneuvered through waters that a skiff couldn't manage.

He wondered how Lazare could have possibly made it this far. Then he remembered how very stubborn his younger cousin had been—and that Lazare had been gone a week.

They stopped for lunch on a fair-size natural ridge—he couldn't see where the water started on the other side of it, at least. He didn't go looking. If Mary said they hadn't gotten very close to the source of the coin yet, then he believed her.

He'd always believed her about psychic stuff like that. He'd known about her abilities long before he learned they were anything special. In his family, TiBoy could fix broken machines, Ralph made friends easily, and Guy excelled at sports. In her family—among the siblings old enough to be interesting, anyway—Simon was a brain, Anne was considered beautiful, and Mary was magic. Just like little Joey had been the angel of the group, and Lazare had been the hellion.

Once beached, they separated long enough to take care of personal matters, then ate peanut/butter sandwiches together—this being Friday, he couldn't have the jerky he'd packed. He'd brought a canteen and a few beers, and she'd brought bottled water and juices; they downed their drink of choice. But they didn't get up right off.

She didn't look like she wanted to move any more than he did. He found himself watching her, glad she'd worn cutoffs so that he could admire her firm, sexy legs. Her blue tank top did the same for her shoulders, and for those relatively new curves of hers that kept surprising him. Bits of sunlight, strained through pine boughs high above them, puddled across her, turning her hair and eyes golden. They hadn't talked much, except for their not-quite-argument about the boys' deaths. But he realized he would be feeling very lonely by now if she hadn't come along.

He just wished her companionship didn't entail such responsibility. He'd made this trip to clean his slate, so to speak. If somehow he managed to get Mary Margaret hurt, too...

He reminded himself that she was a grown woman, that her decisions remained her own. It didn't fully work. He'd been born two years earlier, and she'd always tagged after him, and that made her as much his responsibility as a younger sister. But more dangerous, because she wasn't his younger sister.

He found the strength to cast off again.

The bayou they followed—one of who knew how many uncharted passages threading around here-and-gone ridges and islands—took them into a dead forest by late afternoon. Spanish moss had swarmed so thickly over the trees that they'd died from lack of light, gaunt and gray. The grayness reflected off the water. As if in sympathy, the sky began to dull itself with clouds. The wind picked up, sounding like rushing water through the trees, and drapings of phantomlike moss fluttered and danced.

Eerie. Very eerie.

Mary changed sides with her paddle. Guy switched to the opposite side, to balance them. "Did you know that authentic voudun dolls should be stuffed with Spanish moss?"

Apparently their surroundings had affected her, too. He played along. "Uh, no. I didn't know that." When she didn't say anything else, he had to ask. "You don't know this from personal experience, do you?"

She twisted around in her seat to grin at him. The canoe wobbled. "No," she said laughing. "But remind me to explain to you why voudun's gotten as bad a rap as witches have."

He sighed. "I can't wait."

She laughed again, turning forward. "I bet you can't."

And he found himself grinning, too. As if in response, the channel they followed veered away from the spectral sentinels of death. Though they'd never leave the moss behind, it thinned enough to allow life again. Pods and catkins hung on living cypress; pine trees edged the thin strip of sky above them. Vines—honeysuckle, jasmine, ivy—covered everything.

Mary pointed out an alligator, which rose silently from the brown water like a submarine, exposing first its eye ridge, then its rounded snout, and finally its long back and tail. An eight-footer, at least. Drifter started to bay at it, propping her paws on the side of the canoe, and Guy put his paddle down long enough to yank her back.

Alligators didn't generally attack human adults, especially not when it wasn't their nesting season. But small animals—or children—would be fair game. Not that he'd want to go swimming with one, either, no matter the statistics.

It surprised him that, instead of cringing back, Mary watched the gator for as long as she could. When it sank into the water, vanishing beneath the brown surface, she grinned back at Guy to share her excitement at the experience.

"I bet you wouldn't wear anything made out of gator skin, either, eh?" He dipped his paddle into the water again to hide his admiration of her unafraid enthusiasm.

"Absolutely not," she returned. "I'd be hypocritical if I only cared about the cute animals, wouldn't I?"

He shook his head. He might have to redefine his "bunny-hugger" stereotype of animal-rights folks.

Though their surroundings had brightened, the sky had darkened even more. A rare wind still made the tall, slim pines sway into one another, signaling approaching rain.

Maybe a storm. Great. Didn't that thing they wanted to stop—the thing that might be trying to kill him—like storms?

They finally stopped to make camp on another natural ridge, with enough high ground to support live oak trees, which weren't very water-adaptable—floods shouldn't pose a threat. Guy didn't miss how Mary practically hobbled from the canoe before he managed his tightrope-walker balancing act to the front himself and pulled the whole boat onto land. She started to unload their plastic-shrouded camping supplies before he finished tying the lead rope around a tree.

To lose the canoe, at this point of the trip, would be a very bad, very dangerous thing. Which reminded him of something. "Does anyone know you're out here?"

Her sigh, followed by an "Of course," eased several concerns—both about how her friends might be panicking, and about what kind of a woman she might have turned into. "I had to cancel some appointments at the Wellness Club," she admitted around an armful of trash bag, "so they know. And, well, actually, I didn't mention anything to the family, because they wouldn't expect to see me for another few days anyway. My friends can tell them, if I'm gone longer."

He couldn't begrudge her that. He'd let Rand Garner know his plans, since Rand had let him stay in his cottage last night anyway, but he hadn't called his family, either. How would he explain it? *I think some kind of monster killed Lazare, that Lazare's still haunting the swamp, and that it all hinges on a cursed gold coin. Hope to see you at Easter. Unless I'm dead.*

"Last night I had to convince Cy and Sylvie not to risk their jobs to come with us," Mary continued, depositing the last bag near a vaguely clear patch of land. "Even Brie considered it, baby or not."

He chose the bag most likely to contain the tent, and sure enough, it clanked. A glance toward the sky—what sky they could see through all the trees—warned him to hurry. "How'd you manage that?" he asked as he unrolled it.

Mary picked up two poles and slid them together, just the way they went. "I told them they'd be as much, if not more, help where they are. Which reminds me." She stopped assembling tent poles long enough to dig in to a pocket of her cutoffs. She swiveled her hips in a really sexy way when she did that. Guy couldn't have looked back to the tent if he wanted to.

"Here," she announced, freeing her hand from the denim at last, and held something out to him. "This is for you."

Belatedly he extended his hand for it.

She pressed a stone into his palm—a friendship rock, he realized, one with a hole naturally worn through it. She'd painted a symbol on it, similar to the one that had decorated the shell, like an upside-down peace sign without the circle.

"We charged that last night," she explained—he didn't think she meant like batteries. Or did she? "To replace the other amulet. It's for protection." Magical protection. She was a witch, as were her friends. Oddly, that seemed less disturbing here in the middle of nowhere. Less unlikely, even.

"What about you?" he asked.

"I've got my own protections," she assured him, starting to assemble more tent poles. They heard the plopping noise at the same time, and both saw the drop of water that hit the still-unassembled nylon of the tent.

"Uh-oh," she said, unnecessarily.

Guy shoved the stone—the amulet?—in his pocket and tackled the job of setting up the tent with more fervor. They did *not* beat the rain. Halfway through their rush, water running off his hair and down his neck and arms, frantically staking the tent pins and slipping the tent poles through their proper sleeves, Guy realized he didn't mind. Mary moved beside him, staking and slipping and raising with equal speed, getting just as drenched as he. They worked well together, he thought. They always had . . . but it would have seemed a lot to hope for, for that ease to follow them into adulthood.

Once they'd gotten the tent up, they raced each other to throw their assorted bags and supplies into their man-made shelter before they could dive in, dripping and laughing, bits of pine needles and leaves sticking to Mary's bare legs, to Guy's arms. He whistled for Drifter, who scurried in after them, and only then zipped the tent flap shut.

"It's not just a campout," he panted. "It's an adventure." Then he looked at their cramped, temporary home, supplies strewn every which way, mud already tracked in, rain beating steadily on the nylon above them. Mary had flopped down next to him, against the trash sack containing either his or her sleeping bag, still laughing. Her hair dribbled across her elfin face; her sprawled, bare legs glistened with the wet; her tank top molded far too intimately

over her breasts. He knew he should look away. The heat
that rose in him, despite the chill of the storm outside, made
that clear. If he didn't look away very soon, he was going to
have a really frustrating night.

When she cocked her head at his silence, confused, he
attempted a grin and quickly turned away to rearrange their
belongings so that nothing touched the sides of the tent to
conduct water—and so that he could get a grip on his very
physical reaction to her. He would have a frustrating night
anyway, he decided, because he had had no idea Mary
would accompany him and therefore had not packed with
her in mind.

Even if he had, the mind-numbing exhaustion that crept
through his abused body, now that they'd averted crisis,
should have kept him from suggesting a do-over of the other
night's activities. He wouldn't have counted on it, though.
Even a full day's canoeing might not be enough to keep him
from making promises he maybe couldn't keep, from im-
plying affection he didn't wholly trust, from risking a relationship he wasn't sure he could do right by.

He'd done right by so few things in his life, as it was.

Yet more responsibility he hadn't asked for.

They toweled off, ate a quick, cold meal of sandwiches,
and soon realized neither had the energy to do anything but
crash. They turned their backs to one another, to strip out
of their wet clothes. Mary slid into her sleeping bag wearing only a pair of panties and a T-shirt and, true to her
word, didn't try to peek and see what he wore.

She knew only that once he got into his bag, his shoulders and chest were bare. Seeing his firm, rounded muscles
reminded her of his strength, and how much she had to
count on him, isolated from the rest of the world.

Isolated with a man she'd known only a couple of weeks
since their eleven-year separation.

She exchanged good-nights with him and, as he switched
off the halogen lantern, wished once more that she had more

energy. *More energy to mess up your life, you mean.* Not sleeping with Guy was a *good* thing. A safe decision.

Though she still had Cy's "present."

Entombed in her sleeping bag, Mary decided she'd never ached this badly. She sensed Guy watching her, sensed his attraction—and almost felt relieved when he didn't comment on it.

Almost. Even drunk with exhaustion, stiff and sore and longing for nothing more than the solace of sleep, she also felt a bit disappointed. This camping stuff showed him in a whole new, admirable light. His size and strength and knowledge of swampland had all benefited her in a dozen different ways today, from his spotting her so she could take little breaks to his knowing where they might best camp. She knew herself to be in very good physical shape, but his six-foot-plus height and his broad shoulders and his strong arms gave him abilities she could only dream of.

Assuming that she had happy dreams.

She wanted to roll over again, but knew it wouldn't help. No position would feel comfortable. What she needed was a good massage—but she wasn't up to giving herself one. Or Guy, either, and if anybody deserved a massage...

She yawned. Listened to him breathing, mere inches from her. Listened to the rain drumming on the tent, as if they really had slipped back into the past. Like time travelers, hoping to change history...

She awoke on the echo of a thunderclap. "Guy?"

"Shhh..." His low, rich voice in the darkness soothed some of the panic that had filled her at the blast of noise. "It's just getting worse," he murmured. "That's all."

She didn't think that was all. He didn't sound as confident as she would have hoped. When she reached across the space between them, her searching hand found his sleeping bag, his—ribs? Hip? His hand captured hers, and squeezed it. But she was getting another uncomfortable sensation of déjà vu....

A flash of nearby lightning illuminated the side of their tent—striped with the silhouettes of trees, and something the size and rough shape of a man.

Mary screamed, another boom of thunder shook the ground beneath them, and the world plunged back into darkness.

CHAPTER TWELVE

Several things happened at once. Drifter started baying wildly. Guy's hand tightened around Mary's, and he pulled her, sleeping bag and all, across the plastic tarp of the tent floor and into him. A rush of nylon hinted that part of the tent had collapsed; perhaps one of the poles had given out. And from her dream, Mary remembered only darkness and danger.

She heard a metallic snick, and realized Guy had flicked the rifle's safety off. "Who's there?" he demanded loudly.

I've got my own protections. Mary took a deep breath, gathered the energy of the timeless swamp and the burgeoning springtime and the pelting rain, and channeled it into a protective moat of energy between the danger and them.

Drifter stopped howling, and whimpered.

She felt the thing almost immediately, as she would a slug against her skin. Dirty. Wrong. A soul, or what remained of one, darker and more chaotic than the stormy night outside. Its thoughts—no, its *life force*—felt eaten away from the inside out. She doubted the strongest healer could mend such vast, self-inflicted damage, even if it would allow the attempt.

Even if the healer wanted to try.

Another flash of lightning washed the tent's side, striped with tree shadows and with *it*. As after the burst of a strobe, images lingered, even as darkness swept over them again. A corner of the tent sagging inward. The misshapen, menacing silhouette—a bone-skinny arm, a shoulder lumpy with what could be...leaves? The near-nude Guy beside her, aiming the rifle but not yet fingering the trigger.

Thunder echoed the lightning. Guy echoed the thunder. "Whoever you are, I'm armed and I'm jumpy. Say something!"

Mary's sense of the thing, her horror, eased somewhat. Was it leaving? Or was she just tiring? Her protection fed directly from her own strength. She couldn't maintain it indefinitely.

Guy's breathing, her breathing, the steady patter of the rain, all surrounded her. Drifter whimpered again. Mary felt dizzy. Another strobe of lightning, bright-dark-bright, lit the side of the tent—striped only with trees now.

Guy twisted around quickly, his clammy shoulder catching against hers, apparently seeing nothing behind, beside or above them. After several struggling breaths of darkness, thunder rolled over them. The storm was moving away.

She didn't want to lower her shields—but she felt so tired. More than canoeing-tired. Soul-tired. Reluctantly Mary released her hold on the natural powers that formed their protection. As the energies spread back into the night, the rain, the bayou and the earth, she sank against Guy's side. Safe?

She heard the snick of the rifle's safety, and felt Guy shift as he put the weapon down beside him. His cool arms encircled her, his bare chest became her headrest. His rough cheek pressed against hers from above and behind. "You okay?"

That spell took it out of me. She didn't say that, didn't say anything. Just nodded. She knew he could feel her nod.

More barely discernible words rumbled from deep in his chest. "I think it's gone, but let's be sure."

She nodded again.

They waited, sharing one another's warmth, for the next flicker of lightning. When it came, it revealed only trees, the sagging corner of the tent, and Drifter curled up on Mary's sleeping bag. Mary had caught her breath by then, had grounded herself in the physical realm. But she still felt tired, on many levels. Guy's arms seemed the safest place to sleep.

"I think it's gone," he announced, not so quietly, and her eyes fluttered open again. Thunder murmured in the distance.

"Without you shooting it, either," she noted drowsily.

He made a rude noise. "It could have been a hermit, checking us out. I do think of that stuff, you know?" He paused, shifting positions, and she found herself having to sit up on her own minimal strength. "Or it could have been some harmless drifter, scared off when I mentioned the rifle."

"You think so?" It hadn't felt harmless! And he'd unpacked the rifle before anything happened. Guy had sensed danger, too.

"No, but that sounds better than what we're really thinking, right?" he admitted, humor lightening his low tone.

"Can we use the lantern now?"

"Yeah."

When she turned on the halogen lamp, she could see Guy's blue eyes flashing with ideas. "You know," he said, "it left when the storm left."

She could also see most of his body, clad only in white briefs. Revealing white briefs. Distracting, that. Especially in a small, sag-sided tent. She'd returned to the physical realm, all right. Her throat felt dry. "Uh-huh."

"At Bobby Lee's house, when whatever it was knocked, there was a storm." Guy rolled to his knees, reached for his jeans. Light caught the bronzed hair on his trunklike legs, his broad chest. He didn't seem to notice her noticing. "Could be there's a pattern. It only shows up during storms because . . ."

But there he frowned, stumped. Mary dragged her attention back to what he'd said. "Because lightning is an energy source?"

Guy blinked at her, not getting it.

She decided he even looked gorgeous when he had no clue. "How did Bobby Lee describe this thing?"

"He just saw a hand, but he thought it was skeletal, with mud and stuff on it." Guy's words created an image disturbingly close to the silhouette—and the tarot card. "But Bobby Lee had been drunk on his butt at the time," he added gently.

She smiled at him, at his mussed hair and concerned eyes. "Okay. Say it's true—"

"It's true." He grinned, if shakily.

She rolled her eyes, but returned the uneven grin. "Skeletons can't normally walk around by themselves, right?"

"People don't normally have conversations with their dead kin, either," Guy noted, swinging his legs around to put on his still-muddy Levi's. Mary watched shamelessly as he rolled to his feet and, bending, pulled the jeans up, zipped and buttoned them. She found it almost as erotic as she would him taking them off.

Almost.

"Actually, that *is* more likely." She ducked her head when he stared at her. "From an arcane standpoint, okay? Lazare—or the *couchemal*—uses light and sound. That could be the power of thought alone, his need to communicate with you." This wasn't the time and place to go into an explanation of the physics of magic. She settled for "It could be a kind of illusion. But affecting physical reality— smearing mud on doors, dragging people out of trucks— that's stronger juju. Thoughts can't often kill people, despite what you see in horror movies. Maybe a group of very skilled magicians, with no concept of karma, could do it . . . but I think this thing is acting alone. So it has to complement its own power with something else."

"Lightning?" Guy pulled on a muddy boot.

"Maybe." She could still remember the slimy, diseased feel of it against her shields, and she shuddered.

"Which would mean we're safe except during storms." Guy balanced awkwardly on one leg while he pulled on the other boot.

She hadn't meant *that*. Despite finding strength in the powers of nature, she could do magic without them. Just not as easily. So they shouldn't assume...

She realized why Guy had put on his shoes and pants when he picked up the lamp. Drifter scrambled over to the tent flap and whined. "You're going out?"

"Gotta check the tent." Hunkered beneath the nylon roof, he waved a hand toward the front corner that still sagged. "It'll fill with water and collapse on us if we don't fix it."

"I'll hold the lantern for you," she offered, scrambling wearily to her feet. Unlike Guy, she didn't have to stoop.

His gaze skimmed her bare feet and legs up to where her T-shirt hem brushed her thighs. He swallowed noticeably. "You're...uh...gonna step on sticks or something."

"I'll stand in the doorway," she promised. "Just let's not split up, okay?"

He stared at her a moment, as if he might defend his manly ability to take care of himself, then handed her the lamp. "It'll help to have both my hands free," he admitted, unzipping the tent flap. He bent almost double to step through.

Mary shined the light on the ground just outside the tent, long enough to be sure she'd step only on harmless brown pine straw. Ducking through, she turned the lamp toward the corner where Guy headed. As halogen brightness cut through the darkness of the swamp night, she realized that Drifter hadn't left the tent. She realized Drifter was growling.

It waited.

She zagged the light past Guy—and her voice froze in her throat. Beyond where he crouched, shirtless, at the side of the tent, running his hand over the muddy tent pole...

Beyond him, cloaked in trees and shadows, she saw Death. A skull, at least. Empty eye sockets and nasal cavity, elongated teeth, a smear of mud and a drape of moss.

That hadn't been there when they'd set up camp.

It moved, shuffled nearer. No!

She found her voice.

"Guy!"

He nearly jumped out of his skin, spun to stare at Mary, recoiled from the lantern's glare. Then he placed the horror in her expression, and whirled back around. He squinted, his night vision shot. Movement. Bone white. Holy—

"Tent," he managed to say, straightening from his crouch and backing toward Mary. "Rifle." He could only handle one word at a time. His mind screamed protests. This couldn't be happening.

He glanced away long enough to spot a nearby branch on the ground. He looked back, and the thing had moved closer. How had it moved? How could it? This wasn't real.

Cloaked in shadows, draped in filth, the thing stared at him . . . or not. Faced him, anyway. Guy stayed outside the tent, between it and Mary. This suddenly seemed really stupid, though he'd rather be stupid than let it get her. He didn't look away again as he crouched, groped for the branch, rose with it in his hands.

It felt them *approach. No!*

It hesitated, perhaps five feet away. Guy hefted his rough club. Half-rotten. Still, if it slowed this thing down—

If he'd had any nerves left, the explosion beside him would have finished them. Even before the rifle's report faded from the night air, the skeleton, the *thing*, disappeared backward, into the shadows, as if swallowed.

Silence. Nothing, nobody moved.

Then, thick as a fog, something blew past them. Misery. Despair. Moaning, worse than wind, worse than death. *Too late—always too late.* It surrounded, circled, drowned them—

And vanished, as well. Unbelievably normal night sounds crept into the patter of rainfall. Crickets, banjo frogs, cicadas. Slowly Guy turned to look at the woman beside him.

She stood in the slow rain, wearing only her T-shirt and panties, the .22 rifle still braced against her shoulder. Maybe she wouldn't be so hard to protect after all.

She didn't move. Was she breathing?

Guy carefully took the weapon from her. He ejected the shell casing, flicked the safety on. Mary lowered her arms to her sides, still staring at the patch of darkness that had swallowed the threat.

"I thought—" he winced at how his words seemed to cut the night "—you didn't approve of guns."

"I . . . don't." She shuddered. "I hate them. That doesn't mean I c-can't use one. I was so . . . scared."

Silence only echoed the madness of what had happened. He needed words. He needed normalcy. "Do you think you got it?"

"Maybe," whispered Mary shakily. "You can't kill something that's already dead." Then she ducked back into the tent.

With one last glance around them, Guy followed her, setting the rifle down inside. "We'll take turns keeping guard," he said. "Now that we know it doesn't use the lightning."

Mary had knelt on her sleeping bag, facing away from him. He noticed that she drew an arm across her unseen face before speaking, noticed Drifter hovering near her. "I think it uses the lightning, it just doesn't need it. Maybe it stores extra, like a hibernating animal. If—" A definite sniffle. "If there had been lightning, we'd probably be dead."

He knelt beside her, tried to see her face. "But we aren't, *chère*. We're here, and we're safe. For now. Don't cry."

She glared tearfully at him. "I'm upset! It was *Death!*"

He grasped her shoulders. "C'mon, Mary Margaret. That Grim Reaper stuff, that was Bobby Lee's idea. It's not—"

"Not *the* Death, maybe," she conceded stubbornly. "But death. I used a *rifle!* Who knows where that round ended up? I may have killed something! A deer, or a bird, or—"

"Better them than us."

"Tell that to the deer or the bird!" She shrugged off his hands, turned to draw her knees up to her chest. "I shouldn't have used it, shouldn't scare that easily." She raised her face to his, eyes shiny. "I believe in reincarnation, you know."

Huh. Guy settled more comfortably beside her. "Really."

"My being Wiccan means I believe in magic and karma, in doing no harm. And that God's as likely to be female as male." She added this last as a challenge, her chin up, her gaze steady. *So there,* her posture said. "Maybe more likely."

"That's it?" He'd expected something more dramatic. Darker. Not from Mary, though. Not his Mary Margaret.

She stared at him, surprise and then relief playing across her expressive face. "That and reincarnation," she reminded him, her voice falling as her proud shoulders sagged. "That's why I don't understand why I got so scared, or why I hate death so much. I just..." She hid her face in her knees, but not before her tears spilled over. "Sometimes I miss him."

Joey. She meant Joey. At a loss, Guy drew her against him, hugged her hard. She began to cry in earnest. He stroked her hair, wished he could tell her it was okay, but it wasn't, not that. Losing Joey and Lazare so young wasn't okay, it just... was. Having to deal with it, young as they were, also just was. They'd grown up too fast. But at least they'd grown up.

She shook her head; he could feel her fighting the tears and said, "No, *chère*. It's okay to miss him."

"He was so little," she managed, her voice high and unsteady. "He still believed in Santa Claus. He named—" An awkward, wild giggle. "He named his shoes..."

Oh, God—she *hadn't* forgotten. Guy laid his head on hers, still holding her, not fighting his own flood of emotion. He'd feared she'd amputated that part of her life entirely, that she'd forgotten him, too. It shouldn't matter, but he knew it did. It mattered terribly. Knowing that she hadn't forgotten eased something deep in him. He prompted her: "His favorite crayon?"

"Was white, because he thought we couldn't tell if he colored wrong." Mary's laugh came out half sob. "And he always carried around that dingy little green elephant. We..."

More sobs. He wasn't sure he could hold her any tighter, but he tried, suddenly ashamed. He shouldn't have wanted so badly, so selfishly, for her to remember; he'd just hurt her more. What good did it do for her to recall that they'd buried Phink the Elephant with Joey? What good to linger on memories? She'd seemed happy just a week ago. Now look at her.

His fault?

No matter what he said, he'd probably get it wrong. So he just held her, let her cry until she couldn't seem to cry any longer and she lay, limp and exhausted, across his chest and shoulder. Finally, he laid her down on her sleeping bag.

She blinked up at him, eyes a bit swollen, nose red. The real Mary, he thought, wiping her tears away with a thumb. Witch or not, grown-up or not, this was the real Mary Margaret.

She said, "I think I drooled on you," and he smiled.

"Won't be the first time, *chère*." To his relief, she glared at the teasing. "I'll take first watch and wake you up in a couple of hours, eh?"

She yawned, not trying to hide it. "Too bad," she murmured, fatigue stealing her voice, "that we can't sleep together."

His stomach knotted in—surprise? Excitement? Hope? She probably didn't mean that like he thought. He almost asked, but because she'd fallen asleep, the question proved moot.

Or it would have, if he'd been interested in just a night. *As opposed to?* Guy moved onto his own sleeping bag, rifle within reach, in case that thing came at them again.

A night, Poitiers, might be all you get.

Too late. Always too late. Doomed to an eternity of chase, never to catch up, never to have vengeance . . .

"Chère?"

Mary's anger drained; she felt lost between worlds. The touch on her shoulder felt warm and gentle. Familiar. She opened her eyes to a ceiling of shadowed fabric, to the mild illumination of a flashlight—to Guy's blue eyes. She remembered last night, then realized it hadn't ended. The night, that is.

The air around her felt hushed, despite the night songs outside the tent. How strange, and yet right, that Guy's voice should have drawn her into this humid, shadowy sleep time.

"You were having a nightmare," he murmured, low. She nodded, still gazing up at him. She'd dreamed of a plantation house, dreamed of her fate—no, not hers, but someone's—forever locked to a murderer's. Now she filled her gaze with Guy's concerned face, willing that other image back into the realm of her dreams. She needed the grounding of the physical world right now. And nothing seemed more physical in this tent than this man who wore only a pair of jeans and a tired, worried expression.

"My turn?" she asked, sitting up. Her sleeping bag bunched at her waist. She couldn't remember getting into it.

He nodded wearily. "For a few hours. If you're up to it."

She returned his nod, glancing around her to fully regain her bearings—and to do something other than stare into his eyes, or at his truly fine chest. Drifter lay by the tent flap, her ears perked at them. Instead of the halogen lantern, Guy held a flashlight—to minimize their silhouettes, she imagined. He'd tied their two walking sticks together to prop up the sagging corner. Very clever, her Guy.

Her Guy? *Wake up, Mary.*

"I'm sorry I freaked on you earlier." She climbed out of her sleeping bag, found her jeans—damp from the humidity—and pulled them up her legs. She tried not to notice Guy watching.

"You freaked on me?" He managed a tired grin, then stretched back onto his own sleeping bag. "Sounds kinky, *chère.*"

"Crying over Joey."

"Doesn't he deserve it?"

She frowned at him. Pillowing his head on the biceps of a crooked arm, he mimicked the expression. Okay, so he was right. "I do miss him," she admitted, "but..."

Guy waited for her to finish. She shook her head. *But it was a long time ago* didn't seem to apply in this timeless place. *But not enough to cry like that* implied Joey didn't deserve her grief; surely he did. And her last, most honest reason seemed sacrilegious: *But not as much as I missed you.*

Now here he sat—rather, lay—more handsome than she'd ever foreseen. And tired, sore from a long day of trying to take care of her, as well as himself. His lids fluttered sleepily, then he blinked awake. The visible tension in his body wouldn't shut off automatically, just because he'd ended his watch. And her hands hungered to touch him—if not in passion, then in healing.

He caught her staring, and attempted another sleepy smile.

"Take off your pants," she said.

His eyes widened, fully awake. "What?"

"I'm going to give you a massage," she said with a laugh. "Take off your pants, or I can't do your legs."

He stared at her, then flashed her a half grin. "I appreciate the offer, *chère,* but I'm way too tired...."

"To get a massage?" She folded her arms. "I told you once before that this is a healing practice, not a sexual trick. Fine. I'll just give you a back rub."

Guy sat up, hesitated, then glanced away from her while he unbuttoned his jeans. His fingers fumbled at the zipper; it made a sensuous, rasping noise on its way down. Mary decided to look away, too, or else she would have a hard time proving her point about healing versus sex. The two weren't exactly opposites.

But she didn't want him to think any of her clients turned her on this strongly.

She dug into her duffel bag for the mini mustard bottle she'd filled with oil when she packed; she'd planned for sore muscles. On second thought, she nabbed a towel, too. Were she at the Wellness Club, she would drape a sheet over him and only expose the area she worked on, both for modesty and because the oil would cool him. Out here, they'd just have to rough it.

"Just...lie on my stomach?" Guy asked from behind her, his voice thick with uncertainty.

"Mm-hmm ... And relax." After a deep, strengthening breath, she turned back to him. His six-foot-plus length, clad only in his briefs, stretched across his sleeping bag. He'd folded his arms beneath his head, and watched her with curious blue eyes shadowed by his mussed hair.

She tried to eye him professionally, rather than appreciatively. Though, again, the two weren't completely exclusive, right? She decided not to mention that the massage would go more smoothly if he took off his briefs, too. Neither of them would manage to relax with that much distraction.

"You'll want to let your arms lie at your side," she prompted, rubbing her hands together to warm them. "Close your eyes, let your mind drift. Don't worry about helping me, it might break the flow. If I need you to move, I'll tell you."

"Got it," he murmured.

She squirted some oil into her warmed palms—almond oil, none of that cheap mineral stuff for her. She'd added a few drops of rich cedarwood oil, for its protective properties. "Don't worry, it's not a floral scent."

He grinned at her from the crook of his arm. "Now I can relax." When she looked at his arms, he obediently straightened them beside him.

She leaned over his broad back and lay her hands on him. The warm, tingling sensation as their auric energies met felt particularly strong, increasing as she skimmed her palms up the dip of his spine, over the rise of his shoulder blades. The smell of cedar wafted up at her as it met his warm skin.

Relax? Her uncertainties—whether he'd like it, whether she could concentrate—sank beneath the familiarity of what she loved to do. For her, massage had less to do with manipulating generic muscles than with mingling life forces. No matter who her client might be, he or she shared Mary's humanity. This person—any person—could be a very distant cousin, or a future friend, or a lover from a past life....

From Guy's strong, smooth back, his well-defined lats, Mary worked her way up to his shoulders, then, more gently, onto his neck. She noticed that his eyes had drifted shut. Good. At the base of his skull she traced tiny, hard circles with her fingers, working them into his thick, burnished hair. She preferred giving full-body massages, instead of compartmentalizing people, and she'd learned to massage with her own full body. As she moved back to his delts, she used her weight, not just her hands, to apply pressure. She tried to feel him, tried to listen to the body beneath her touch—as she would any body.

But this was Guy's body. She recognized the slim, pale scar over his shoulder where he'd caught himself on a barbed-wire fence. She knew, as she worked her way down his left arm, that she would feel a faint ridge along his radius, where he'd broken it falling off the roof. She knew so much of his body from childhood. But this was no child's body.

Once she started, she never removed both her hands at once; she wouldn't willingly break the tidelike flow of their energy. When she needed more oil, she turned one hand over on him, and used her free hand to fill her palm with more cedar-scented lubricant. She kneaded his biceps and triceps, then the flexor of his lower arm. She used her thumbs to work his palm, then paid attention to each of his fingers before smoothing her hands again over his back, and the other arm. More oil. She disliked having to skip his gluteus, but client modesty often imposed the same handicap; she knew how to move one hand to his thigh, then the other, before starting work on his legs. Hamstring. Soleus. He felt so real. So very alive.

After thoroughly kneading the muscles of each leg and foot, she returned again to his back, using the heels of her hands, then the underside of her closed fists, easing the last of his tension away. Considering the night they'd had, *that* was magic. She could feel what a good massage this was.

She paused to catch her breath, her hands spread across the pliant firmness of his delts again. "Time to roll over, Prince Charming," she told him.

His eyes didn't open. Still resting, hands spread on him, she looked more closely, then let her shoulders sink. He'd fallen asleep. She hadn't done his abs or pecs yet, or his quads or his other front thigh muscles. She still hadn't massaged his face. This sometimes happened at work; if he'd paid for a full-body massage, she would wake him as gently as possible and continue. But he hadn't even asked for this much—and he likely needed the sleep more. She should stop touching him now.

Mary cocked her head, noticing how the gleam of oil, in the faint illumination of the flashlight beside her, highlighted the contours of his muscular form. Now that she'd officially ended the massage, her professional mantle slipped a bit. She still wanted to touch him. Very much.

Right hand on his back, she slid her left hand, her receptive hand, lightly to his neck. She turned her wrist so that the back of her fingers skimmed his jaw, then played into the burnished curls of hair that brushed across them.

In the absence of professionalism, her breath had fallen short. Her pulse sped. A sweet warmth, completely different from the scent of cedar oil, filled deep recesses within her. She considered waking him up for less philanthropic reasons. Attraction? What an understatement. She wanted him, as surely as she'd wanted anything in her life.

Just because he looked good? She closed her eyes, but that felt fake, so she reached over and turned off the flashlight. Complete darkness filled the tent. How many miles had they traveled from the nearest electricity? She listened for a moment, ascertained that the night songs hadn't broken for any unnatural intruders, then turned her attention back to the living, breathing, unseen man beneath her touch.

She still felt attracted, more than ever. Frustratingly so. Achingly so. She could remember what *his* hands felt like on *her* body, after all, and what his mouth felt like, too. What the unspoken promise of his lovemaking had excited in her, back on her houseboat's sofa, before they'd been so rudely interrupted by pragmatism. He'd napped awhile. Maybe he wouldn't mind—

A giggle interrupted her amorous thoughts, chilling her deeply. A child's giggle. Mary turned her head in the blackness, as if she could see. She didn't. She didn't want to.

Another giggle. A soft voice, distorted, as if through time and space, or underwater. "Hi, Mary. Hi, Mary. Hi, Mary."

Oh, Lady—what if this was Joey?

CHAPTER THIRTEEN

Mary groped for and found the flashlight, which felt cool and unnatural to her warmed palms. Her oily fingers fumbled at the switch—there! The single beam seemed like too little light. Anything short of full dawn would be too little light.

Was that movement? She spotlit the dog, which had lifted its head, ears perked toward another giggle.

Drifter heard it, too? Her breath caught in her throat. Desperate for distraction, she grasped her sleeping bag and drew it over Guy as a makeshift comforter, up to his ears, her hands suddenly clumsy. She didn't want him to get cold while he slept—and she certainly didn't want to wake him. Not to this.

If he, too, thought it was Joey, that would make it more real. She couldn't bear for it to become real.

The voice returned, wavering in volume and consistency. "Hi, Mary, hi, Mary, hi, Mary." It wasn't going away—and she couldn't.

Reluctantly she crawled to the tent flap, unzipped it as quietly as possible. She poked the flashlight out ahead of her, like a light saber. Its beam cut across wet pine straw, vines, and tree trunks, and glistened off water.

Nothing...except another coy giggle.

Her free hand gripped the nylon flap, so that if anything did grab her, she'd bring the tent down as she went.

Nothing grabbed her.

The night sounds had been silenced since the giggle, replaced by a strangeness in the air, thicker than humidity, more chill than darkness. Hand trembling, she switched off the flashlight.

Residual blurs of light danced across the blackness. And then, slowly, she realized that one wasn't a residual blur. One of them hovered like a blue-green smear of...what? She raised her hand to the pentagram around her neck, willing herself not to panic. Her circlemates wouldn't panic, would they?

Echoing, hollow, the little-boy voice repeated: "Hi, Mary."

She shook her head.

"I saw you watching me. Come see. Come see what I found."

Recognition, despite the words' distortion, suddenly eased the worst edge of her fear. Lazare. Lady praise! That wasn't Joey's voice, but Lazare's.

She immediately felt shame at her relief.

"I found it." Definitely Lazare—petulant. Insistent. "I found it, Mary. Come and see." And then the pulsing light that danced nearer, then drew away, began to change. Its bottom extended; its edges drew in. It didn't become a boy, exactly. But it had the hint of arms, legs, a head. It had depth. For the first time, she could almost make out a human shape to it.

Almost, in this case, counted.

"You gotta," whined the voice, this time wavering from more than ethereal distortion. "You gotta help." Unfair blow. She and Guy were already helping him!

She gripped the tent flap tighter, managed to space her breaths, tried her voice. "Help you . . . what, exactly?"

"Home." His voice went higher at the end of his plea, and from more than its strange distance. She could no longer see it—him?—so clearly. He had begun to fade. "Help me go home."

Oh . . . Her knees failed, and she sank to the tarp floor, catching herself with her flashlight hand on wet pine straw outside the tent. She didn't want to know this, wanted her world to stay light and future-oriented. The past should remain in the past, the dead should remain dead.

So tell him: You're dead. You can never go home again. Her chest tightened unbearably, cramped with unshed sobs. She couldn't do that to him. Not to Lazare, not to anyone.

"Home," repeated the thin voice. Its ethereal form faded slightly. She could see previously invisible outlines of trees, of the canoe; why couldn't she see Lazare? "I wanna go hoooome."

Her fingers ached to reach out, to touch him. She tasted salt in her mouth, tears. "If we follow you—"

A sharp, high note startled her; then she recognized the birdcall. Another whistled back through the morning silence.

Morning? She blinked, her lashes sticky, and searched for the ghost. She saw only trees and the canoe, which gained depth with increased visibility. Blackness had faded to a steely slate color... taking Lazare with it. Did she imagine the last sigh, faint through the humid air, of *hoooome?*

Another birdcall cut the stillness. Then more chirps; the sharp tapping of a woodpecker after its breakfast. Even before the sun showed itself, dawn in the swamp began.

Mary drew the back of her hand across her eyes, wiping away most of her tears, nearly hitting herself with the flashlight. She uncurled stiff fingers from the tent flap, scooted farther inside. She began to shiver uncontrollably. She called herself a healer—surely she could help the boy who had been almost like a baby brother to her? Lazare just wanted to go home.

Don't we all, Lazare?

Her tear-blurred gaze found Guy, shrouded in tent-filtered shadows as surely as in her sleeping bag. When she leaned nearer, planting her hands on the gritty plastic floor, she could almost make out his handsome face. His parted lips. The dark smudge of his short lashes. He looked softer, asleep. Younger. More like her old Guy—but with beard stubble.

She could very easily lift the edge of the sleeping bag and slide in with him. Catch a little more sleep, gain strength for tomorrow. Maybe wake in his arms, finally, and maybe—

Lazare wanted to go home.

Mary turned away from the attractive image. She would pack together what she could, so that they could leave as soon as he woke again. She couldn't put this hell off any longer.

Not even for heaven.

From the back of the canoe, Guy steered them around fallen logs surrounded by flecks of duckweed, past stumps scabbed over with mushrooms, between trees green with ivy or gray with Spanish moss. He felt alone in the boat. Even with visual proof of Mary ahead of him, leaning forward and then back with each stroke to wring every bit of power from her motions, he felt alone.

She had barely spoken to him this morning. He'd gotten a distracted "You're welcome" when he thanked her for the massage—so distracted, he'd decided to keep further flirtatious commentary to himself. When he asked what was wrong, she'd admitted she'd seen the *couchemal*. Lazare's ghost, she'd said.

And when he caught her arm, slowed her bustling for a moment, and asked if she was okay, she'd held his gaze, looking so very vulnerable he'd wanted to pull her against him, stand between her and all the horrors of the world, kiss her painful memories away, even if it meant ridding her of his memory, as well.

But she'd dropped her eyes, nodded, and he'd let her go.

She didn't look vulnerable now. Her tanned arms trembled with exertion; strands of honeyed hair stuck to the nape of her neck. Surely she would need rest sometime. He was the one who'd gotten a massage.

Better not to remember that. But his every easy movement reminded him. Muscles in agony last night were today revitalized from Mary's magic touch, her sensual fingers, her firm strokes. And that was her being professional. Imagine her being personal! Or not. With at least five feet of unstable canoe between them, such thoughts could, well, rock the boat.

Mary stopped in midstroke, then lifted her paddle from the water. Her head came up, as if to sense the air. Then again, she might just need to draw a clear breath. Muggy humidity surrounded them, flavored with the thick odors of flowers and rot—thank God it was early in the year for mosquitoes. The sky had remained gray all morning, claustrophobic under low clouds.

"That way." She extended a slender arm. Guy couldn't tell if it was a channel or not. He didn't think they were on any particular channel anymore, anyway. "We have to go that way."

So he put his back into getting them "that way"—and keeping up with her.

The water became more stagnant. A thicker carpet of duckweed swirled away as the canoe cut through it, washed back in their wake. Slimy, pod-tentacled weeds surfaced in the water moved by their paddles, only to sink again. How deep into the swamp were they? They passed a huge cypress, far larger than any he'd ever seen before. Most of the big trees, except those very deep in the swamp, had been cut for wood long ago.

This one, he thought as he used his paddle as a rudder to circle the tree's huge, flared bottom, meant they'd gone very deep. He twisted to watch it, even as they glided forward—and when Mary's breath caught, he nearly capsized the boat. Drifter stumbled, paws scrabbling on aluminum. The cooler tipped. Mary grasped the side of the wobbling canoe, he did, too, and together they managed to regain their precarious balance.

"What?" Guy demanded, more angry at himself than at her. Trust him to nearly dump Mary, their supplies and the dog into a gator-infested swamp.

"Hyacinth," she announced. As they came around a copse of cypress the moss seemed to draw away, like curtains from a stage, revealing a wide channel of dormant water, filled almost bank-to-bank with floating greenery and purple flowers. Water hyacinth—the plant that had nearly destroyed the Louisiana waterways. A tugboat couldn't break through the interwoven underwater roots once they took over a channel. The shallow draft of the canoe might help them. Maybe. But as they began to glide between one or two of the flowering plants, then clusters, Guy suspected they couldn't get very much farther.

He stared, appalled, at the horrible beauty before them. How could they help Lazare if they couldn't get through? "Do you think you could find another way, if we went back?" he asked, knowing that Mary would hate the idea. She'd all but cracked a whip and yelled stroke, stroke, since they'd left this morning.

"The water isn't moving, is it?" she asked from the front of the canoe, watching the flowers bob by their prow as the canoe's momentum slowed, and then stopped. Drifter leaned precariously over the edge, as if to sniff one.

Guy surveyed the area around them again—a definite channel, or at least it once had been. The land across from them rose decidedly from the water. He could spot oak trees further inland, past the birch and willow that crowded for light at the bank.

"Dead lake," he decided. When her back stiffened, he regretted his choice of words. "An oxbow lake. One of the rivers probably looped out this direction, then doubled back. Over time the river cut a new channel, so the old channel became a lake of dead—uh, *still* water." Water filled with hyacinth, like a meadow of flowers for as far as he could see. "We can't go on through this." Surrounded, they bobbed atop the water, going nowhere. "If we go back..."

"We don't have to go back." Mary turned carefully

on her seat up front, flushed with excitement and ... apprehension? "We just have to get across. It's there."

The bank. The oaks. Real land. "There?"

"There." She dipped her paddle into the water again to wrangle some of the hyacinths out of their way. "The coin came from up there." She took a deep breath. "Somewhere, anyway."

He definitely sensed apprehension off her. "You okay?"

"Me? Uh-huh." As if realizing how lame that sounded, she paused in battling flowers to smile at him. God, she had a pretty smile—and a determined set to her delicate, T-shirted shoulders. Like the hyacinth, he thought. A lot stronger than she looked. Better able to take care of herself, too.

Which didn't mean she couldn't use all the help she could get. He followed her example, putting his back into forcing them through the tangle of water weeds.

They could *both* use all the help they could get.

"There was once a plantation here," Mary said, trying to match the thick, overgrown wild around her with half-remembered images from last night's dream. She glanced toward the water, barely visible through the black willow and tupelo gum trees that crowded its banks. "There used to be a dock," she decided, catching a brief glimpse with her mind's eye before turning away from the water to forge her way deeper inland. Lucky she'd worn jeans today; vines and briars fought them and their walking sticks for every step. "The plantation house was this way. See that big old oak there? And the one farther on? They lined—"

"A drive," Guy finished for her, and she stopped to stare at him. Could he see it, too?

He'd been pretty quiet all morning. Now that she'd talked to Lazare, though, she understood Guy's need to end this. She couldn't expect him to play at romance with her while his cousin's spirit wandered through an eternity of nightmares. Still, she liked the idea of him seeing the same scene she could. Though not exactly in the way she could, she decided. Guy squinted from one tree to the next, as if putting pictures together more from educated ideas than instinct. Just as well, too. Her own instincts weren't cooperating in narrowing her field of search—as far as they were concerned, she'd already found what she'd been looking for. This was where the coin had come from . . . more or less.

Drifter, who'd been scurrying back and forth since they'd landed, began to bark furiously, maybe ten feet ahead of Mary.

"Not much left of the house, I bet," Guy noted, darting forward and jabbing his walking stick into the brush. Mary waited while he scooped up a snake and tossed it well clear of their path. Her inner revulsion—she tried to love all creatures, but reptiles took more effort—mixed with gratitude while he stopped to pet the dog. There he went, taking care of her again.

Had he said something? "Fire, I think," she realized, fighting to remember the dream. "Something violent."

"Hey!" Guy waded farther through the weeds, then waited for her to catch up and see what he'd found. The crumbled ruin of a brick wall rose perhaps a foot high before him, running southward only to vanish amid more growth. Vines crept along it; weeds grew out of cracks between and within the bricks. This used to be a grand plantation house, she thought again, staring in horror at the decay. Someone used to love this place. And then—

Him.

She closed her eyes against the image. She didn't want to—

"Mary?" Guy's hand touched her shoulder, strengthening and steadying her. "What's wrong?"

She opened her eyes, met the concern in his. For the second time in twenty-four hours, Guy's face replaced the man—the murderer—of last night's dream. "He ruined it." Him—and time.

"Who?"

"I don't know." She didn't blame him for his slanted, curious eyebrows. Could she explain that she didn't *want* to know?

He waited for her, restless, but with a good-naturedly patient smile, blue eyes warming her despite the overcast skies. She couldn't explain it to him, because she couldn't justify it to herself. She didn't want to know because it *felt bad?* Compared to Lazare's suffering, how could she tell Guy that?

She whispered, "Hold me?"

A moment of confusion flickered across his face, but that surely didn't stop him. He gathered her smoothly into his arms, drew her against the solid safety of his T-shirted chest. Her own arms instinctively wrapped around his waist before she remembered she'd only meant for him to anchor her while she looked into the past. The present suddenly seemed more important. *Go with the flow.* She laid her cheek against his heartbeat; felt his suddenly strained breath on her hair.

He felt so warm and alive in her embrace. *Just as Lazare and Joey had once been alive.* Stable, and permanent. *Just as this plantation had once seemed permanent.*

Mary felt suddenly ill. This feeling, this bond between her and Guy, wouldn't last, either, would it? Nothing did. She tipped her face toward his and realized even as he froze, dismay and then embarrassment playing across his face, that he'd meant to kiss her. A moment ago, she would have wanted it. No—worse. She still wanted it, desperately, *because* it wouldn't last.

But her expression of horror had surely killed the mood. "I'm going to try a trance," she explained, suddenly self-conscious, and tried not to notice how he slowly straightened again, how he pretended nonchalance. "I'd like you to hold me so that I don't get . . . lost." Maybe he understood, maybe not. He agreed with a nod and a shrug, in any case, so she turned in his embrace to stand with her back to him, wrapped in his arms, gazing off across the stretch of swamp.

She took a deep breath, then another. Forced her mind to go in reverse—widdershins. Probed the energies of this place, in search of what had happened before...

The face—oddly handsome, narrow. An angry man, leading other men. A flatboat of some kind, from which he raided other boats, and riverside homes. He was captured, branded. His anger pulsed around her for a moment. Free again, he robbed and burned cabins, plantations. He destroyed this place, returned to hide things. A lynch mob ambushed him... so very angry.

The image of him kicking, then dangling from the branch of a huge oak, held Mary's mind too long, and she whimpered. She heard something deep and soothing outside the images, steadied herself with the warmth that surrounded her, made herself look just a bit farther. She saw the same angry man. *Frustrated. Furious. He couldn't get at what was his, had worked so hard and now he couldn't have it—because he was dead.*

A fetid chill rushed through her, so very cold, and Guy's arms tightened around her. "It's all right," he murmured; she realized he'd been murmuring that for some time now. "It's all right, *chère.* I'm here."

But how long could she count on that? How long until he left her again? He might not even make it out of this swamp, much less— She caught back her fears, knew better than to grasp at the future so quickly after seeing the past. Like dating on the rebound, it wouldn't help. Or that was what she told herself.

"A river pirate," she said, and Guy stopped murmuring. As his hold on her loosened, she turned within his embrace, spread her hands on his chest and looked up at him. She liked the feel of his heartbeat beneath her fingers, no matter how temporary, and clung to it. "Some kind of river pirate, from way back in the early 1800s, left something here that he wants, and he can't have it. So he won't let anyone else have it, either."

He didn't question her information, just went with it. "We really *are* after pirate treasure?"

"Just not Jean Laffite's," she agreed, trying to smile despite residual horror. How many lives had the man—the Reaper?—ruined? What kind of misery must surround that bastard?

Enough misery, obviously, to last almost two centuries since his violent end.

She stepped away from Guy's strength, his familiarity. They had work to do—and she feared they had some terrible deadline. "If you were a pirate, where would you hide a treasure?"

"You don't know?"

"Just that we're warm." She followed his gaze, able to pick out bits of the wall more easily since her trance. Wandering perhaps twenty feet, she began to find remains of stone flourishes that had once topped the capitals of pillars long since rotted. They would never find anything amid this decay!

She glanced back at Guy and caught him looking at her. She felt watched after. It reminded her she wasn't in this alone.

Maybe he read her uncertainty, because he glanced down at his wristwatch, then back at her. "It's not even noon," he pointed out. "Don't worry. We've got time to find it."

Within two hours, they'd given up. Guy had half expected it of himself—he did great work, but hated holding jobs for any amount of time. He had liked college, but lost his scholarship. He surely hadn't managed a successful relationship! Why had he thought he could see this particular quest through to its end?

Just because it somehow meant his salvation, that didn't mean he could actually do it.

"It's too big," Mary decided, checking a fallen tree trunk for snakes and bugs, then sinking onto it. "It's just too...big. We'll never find where the coin came from."

"Lazare found it," Guy pointed out, surprising himself. He was the quitter of the pair, right? Still, he had a point here. "If Lazare found it, then it can't be hidden that well."

"That," Mary pointed out, "was eleven years ago."

He glanced toward what he could see of the sky through the trees. Still overcast, it told him very little, so he glanced at his watch. They had maybe four hours until sunset. When the sun set, their problems would get a lot more complicated. "Let's make a floor plan," he suggested, not even trying to find a spot of dirt clear enough to support a map. Instead, he drew a rectangle in the air. "The main house was about where we're sitting, right?"

She cocked her head at the imaginary drawing. "Uh-huh."

He nodded approval. "You found the remains of some kind of smaller stone building that way—that's probably the kitchen."

"You think?" She stared at him, as if she didn't know that old buildings had once had separate kitchens from the main houses.

"Kitchens burned down a lot," he explained.

She nodded again, leaning forward. "What about those bits you found way back there?"

"Uh . . . slave quarters?"

Her eyes went still, as if she could see it. She probably could. When she focused again, on him, she nodded. Eerie, that.

"They wouldn't have roads," he continued, realizing that through his interest in old houses he'd absorbed more than he would have thought. "The river was their road. Whatever they raised, they would have been self-sufficient. No doctor, or priest. Cemetery would be nearby."

Mary grimaced, as if hating the very thought of cemeteries. Then she looked back up at him, startled by an idea.

Guy blinked. The cemetery. Something seemed important about the cemetery. He just wasn't making the connection.

She made it for him, and grasped his arm with both hands. "He can't get to it!"

"He's dead," Guy reminded her. "It's not like he'd have pockets to put it in if he could get to it."

"No," she protested with an elfin grin. "The remains of the pirate—that's the Reaper—he can't *get* to his own treasure. That's why he needs other people to take it, so that they'll bring it where he can reach. He hid his money somewhere that he couldn't get back to once he died!"

"A church...or sacred ground." Guy shook his head even as he tried the idea. "But...don't cemeteries have ghosts?"

"Probably. But if this man was an unrepentant murderer—"

"His soul is damned, and they wouldn't have buried him in sacred ground!" Guy laughed, and grabbed Mary at the waist to lift her high into the air. She smiled back down at him, her eyes sparkling like water at sunset. A touch of sunburn blushed her nose and cheeks. So pretty, and ethereal—and witchy. Belatedly, he returned her carefully to the ground. But he didn't take his hand off her waist. "Do you believe in that? Eternal damnation?"

"Not as a final destination," she admitted, the ease of her answer relieving him more than any particular response could. "Karma's similar. But it doesn't matter what I believe."

"It doesn't?" She'd acted like it did.

"We create our own hells, *chère.*" The endearment slipped from her lips like honey. "What matters is what the river pirate believed."

"So we find the cemetery."

"My favorite place." She tried to grimace and yawn at the same time, then matched his stride as he started toward one of the few adjacent areas that they hadn't already explored.

If she didn't like cemeteries in general, she really wasn't going to like his next suggestion. "If it's fenced in, we need to see if there's a clear area—not on top of any graves—to set up the tent before we start hunting treasure.''

He heard Mary stop beside him. "In a cemetery?"

"It may be the closest thing we'll get to a Do Not Disturb sign," he pointed out. Then he realized how that had come out sounding. He'd meant, to make it through the coming night alive, not necessarily happy. Mary continued to stare at him.

"We haven't even found the place yet," he pointed out, impatient, and headed on. In a moment, he heard her hurrying through the brush beside him again—just like always.

CHAPTER FOURTEEN

To Guy's obvious delight, and Mary's quiet dismay, they found the cemetery. Rusted remains of an iron fence surrounded an overgrown patch of land, guarded by a sprawling oak and dominated by a huge tomb. Its time-stained, moss-colored stone frieze read Famille Valmont Beauvais. Taller than Guy, it looked like it held perhaps six... well...bodies.

Three smaller tombs clustered near the main one, gray in the shadows of trees, beneath a grayer sky. Any designs that had once been molded into the plaster had worn down to vague images—a chalice, a cross—or flaked away to reveal patches of brick. From cracks in the plaster grew bright green ferns. Weeds sprouted, high, like a grassy sea around four stone islands.

Mary leaned against the base of the sentinel oak, wide as a Volkswagen Bug, watching Guy set up their tent and feeling useless. They'd searched—along the perimeter of the fence, around each tomb—but found no stash of doubloons. Snakes, bugs, lizards, and a disgruntled possum that had snarled at them before Drifter chased it into the woods, yes. But no gold.

When Mary tried to sense it, tried to go still inside to feel the inner tug from the coin's source, she felt the treasure's nearness—*hot, so hot you're burning up.* But she couldn't place a direction; she felt the tug no matter where she faced, from whatever corner of the graveyard. The inner tug soon began to feel like an upset stomach. Recognizing how her efforts drained her, Guy had suggested she rest while he raise the tent. She had complied, though more from distaste than from exhaustion.

How would she manage to sleep in a cemetery? Guy couldn't even assure her he wouldn't put the tent atop a grave. While they searched for buried treasure amid the tombs, and around the base of the fence, they'd made out three different dates, all of them from the 1830s. Guy had admitted that any wooden markers would have rotted away by now.

Closing her eyes didn't chase the idea away; it just made her more aware of the drowning humidity, the buzz of insects, the low hooting of a wood owl somewhere nearby.

An owl? She opened her eyes fast, as if expecting to catch something in the act of... what? Stealing Guy away? He crouched at the edge of the tent, pushed a stake into the soft ground with his hand, then duck-walked a few feet and repeated the motion. Superstition, she reminded herself.

She didn't believe in bad omens. Even if she had dealt him the death card, she was trying to change that reading, right?

Still, she hated cemeteries.

"I'll bring up some of the supplies," she called, and practically ran out the open, one-hinge-left gate that gaped amid the rusty, vine-covered flourishes of the fence.

By time she'd carried up the last of their supplies, Guy had completely erected the tent, which now had a lovely view of the Valmont Beauvais family tomb. They ate in silence, her leaning against the oak tree and him propped against a tomb. Silence seemed fitting, in a cemetery. Birds sang. Somewhere in the swamp, a loon giggled hysterically. Squirrels chittered.

And dead people lay rotting beneath their feet.

"Maybe we were wrong." Guy fidgeted with his jerky wrapper—this was Saturday, he could have meat—then stuffed it in his jeans pocket. He squinted up at the cloud-covered sun. "Maybe nobody hid any treasure here. Maybe there isn't even a treasure. Maybe we imagined all this."

Good. Then we can go home. Mary knew better than to say that. "Sacred ground makes sense, though," she admitted reluctantly. "It felt right, you know?"

"Yeah." He sighed. "I know. I just—" His free hand clenched into a fist. "We're so close, Mary. I can feel that, too. But what if we don't find it?"

Then other people might get lured to this place and die. Then we won't be able to stop the greedy son of a bitch who started all this. Then your cousin—and maybe my brother—could wander these swamps for eternity.

Lazare. "Lazare might show us," she said suddenly. "He's been trying to all along, right?"

Guy raised his eyebrows, pointed at her. "Now that we're here, maybe he'll just point the treasure out and we can..."

He stared at her, his face suddenly blank.

She stared back at him. Oh. Oh, my. They didn't have a clue as to what to do next, if they did find the treasure. Lazare wouldn't make an appearance before nightfall, they didn't know what to do if he did—and by then, they might have other creatures to deal with. What were they even doing here? What did they hope to accomplish?

Guy boosted himself away from the moldering tomb and strode on long legs to the tent. "I can't think anymore. I've got to get some sleep."

She would have said, "Help yourself," except that his voice shook. He'd probably had the same thought she did— what *did* they hope to accomplish? But it meant a lot more to him.

Maybe life and death.

She followed him into the tent.

He'd already spread his sleeping bag and sprawled on it, fully dressed, an arm draped across his face as if to block out the weak daylight. Or to mask his expression. He couldn't hide his mouth, though, and it telegraphed his discouragement. She'd always been able to read Guy's feelings, more or less—and she didn't even consider herself an empath. She... knew him.

Helping Lazare wasn't just something he felt he should do, she realized. Helping Lazare meant everything, *was* everything, to him. Icy tricklings of dread spread from her spine at that idea, wrapping around her ribs, chilling her neck. She drew several breaths, tried to picture him a week into the future.

Nothing.

Several days into the future.

Nothing.

She had an existence planned past this trip. She had a job to go back to, friends sending magical aid, Betsy's wedding to attend. But Guy had nothing past helping Lazare, assuming he even managed that much. He had planned nothing past it. Counted on nothing past it.

She remembered the skeletal Death card.

Was he going to die here? She didn't know. She might not be seeing things because, on some level, she just didn't want to. Fear, again with the fear. But that didn't have to mean death.

She didn't want him to die. The existence she'd planned past this trip suddenly seemed insignificant, if he couldn't have any part in it. She'd learned to get by without him once... but could she manage it a second time?

"Stop staring at me, Mary Margaret," he muttered, not moving his arm. "Get some sleep. We can't think if we're exhausted."

"I'm too tense to sleep." Her voice trembled, too. She hated being in a cemetery. The whole plantation felt like one.

Slowly Guy moved his arm from over his eyes. Could he see into her as deeply as his blue gaze promised, warned he could?

"Lie down next to me," he offered finally, huskily. "I won't let anything happen to you."

"It's not..." But she couldn't explain without going into her perhaps irrational phobia about death again. So she freed her own sleeping bag and spread it to overlap Guy's.

Then she stretched out beside him to gaze up at the top of the tent, fully dressed herself. She tried to think of something other than the tombs just outside.

With surprising ease, she did.

She'd never felt so aware of another person in her entire life. A small shadow darted across the tent—a flying bird, probably—and she heard the wood owl, again, and the muggy air felt thick as water in her lungs, but suddenly the only thing she could concentrate on was Guy's body, inches from hers.

His live body. The back of which she'd explored so thoroughly last night.

She reminded herself that they were fully dressed, and in a cemetery. He'd probably fallen asleep already.

She rolled over to look at him.

He met her gaze, still wide-awake. "You can handle the canoe okay," he said quietly, his voice low. Was it a question?

She nodded, just in case, feeling his warmth brush her skin even through their jeans and T-shirts.

"If you had to, you could get out on your own, right?"

That was when she realized what he was getting at. "Shut up."

He rolled onto his side, his head pillowed on one bare arm, to look more directly at her. "I'm not saying you'll have to."

"Don't even think it." She wanted to knock on wood, or cross her fingers, or do something to take any power out of his words. She wanted him alive, damn it. Alive, and with her. "Are you spending Easter with your family?"

He didn't answer. He just looked very, very sad.

No. She wouldn't accept that. Maybe he was getting premonitions—everyone was psychic—but he had to be misreading them. Or they were mere warnings of something that could be avoided. They had to have a future together; they just had to.

Or else—?

She didn't want to cry again. If they didn't have a future together, even as pen pals or just friends, she would have plenty of time to cry when—if—that happened. If they didn't have a future together, all they had left was now.

Guy's gaze drifted slowly over her, as if absorbing her, memorizing every bit of her.

She put her hand on his waist, near his hip, and the rightness of their mingling energies washed over her.

His gaze stilled on her face.

She slid closer, so that her sneakered toe touched his boot, and one of her knees brushed his, and one of his arms lay caught between them. She had to tip her head to hold his gaze.

He continued to stare at her. Maybe he didn't understand what she wanted. Maybe she didn't fully understand herself, but she'd read books and seen movies. She had a really good idea. She wanted him. Wanted to be with him, as fully and completely as possible, while she still could. Wanted to consummate the partnership, the friendship, the constant companionship they'd shared between them for so long as children. If he hadn't gone away, they would probably have ended up married. Maybe had a baby or two by now. Maybe been blissfully happy.

Even separated, they hadn't found anyone else. She couldn't imagine them in other relationships. Not as fully as they'd already given themselves to one another. They hadn't shared their bodies, but they'd shared their thoughts, hopes, fears. Far more intimate elements of themselves. Their souls.

Their bodies... This was just an afterthought.

Guy leaned nearer, and kissed her.

Mary's eyes fell closed at the brush of his lips on hers. Yes. He felt the bond, too. Even if they'd spent nearly half their lives apart. Even if they couldn't count on anything past this moment, either because of swamp zombies or because of his inability to stay around. Even if they had nothing else, past or future, they could try stop time and have a long-overdue now.

He freed his hand from between them and ran it up under her arm, down to her knee, up to her breast again. The biceps he'd used to pillow his own head, he now used to pillow hers, freeing that hand, behind her, to play across her back, to gather up handfuls of T-shirt and slide beneath its hem.

She arched against the touch of his callused palm to her bare back. When he rolled against her, covering her mouth for a far more thorough kiss, she lay back and let him. He was the expert here, right? Which didn't keep her from giving as good as she got—pressing her mouth eagerly against his, meeting his playful tongue with her own.

"*Chère,*" he breathed, his voice hot across her cheek, before their passion muffled him again. She wriggled impatiently against him, surprised and delighted by the sensations that fountained through her at his touch—and the anticipation of his touch. She copied his technique with the T-shirt, yanking his free of his waistband to slip her hand beneath, to feel the now familiar contours of his lats. It wasn't enough. She threw a leg over his, as well, pulled him closer.

He rolled, and she found herself more beneath than beside him; good. She used both her hands to wrestle at his T-shirt. With his assistance, she managed to pull it up over his head, giving her an up-close-and-personal view of his beautiful chest, which she'd missed out on last night. She spread her hands across his pectorals, skimmed them up to his delts, marveled in the hardness of him. Definitely worth the wait.

He lowered himself for another long, languorous kiss. And another. And another. Very soon, or was it?—she'd lost track—he'd lowered his chest onto hers, and his legs straddled hers, and his hips brushed erotically across hers. He rested most of his weight on his knees and elbows, both of his hands cradling her head, so she didn't feel at all in danger of being crushed. But his kisses and his gaze stole her ability to breathe for herself. The rhythmic rub of his loins against her abdomen, held just too far off her for her to really *feel* anything, had her holding her breath anyway.

Enough of that. She wrapped her arms around his torso, her legs around his thighs, and pulled him more firmly onto her. Now she felt him, all of him, hard and hot and wonderful even through two layers of denim, and she moaned.

He maintained the rhythm atop her, but more firmly, and she really resented those layers. She had to do something about that, but when she slid her hands from the back of his waistband toward the front, she couldn't squeeze in between their bodies. A dilemma. She didn't...mmm...want him to move off of her, either.

She ran her hands up his arms to his shoulders, then back down, thrusting herself against him each time he pressed down onto her. At least she could get off her own shirt, right? She only broke their rhythm maybe a beat or so, yanking the soft cotton up off her chest, breaking their kiss just long enough to get it over her head and then let it fall wherever.

Guy moaned, and kissed from her mouth to her neck to her collarbone to her breasts. Then he kissed each of them as thoroughly as he'd been kissing her mouth. He seemed to like that she didn't wear a bra; at this moment, she really liked that, too. His tongue on her nipples set her writhing beneath him, anxious, hungry, thirsty, needy. For him. All of him. His body, as well as his soul. She tried for his jeans again; managed to squeeze her hands between her thighs and his waist, managed to ride his swaying against her while she unbuttoned and then unzipped them. He raised his head from her breasts, and she whimpered a protest.

"*Chère*." He didn't say the word with his usual smoothness, either; it ground out of him. When she met his upward gaze, she saw desperation on his face. A need equal to her own embattled self-control. "We shouldn't," he

managed to say, even if he couldn't still his slow...
mmm...writhing.

"That's your morals, not mine," she gasped back.

"Not morals..." His eyes closed as she slid her hand into
the waistband of his briefs and felt the hardness of him—of
a man—in her palm for the first time. Hotter than she'd
imagined; more real, more pulsing. More alive.

He'd slept with other women, shared all of himself with
other women, he'd admitted that himself. Surely he didn't
mean to deny her. He felt the same way she did, didn't he?

"I didn't...bring anything," he managed to moan into
her collarbone, and suddenly she understood.

"I did," she assured him distractedly, still exploring the
length of him, testing his thickness. After a moment in
which he seemed to have trouble breathing, Guy slid back
up her and kissed her full on the mouth, so thoroughly that
she forgot to do anything with her hands. How could the
mere meeting of lips and tongues thrill her like this? When
he nibbled on her lower lip for a moment, she felt herself
melting into liquid beneath him. He would have no one with
whom to make love. She would turn into a mere puddle of
pleasure.

"So can we?" she whispered, the words muffled by his
ministrations, but he seemed to understand.

"Well..." He stretched the word out, his voice rumbly
and low. "If you truly want to."

She nodded.

"I mean, if you really, truly want to."

She narrowed her eyes at him.

He kissed her again. After that, sensations began to blur
into one another. They skimmed out of their jeans, leaving
only his briefs and her panties, bare chests pressing together and pulling apart, bare legs entwining. They explored one another with hands, with mouths. At some
point, she managed to talk him—in gasping monosylla-
bles—through her duffel bag to the appropriate package. By

then she was already pulling off his briefs, more than ready to see all of him.

He rolled onto his back and let her.

Exactly what she'd expected, really, she thought, running her fingers over the smooth length of him to admire nature's cleverness, then slipping her hand between his legs to investigate the rest of the setup. Guy gasped, but when she checked on his expression, he was grinning at her. Yes, he definitely liked that. What she'd expected, and yet so much more real, she decided. Real, because he was here, with her, because he was hers.

Sort of. In every way that counted. For now.

His thumbs snagged at the waistband of her panties, and she wriggled her hips to help him, then lay across his hard stomach to lift her knees so that he could get the underwear the rest of the way off. Now they had nothing between them, nothing at all. Was she supposed to do anything specific—

He eased his big hand between her legs, stroking the delicate skin of her inner thighs, and she stopped thinking and merely focused on not falling over. His fingers explored her as she'd explored him, feathery touches sending ripples of pleasure through her. "Lie down," he murmured, and she did, the cotton of the sleeping bag beneath her strange and wonderful against her bare skin, but not as wonderful as him.

Leaning over her, he began to do intimate things with his hand, a lot more thorough than her explorations had been. He watched her face the whole time, held her gaze even as he brushed his thumb against her, its rhythm somehow matching the instinctive swivel of her hips. She felt something pressing at her, then felt him—his finger—slide inside her, and she gasped.

He paused, his eyes showing his concern.

She shook her head. "Don't you dare stop."

So he didn't. Soon—soon? she'd really lost track—she was fumbling at his hard arousal with clumsy hands, managing to make him gasp through their kisses, while he did a far more dexterous job with her. She arched against his hand, wanting more, wanting all of him, wishing he wouldn't put it off. Then sensations, new and wonderful because he gave them to her, pounded against her like surf, then broke over her, and she felt herself caught in an undertow, pulled under, drowning in the most wonderful way.

When Guy moved his hand, she felt lost and cried out. His kisses and soft murmurings assured her he was still there. She wrapped her arms around his waist to hold on to him, even so.

"I don't want to hurt you," he whispered at her, his eyes full of sincerity and desperation.

"You can't hurt me," she insisted, trying to touch him with all of herself, her legs and her belly and her breasts and her arms. He groped for something near her head, then shared a bashful grin with her as he tore the foil packet open with his teeth. Something else new—she took the slick rubber roll from his fingers, then softly slid it on him, smoothing it slowly down the length of him.

Guy sagged onto his side, eyes falling shut with frustrated appreciation. "You're sure you haven't done this before?"

"Not in this lifetime," she assured him, her own voice odd and hushed in the late-afternoon shadows of the tent. "Who knows about other lives?"

He played along, regaining strength to lever himself beside her again. His wonderful fingers played at her breasts, swirled around her belly button, then drifted between her legs to work more of their magic. "You mean maybe we've done this before?"

That would explain a lot, wouldn't it? "I wouldn't be . . . ahhh . . . surprised." She didn't want just his fingers anymore, and she pushed his hand away. For a moment, he looked surprised, but then comprehension dawned and he kissed her. Chest to her breasts. Mouth hot against her ear. His knees nudged hers farther apart; she felt his hardness against her thigh. Please. Soon—

Oh, my.

He slid into her, slowly, and her eyes widened in awe at the sensation. Pushing, stretching. It didn't hurt, really, but...oh, my. She kept thinking there couldn't be more, and then—

"Hey there. You all right?" His question tickled hair away from her ear. She realized she'd squeezed her eyes shut, and she opened them. She loved opening her eyes to his concerned face. The most familiar, most important face she'd ever beheld. Their souls had married long ago.

She nodded, not trusting herself to speak. He held her gaze a moment longer, making sure she wasn't lying—he could always tell if she lied—and then he nodded, kissed her...began to move.

Inside her.

She held tighter, not exactly uncomfortable, but still very relieved when little waves of desire began to lap through her once again. She relaxed, let herself float on the sensations, moved her hips languidly with the rhythm he'd set. She liked this. She definitely liked this. She'd like it even more if they went faster.

They did.

She laughed, then feared she'd hurt Guy's feelings or something, but he grinned back, brighter than the sun, not trying to hide his own relief and pleasure. After all their shared smiles over finding turtles or getting jokes, this one seemed particularly ironic, which only made them smile wider. He kissed her again, a wonderfully sloppy, hungry kiss, and began to move even more desperately against her and in her. When his thrusts got intense, she wrapped her legs around him, held on to him and trusted. The sensation of lapping waves became breakers, almost crashing over her, but drawing back; coming even closer, only to pull out again. Teasing, taunting. It followed the same rhythm as his thrusts, a slightly different excitement from what he'd given her with his hand. Better. This was all of him, every inch of him, skin and bone and muscle and heart and mind—

When the wave finally did break over her again, she let herself gasp and cry out, not afraid of drowning, because Guy wouldn't let anything happen to her. He'd said so. Their voices mingled, joyous, ecstatic, as their bodies lurched together at the swirling, explosive sensations they shared.

And then they lay, almost still. But even as she caught her breath, even as her vision cleared and the rushing sound faded, she moved slowly against him. Remembering this.

He slid out of her too soon for her liking, murmuring something about the condom. She didn't mind so much, since he gathered her against him, and she curled into his embrace. They cuddled together, warm and wet and sated, drifting with the buzz of insects outside, the songs of toads and frogs. A loon laughed again, somewhere in the distance—and thunder rumbled.

The wood owl hooted its own mournful call, very close.

They both remembered at the same time; Guy could feel it in the sudden tightening of Mary's embrace, as surely as he felt it in the pit of his stomach. Despite the ecstasy they'd just shared, they weren't simply two lovers, discovering each other for the first time on an innocent campout.

Nothing so safe as that.

"Where's the dog?" she whispered abruptly, wriggling from his arms to sit up. "Guy, where's Drifter?"

He propped himself on his elbows, more chilled by her sudden departure than by her widened eyes and suddenly shallow breath. "She was outside, last time I knew."

"Why hasn't she barked?" Mary scrambled to the tent flap to unzip it, standing for a better vantage point. "Drifter! Here, girl!"

Guy liked that she didn't pull anything over her beautifully fit body in a belated show of modesty. He wondered if she remembered that this wasn't the first time they'd seen each other nude. It didn't matter; they'd looked a heck of a lot different twenty years ago, and they'd had a lot more fun this time.

No, more than fun. Fun was the least of what they'd shared in this tent. By joining with her, making love to her, he'd participated in something a lot more momentous than mere enjoyment. He'd admitted something, to her and to himself, that he hadn't wanted to admit yet.

Something about how important she was, always had been and maybe, possibly, always could be to him.

At her gasp, he rolled to his feet and bent to her side to see what had frightened her. And she did look frightened, her normally fluid form stiffening at what she'd discovered. He expected something horrible. Maybe Drifter's mutilated doggie corpse lying at her feet. But Guy had to study the tombs, the oak, the rusted fence of the cemetery, before he finally got it.

She'd forgotten the cemetery was out there.

"Chère," he murmured, wrapping his arms around her from behind, hoping to relax her. God, she felt good against him. She felt right. A woman had never felt so right in his embrace. "It's all right, *chère.* They don't mind." She just shook her head; he brushed his cheek against her ear and murmured, "If you don't believe me, just ask them."

"No!" She squirmed away from him, fell to her knees on the sleeping bag and began to gather up her clothing and pull it on. "I don't do séances."

He sat back in surprise, wished she wouldn't get dressed. Not that he was up to a do-over just yet, but he'd kind of wanted to savor their intimacy a little longer.

Just in case.

He'd been teasing, but now that she mentioned it... "Is that a hard-and-fast rule?" He tried to keep his voice gentle.

"I don't do hard-and-fast rules, either," she murmured, rolling her shoulders before shrugging into her T-shirt. She'd already put on her jeans. Her sneakers came next.

He began to feel underdressed, and started to half-heartedly gather his own clothing.

She'd tied both shoes before she paused, shoulders dropping in defeat. "Why do you ask?"

She wasn't going to like this. Still, he really wanted to know. He and Mary didn't have secrets, right? They didn't have to play games. Anything he couldn't say to Mary could never be said, in this lifetime or beyond.

He cleared his throat; wished she didn't look so worried as she met his gaze.

"Could you find a way for us to say goodbye?" he asked. "If—if I died, I mean."

She stared. Well, he'd figured she wouldn't like it.

He hadn't realized she'd run out of the tent.

CHAPTER FIFTEEN

He pulled on his jeans without briefs, his boots without socks, and managed to follow Mary out in barely a minute. She hadn't gone that far—just past the remains of the iron fence, just far enough to be outside the cemetery. He couldn't see her face, but he could tell she was hugging herself like he wanted to hug her, could tell she'd bowed her head as if in prayer.

Or defeat.

Idiot! He shouldn't have let her come along, certainly shouldn't have let their first time be in a graveyard, *definitely* shouldn't have joked about—then asked her about—doing a séance.

Even if he'd really wanted to know.

The sky hung close to the treetops, its deepening gloom announcing the approach of night and storm. The air felt thick and eerily still, maybe for the same reason.

"Hey there," he said softly, after wading through weeds to reach her. Should he touch her? He wanted to, wanted to hold her and never let go...but fate and whatever lurked in the coming storm might have different plans.

Mary didn't reply with her usual "Hey yourself." She did look up at him, though, her eyes brimming with tears. Okay, so she'd always cried easily. But this time it tore at him, like a skeletal hand squeezing his heart.

He said, "The dog's out here somewhere." A stupid change of subject, but at least it kept the muggy, darkening silence at bay. "She's probably off chasing rabbits or something."

Maybe that wouldn't comfort her. After all, dogs chasing rabbits was what had started the whole Sneezy Bunny incident. He decided to give up on witty conversation, and instead whistled through his teeth for Drifter.

The sound cut the twilight, sharp and clear. Then the twilight seeped back, so thick he almost didn't hear Mary's whisper of "Please don't leave me." When she blinked, the welling dampness in her eyes spilled over and ran down her face.

He almost didn't hear her. But he did.

Without hesitation, he pulled her into his arms, against his bare chest, hugged her so tight that if he hadn't trusted her to protest he might have feared hurting her. But Mary really could take care of herself. As a kid, she could run and jump and climb with the best of them. As an adult, she had already built a better life than his...despite her broken-down houseboat.

Another subsonic rumble of thunder, as audible in his chest as his ears, sounded vaguely nearer. If he *did* have to leave her—if he maybe died—she'd be okay, wouldn't she?

"I don't want to." He longed to promise more than that.

"Then don't. We don't have to do this, do we? We're safe for tonight. We could stay here, then go tomorrow. If you leave the coin here, that thing should stop coming after you, right?"

He didn't say anything. He could tell by the catch in her voice that she knew, as surely as he did, that they couldn't just quit. As Lazare's cousin, he couldn't ignore the spirit's pleas. As a human being, he couldn't leave this creature to possibly kill again. And as a man...

As a man, he had to finish something for once in his life. If he gave up yet again, just to buy a little more time with Mary Deveraux, then he wouldn't be someone she could love, anyway.

Assuming she could ever love him.

Assuming she should.

A rustling in the underbrush caught his attention, and he turned with Mary to see Drifter running toward them, tail whipping excitedly at the summons. The dog stopped several feet from them, then crept closer, as was her habit. Guy left one hand on Mary's waist as he crouched into the weeds, scratched behind Drifter's ears, let her sniff his fingers and warily lick his hand. He glanced at Mary, saw that she'd extended a halfhearted hand toward the dog, too, but hadn't bent to actually reach her. When Mary saw him watching, she dropped the hand to her side and simply smiled faint relief at Drifter's return.

Impersonal reaction, for someone who'd been so worried. Then again, she didn't keep pets—for a reason, right? She'd rather not love Drifter than love her and lose her.

He stood, turning his attention away from the dog and back to the companion who really mattered. "You wouldn't really want me to give up *now,* would you?"

She shook her head, hugged herself again. "It's just that you keep leaving me," she admitted, not quite meeting his gaze. "You did after Joey and Lazare...after..."

"My whole family moved, *chère,*" he reminded her.

She shook her head. "But you barely wrote. You didn't call. You didn't just physically move away, Guy. Inside, you left me, too. And I still don't know why."

Because he'd been a kid? Because he'd known he would remind her of her brother's death? Because—oh, heck, he didn't know why he'd let go of her. He just...had.

"I'm here now," he reminded her gently, reaching for her. But she backed away, the way Drifter might.

He didn't understand. Still half-naked, he felt weak and sated from what they'd been doing in the tent—which, by the way, had been something he would remember for the rest of his life, even if that turned out to be blessedly longer than he feared. Mary's tousled hair, and slightly swollen lips, also bespoke their recently shared passion. She'd wanted it as much as he had, enjoyed it as much as he had, so why—?

Maybe his eyes asked the same question, because Mary hesitated before meeting his gaze. "I'm afraid you're going to leave me again. I was afraid before you went to Bobby Lee's, and then, after you showed up at my place and we almost . . . made love . . . well, then it hurt even worse."

"What hurt?"

"My being afraid," she explained. "And now it hurts so bad, I don't know if I can stand it. I don't know if the pain is worth it, Guy. It hurts too much."

He stared, and finally realized why he hadn't kept writing. He'd tried to stay away from her. He'd thought—maybe foolishly, maybe not—that he wouldn't be any good for her. Even after returning to Stagwater, he'd fought this overwhelming bond between them, because he'd sensed that somehow he wouldn't be around much longer, whether he wanted to or not.

But she'd insisted on coming along. She'd made love to him. He'd lost the fight, and now that he just wanted to spend what time he might have left in her arms, she didn't want to be with him anymore, just because there was a good chance it would end.

What really twisted in his gut was the realization that even if his sense of foreboding was wrong, and even if they did both make it out of the swamp, her reluctance might remain.

After all, everything ended.

He didn't know what he could say to comfort her. He'd never been that good with words anyway, and now he had ghosts and swamp zombies and the possibility of imminent death to distract him.

"All you have to do is completely forget me, like you did last time," he told her, and headed back into the cemetery, back to the tent, to get dressed properly. He paused again. "At least stand inside the gate?"

She didn't look at him as she complied, moving to safety. The Reaper hadn't actually needed lightning to appear. It might not necessarily need storms or darkness, either, though they were obviously about to have a heaping dose of both. Guy stalked over to the tent, Drifter scampering at his heels, leaving Mary outside, where she wanted to be—alone.

Good thing she hadn't let herself get attached to the dog, either.

Long rolls of thunder echoed over the plantation grounds, on and on, until Mary thought it would never be quiet again. She wanted to cover her ears and scream, but Guy might hear.

Though it was so loud he might not.

Finally the thunder rumbled out—not exactly to silence, though. An unnatural wind had kicked up, making the loblolly pines bend and sway against the dark sky, making the Spanish moss across the channel sound like rushing water. Different bird cries mingled—warblers and herons and blackbirds and ducks—distraught at the approaching storm.

She caught a flash of movement and glanced toward the shadow-shrouded tent. Guy, checking on her again. He turned back inside, but not before she noticed that he was holding the rifle. Getting ready. Just like her.

She hated waiting. She hated knowing that something horrible could happen at any moment, and having no idea how she might counter it. Well, no more idea than hiding under her sleeping bag in the tent and churning out protective energy until whatever it was was over. Without Guy, the sleeping bag wouldn't be all that great, and not just because of how he'd made her body feel—how her body still felt. Without Guy, nothing would be all that great.

Besides, when she peeked out tomorrow, the situation wouldn't have improved. The Reaper wouldn't leave on its own.

She'd known Guy wouldn't agree to wait it out and leave things unfinished. She probably would be disappointed in him if he had. But after discovering the ecstasy of loving him, she would be willing to put up with a lot of disappointment if it meant he stayed. She really wanted this man in her future.

But without any assurance of that, having him in her present really twisted up her insides something awful.

Lightning laced the southern sky, all corners and forks, and then vanished to darkness. One Mississippi, two Mississippi, three Mississippi, four Mississip—

Another roll of thunder struck and echoed, as if the sky were a bowling alley... and she a pin. The rush of the wind sounded even louder, and she turned to look over the tops of the plastered tombs, vaguely visible as squares of lighter gray against the dark, toward the sound of it. That was when she recognized the sound as rain, coming at the cemetery in a wall of sheeting water. The tent, hardly visible anyway, vanished in a wet blur. The downpour kicked up a mist off one of the low tombs, then another, then all of them.

In a moment, Mary was drenched. She raised her hands over her head to fend off the battering rain; even with a forearm sheltering her eyes, she could barely see two feet ahead of her. She could probably find the tent—but if this wind kept up, the tent wouldn't be so safe, anyway.

And what they hoped—or at least needed—to see tonight wouldn't show up in the tent.

Mary ducked for the best immediate cover—the wall of the high stone tomb of the Valmont Beauvais family. Against one wall, she merely shielded the tomb from the downpour, instead of it her. But when she circled it, her jeans sodden and heavy against her legs, her hair dripping into her eyes, she found some measure of calm in its shelter.

There are dead people in there.

She tried not to think about it. She shivered; the storm had brought an incredible chill for almost April. Hopefully the tent would keep their clothes and sleeping bags dry. They hadn't found, and wouldn't find, any dry wood for a fire on *this* trip.

At a sudden flash of light, her breath caught in her throat—but then she recognized threads of lightning.

One Mississippi, two Mississippi, three—

Thunder slammed across her like a blow, shaking the ground. She pressed herself more firmly against the patched plaster of the high-walled family tomb. *Forget that there are dead people in there, Mary.*

The deluge beat flat the weeds in the semiopen patches of the cemetery. The storm's power felt tangible, buffeting the swamp with such strength, she questioned her ability to even try harnessing it. It felt destructive—much of nature had to be, she reminded herself. That was what kept things going, right?

Tell that to the dead people behind you.

Fingers touched her shoulder. She screamed.

"It's me!" The sudden brightness of the halogen lantern filled the shadows on their side of the tomb; despite the fact that its glow held no real warmth, Mary absorbed the security of the light with her whole being. The security of Guy's solid grip felt even better.

He seemed to be fighting a grin, probably at how easily he'd scared her. "Why didn't you go into the tent, where you can get dry?" He had to yell the words over the rush of the storm around them. "I can watch for Lazare by myself!"

"Like hell you will!" She jumped as a bright lightning bolt suddenly punctuated a series of strobing flickers. One Mississippi, two—

Thunder swallowed them. She covered her ears, ducked against Guy's chest until the noise echoed away—and she realized he'd strapped the rifle over his shoulder.

When she lowered her hands, he pressed something into one.

"You keep this!" As he released the lantern, his gaze gauged her for a moment, as if reconciling her closeness with her previous rejection of his touch. She considered telling him that, chilled and frightened as she felt, she would huddle against any human, male or female, just as anxiously.

She said nothing. Maybe she *would* take shelter with just about anyone, but it wouldn't feel the same as taking shelter with Guy. When he put his arm around her with careful, buddylike nonchalance, she smiled her gratitude at him and tried not to snuggle even closer.

He shrugged, glanced into the incessant torrent of rain . . . and his face paled. He said something.

"What?" She tried to follow his gaze, couldn't see.

"Turn off the light!" he repeated, louder. Reluctantly, she did. The lantern hadn't helped her night vision, but she could see, through the curtain of rain, what might be a churning brightness, a bluish green smear of light.

Her chest froze, and she realized she was holding her breath, waiting for the giggle. She'd never been so thankful for anything as she was for Guy's solid, warm presence beside her, for the heavy arm that tightened around her.

Especially when lightning hit again, so close she heard it hiss and strike, smelled the ozone, barely started counting before thunder crashed on top of them—and they saw Lazare.

Not the *couchemal*. They saw Lazare.

Blue-green light still made up his mass, but it had to be more than light, since it didn't vanish in the flash of lightning. As darkness washed back over them, they could still see the small, self-illuminated figure that pushed between iron bars in the decrepit fence. It—he—cringed, young shoulders huddled beneath what looked like a T-shirt, as if the rain were buffeting him as mercilessly as it did them.

But it couldn't, could it? He was a ghost!

Another swoosh, then a crack of lightning, amid its accompanying thunder, sparked an explosion somewhere across the channel of hyacinths. Mary looked, despite her horrified fascination with the ghost. She guessed the lightning had blown the top off a cypress tree. Guy's fingers dug almost painfully into her arm, and she reluctantly looked back.

The ghost ran toward them, ducking and weaving in the rain.

She pressed a fist to her mouth, not wanting the moan that built in her chest to find its way out. It was Lazare! She recognized him, as clearly as if she were again thirteen years old. His slightly overlong, curling hair. His gangly build. His flared brows, and serious nose. She even recognized the baggy jeans he wore as hand-me-downs from Guy.

A much younger Guy.

It—he—ran closer. She found herself pressing back into the tomb, into Guy, wanting nothing more than to run in the other direction, despite the rain. Guy wouldn't move; she was trapped.

Lazare, or his oddly lit ghost, reached their side of the tomb, perhaps three feet from her, and leaned against its wall. He hunkered against the cracked plaster, then sank into a crouch, clearly drenched, exhausted, and frightened.

Mary wanted to shut her eyes. Seeing that he had scratches all over his arms, and how he sucked on his hand, which seemed to have blisters, only heightened her desperation to try, against impossibility, to help heal him. She turned her own hand, not surprised that she shared similar wounds from a day and a half in the canoe. Of course Lazare couldn't have gotten this far without a boat.

He doesn't need a boat, part of her protested. *He's a ghost!* But he wasn't a ghost, she realized, when this happened.

"It's a recording," she whispered, cringing inwardly when the ghost began to cry. The ghost? No, it was just a little boy crying. A little runaway boy—eleven years ago.

"Lazare!" Guy's voice surprised her; she jumped, despite his arm around her. Lazare went on crying. "Lazy! I'm here!"

She shook her head. "It's a recording!" A strobe of lightning lit Guy's confused expression. He didn't know how the elements around a place—the trees, the ground, maybe in this case the tombs themselves—could hold images of what had once happened . . . and sometimes of what would happen in the future.

"Like a videotape!" she explained. "We're watching the playback!"

Thunder rolled over them, louder and louder, until it echoed into silence. The wind had died down enough for them to hear the sound of the rain on the ground, the tombs, the leaves of the trees and vines and bushes around them.

Enough for them to hear Lazare's ragged, broken sobs.

Guy groaned, deep in his chest, and let go of Mary. She caught at his arm as he stepped around her, but let her hand slide free, didn't dare follow him to the ghost's side. She could only watch, frozen, as he crouched beside the child's figure. Wrong. It looked all wrong to see Guy, grown and strong, beside Lazare, forever caught in childhood. It looked as if someone had pasted two pictures together.

"Lazy," Guy repeated, and reached out for the boy's glowing shoulder. His hand slid right through it, as if through an image from a projector, and Guy closed his eyes against an inner agony Mary could only guess at. "Oh, Lazare . . ." His voice grew thick. Husky. She could barely hear him, even over the slowing rain. "I'm sorry, *chère*," he said to the boy. "I'm so sorry."

Sorry? Why would he be—?

Lazare wiped his eyes, glanced up—and stiffened. For a moment, Mary thought he finally recognized Guy's presence; from Guy's expression, he thought so, too. But Lazare looked right through him, then wiped off his face with the back of his hand, pushed dripping bangs from his ghostly forehead, and stood.

Eyes on something, he walked right through Guy.

Mary dodged out of the way before he could reach her; even so, she felt a cold far worse than the storm's chill as he wafted by her. The cold helplessness of death. She shuddered off the sensation before turning to see him heading toward the huge live oak tree that stood sentinel over the cemetery.

She looked at Guy, who looked at her, and they followed.

The rain fell steadily, but without its previous violence. A flare toward the north signaled lightning, and made Lazare's glowing form seem suddenly solid and real for a brief, too-brief, moment. With darkness's return, he became a ghost again.

One Mississippi, two Mississippi, three Mississippi, four Mississippi... Thunder halfheartedly echoed the lightning.

Lazare reached the tree, his head cocked. Then he plopped onto his knees, with childlike disregard for mud or stickers.

"No." Guy breathed the word, beside her, and Mary turned from the ghost to look at him. Horror played across his face as he realized... what? "God, no. Lazy, wait!"

He ran past her, toward the tree. Drifter chased after him, from whatever shelter she'd taken during the worst of the storm. Mary scrambled to catch up, circling the tree—and the ghost—to stand beside the corroded iron fence.

Guy dropped to his knees beside Lazare. "No," he repeated, loudly. "Lazare, leave it. You've got to hear me. Leave it."

Of course, the ghost didn't hear. It reached into the roots of the tree, and withdrew...nothing. She squinted—was she just not seeing? Lazare seemed to think he had something. He held it with evenly spaced hands, set it to the ground as if he could barely heft the weight. Delight played across his translucent face, that devilish mischief that had suited him so well. An adventure. He'd found an adventure.

She realized what Guy already had. He'd found the treasure.

"No!" Guy shouted it now, right in the ghost's ear. Lazy, oblivious, fiddled at something with his fingers, then lifted a nonexistent lid. His mouth fell open.

Guy stared up at Mary. "Stop him!"

She stared back. "He's already done it! It's the past. How can we change—?"

His jaw set; his eyes poured desperation out at her. Anything was possible, wasn't it? The fact that the three of them were clustered together, in an abandoned cemetery, proved that.

Quantum time. She snatched a pine branch from the ground and, as quickly as she could, traced a circle around them and as much of the oak tree as she could reach. The sodden branch broke twice. She used its shorter version, getting a palmful of dirt and bark, envisioning blue light pouring from the tool. It made a sphere around them—a magic circle. Quickly she murmured the words she always did—*this circle, bound in power*—placing them between the worlds, magically speaking, in a placeless place and a timeless time. A *timeless* time. She held her breath.

Lazare reached toward the opened box which she now, suddenly, saw. "No!" commanded Guy, yet again.

Lazare leaped up and backward, like he'd been thrown. Then he stared, not quite focusing on them. "Wha—?"

His voice echoed, surreal, like the *couchemal*'s giggle.

"I don't think he sees you," Mary whispered to Guy, who'd started at the boy's reaction himself. "Try to picture yourself as being made out of light, like he is."

"What?"

She did it for him. Lazare stared. Well, how was he supposed to recognize—

"Gilly? Is that you?"

She didn't believe it. How could he know? He was nine years old; to him, Guy should be a lanky fifteen-year-old.

Guy had to swallow, hard, before he said anything else. "Yeah, kid, it's me."

"Look what I found!" Lazare gestured toward the translucent box in front of him. "It's got money in it! I'm gonna bring some back so Mama and Papa won't fight about money anymore!"

"Don't bring it back, Lazy."

The little boy reached for the treasure. "I can't carry a lot, but if everyone treats me nice, maybe we can come back for the rest together, eh?"

"Don't touch it, Lazy!"

Lazare frowned, obviously disliking Guy's tone. "You can't tell me what to do. You aren't even you! You're all grown up."

"Yeah." Guy's voice broke. Mary felt tears mingling with the rain on her face, crying for him. "I'm all grown up, Lazy. And you aren't."

Lazare stared. Somewhere, from the woods beyond the fence, a wood owl hooted in the rain.

"That money is cursed, Lazare. It's going to kill you, and Joey Deveraux, too. You've got to leave it alone, do you understand me? For the love of God, Lazare, leave it alone."

Mary knew the stubborn set of Lazare's chin. He never had taken very well to being given orders. She held her breath...and released it only when he sat back on his heels.

"Joe-baby, too?"

Don't call him that. He hated it when you called him that.

"The money's cursed. I wouldn't lie to you about that, would I?" Guy spread his hands, holding the ghost's gaze, obviously relieved when Lazare shook his head.

"Nah," said the little boy. "I guess you wouldn't. Not 'bout something as 'portant as this."

"Go home, Lazare," Guy said. "Please, put the box back, and just go home."

The child pouted. "Not even one coin?"

Guy shook his head. And the little boy, with pouting, overexaggerated reluctance, shut the lid on the box and tucked it into its shelter, mostly hidden beneath the roots of the tree. He stood, brushed off his knees, cast another longing glance toward the tree . . . and then laughed at Guy. "Bet you can't catch me!"

As the child bolted away from them, Guy scrambled to his feet, looking almost as if he'd follow.

But they couldn't see anything for him to chase.

Quietly, surreptitiously, Mary removed the magical circle, mouthing her usual chant—*ever the circle continues*—to herself. She felt strangely, eerily calm. Shock, she supposed. Even though she'd seen it happen... "I don't understand."

Guy continued to look through the steady rainfall, searching for another sight of his cousin. He wasn't, she knew instinctively, going to catch it. Lazare had gone.

"I don't understand," she repeated, turning on the halogen lantern and setting it at the base of the tree. "I want to believe we changed the past, but we wouldn't even be here if Lazare hadn't died, would we? Is it possible—?"

The idea was too wonderful, too incredible, to risk by saying it out loud. Guy, meeting her gaze with his own, blue eyes full of tentative hope, obviously felt the same way. And yet... She believed in magic, but this!

He dug into his back pocket, yanked out a worn wallet. Crouching beside the lantern, he flipped it open. She looked over his shoulder at Tiboy's wedding photo, then a picture of his parents. An old snapshot of them—Mary and Guy—laughing in Mary's backyard. Before she could register that he'd kept that, that he'd carried it all this time, he'd flipped past it to a family portrait. He closed his eyes, shoulders dropping, disappointment washing across his features.

His parents, his two brothers, his tante Eva, and himself. Tante Eva looked drawn, broken, just as she'd looked ever since Lazare drowned. They hadn't changed the past. Not *their* past.

Guy closed his wallet abruptly, shoved it back into his pocket, and turned to the oak tree. He reached under the roots, disregarding any danger of snakes or possums, and pulled out an already familiar box, crusted over with dirt. He jabbed at the latch, tried again, then hit the box angrily.

"Guy!" She fell to her knees beside him, grabbed at his arm. He shrugged her off, pried the lid open, stared at the coins that filled it. Treasure. If double eagles were worth twenty dollars, there could be a thousand dollars in this chest, not counting increased value. A thousand dollars must have been worth far more, a hundred and fifty years ago.

But not worth human lives.

"Son of a bitch," muttered Guy, and Mary realized it was the first time she'd heard him swear—recently, at least. "Goddamn son of a bitch! All for this. All for this lousy—"

"Guy!" She grabbed his arm again, and this time held on until he glared at her. "It won't help! We did everything we could. We couldn't change our own pasts, our own lives, but that doesn't mean that maybe, on some kind of alternate timeline, Lazy and Joey didn't die. Maybe somewhere else, in another realm—" Maybe she and Guy had never separated, had gone to high school together, to the school dance like they were supposed to. Maybe they'd fallen in love, gotten married, even had children by now.

Staring into his handsome, angry, familiar face—as familiar, she thought, as her own, as familiar as the soul beneath it—she dismissed that thought. No maybe about it. Somewhere, on another timeline, they had definitely done all those things.

"It's okay," she insisted. "Lazare's going to be okay. That's why we came out here, right? To put Lazare to rest?"

Guy slammed the box's lid. "That's one of the reasons."

She frowned. Then she understood. The treasure. They couldn't just leave the treasure here, for anyone to find. Not with that thing—the pirate, the Reaper—waiting somewhere in the rain-drenched darkness for the next unwary soul to trade his life for a handful of coins.

"Are you sure," asked Guy, low, "that we can't kill something if it's already dead?"

She shrugged, disturbed by the edge to his voice and very aware of the rifle over his shoulder, but still not letting go.

"I don't do hard-and-fast rules, remember? It makes sense, though."

"What about vampires? They're dead, right?"

Like Count Dracula? "I don't know! If Sylvie were here, maybe she could help, but she isn't. Maybe you *destroy* undead things, instead of *killing* them."

"What's the difference?"

"Guy, I'm just a witch, I'm not an encyclopedia of the occult!" When he glared at her, she glared right back. "You know as well as I do that we aren't dealing with something natural, here. It was bones, remember? A skeleton. Steve Peabody said that even Lazare's skeleton could only have survived eleven years by being stuck in a tree. Do you think this guy's bones could have hung around for over a hundred and fifty years, if Lazy's couldn't make it eleven?"

"Considering that it's walking around without muscles, I don't guess it's behaving naturally, no," Guy agreed.

"Which means it can't be destroyed like something natural could," she insisted, torn between hugging him and smacking him. Being a healer, she decided on the hug— which he didn't return. She tried not to feel disappointed. She was the one who'd backed away from his hug, just this evening.

She'd forgotten that destructive emotions, like hurt, could just build more destruction. Only positive emotions had any real power. Which gave her an idea. "Guy, what we really want to do is stop this thing, right? Not necessarily destroy it?"

He eyed her warily. "What's the difference?"

"I think I know a way we can keep this pirate thing, this Reaper, from going after anyone else. But I don't know if you're going to like it."

He already didn't like it; she could tell. His voice dropped, low, almost threatening. "Cough it up, Mary Margaret."

She liked her old-fashioned-sounding name, from his lips. It wasn't just a Catholic name. It was her, her youth. "He's killing people to get at his treasure, right?"

Guy nodded. "Right."

She didn't have to be a psychic to know he *really* wasn't going to like this. "So we give him back his treasure."

CHAPTER SIXTEEN

Guy said, "You're joking." It wasn't a question.

In the light of the lantern on the ground beside them, Mary held his gaze. Her hair was slicked over her face; her T-shirt had soaked dark and clingy. "I am not joking. You weren't going the keep the money, right?"

He shook his head. He could do a lot with that kind of wealth, sure—if he lived to spend it. But it was blood money.

"Is it that you don't get to kill anything this way?" she asked, concerned now, lowering her voice as the rain around them softened to a patter.

"No! I never wanted—I don't want to kill anything. But you're asking me to give in. How can I do that? If this thing really killed Lazare, it should be punished." He wished he could see her expression better—had she scrunched her face up with displeasure, or was she merely squinting through the rain? "That son of a—" No. He'd gotten that out of his system. "That low-life murdering *pirate*—" he spit the word out as nastily as the worst curse he knew "—ought to be punished."

Mary continued to blink up at him, and even if he couldn't see her expression, he could see her calm golden eyes. "By us?"

He stared back at her and swiped a handful of wet hair out of his face. "Someone should pay."

"We already have!"

Huh? He shook his head, sure he hadn't heard her right. She grabbed his hand, and the charge that ran up his arm—was it safe to touch a psychic in the rain?—felt very real. He could see her face more clearly then, for some reason could see everything more clearly. A huge rising moon, still haloed behind mist, peeked from behind heavy clouds to the east.

He could tell from the determination in her expression that she'd meant exactly what she'd said.

"You've been punishing yourself since it happened, Guy," she insisted. "That's why you stopped writing me, isn't it? Someone had to pay, and since we didn't watch over Joey and Lazy, it might as well be us."

He shook his head. Ridiculous. But his breath fell shallow.

"You've been punishing yourself," she insisted, as earnestly as when she'd announced that the human remains were indeed Lazare's. She knew it, the way Mary knew anything else she set her mind to. "Because you were with me instead of Lazy that day. Why else would you screw up your scholarship? Why else wouldn't you build yourself any kind of life?" Her face tipped entreatingly toward his, washed in the delicate glow of the half-hidden moon. "Why else would you stay away from me?"

He stared down at her, barely able to breathe, chilled by far more than his wet clothing. She was right. Of course, it couldn't be that simple, but on one level, at least—one deep, resonant level—she really was right. Merciful God in heaven.

"It wasn't our fault," Mary insisted, still holding his hand in both of hers. "And even if it had been, we paid enough. You punished yourself, because people do that. So did the Reaper, by hiding the treasure where his spirit couldn't get to it. If he's really guilty, he'll keep on punishing himself. Maybe your God will help, who knows? But at least we can keep him from killing other people as part of it!"

And that, really, was what they'd come for.

He stood, then used his hand around hers to help her up. They were a mess, soaked and muddied and both trembling from their recent encounter. "I'm not just handing the treasure over to it,'' he told her. But he could tell when her eyes lit that she heard the *maybe* in his tone. ''It's not like it can pick it up and carry it off, even once it's off sacred ground, right?''

''No pockets,'' she agreed with a hopeful smile.

''Right, no pockets.'' He looked toward what he could see of the sagging gateway in the rusted iron fence. He tried to remember the distance to the dead lake. A hundred yards, easy—maybe more.

Mary followed the line of his gaze, then looked back to him, suddenly nervous. ''The bayou?''

He attempted a grin. ''No lungs, either. No reason this pirate guy can't baby-sit his treasure at the bottom of the bayou as easily as he could out here. And nobody else will find it.''

''But—'' Her hold on his hand tightened. ''It's so far. If the Reaper's around, you'll have to get all the way to the water without him...without...'' Suddenly her face brightened, as if washed by a streak of moonlight. ''Wait a minute. We can do it tomorrow! It will be daylight then. You'll be safe—''

''If it's storming?'' Tonight's storm had hit before sundown—not that he would have known that without looking at his watch. ''How do we even know it isn't manipulating the weather? I can't keep waiting, *chère*. I can't keep putting this off!''

He needed this.

She shook her head.

''I've sprinted that far before, lots of times,'' he reminded her, not mentioning that he hadn't sprinted through tangled underbrush in the dark, or with that kind of weight. He'd known the risk from the first night he'd seen the *couchemal*, the night that had brought Mary back into what might be all that was left of his life.

She'd also known the risk, fairly soon after that.

He gazed down at her in the rain-drenched gloom. He'd been an idiot to stay away all these years. If he'd come back right after high school, they could have had so much more. She was right. People did create their own punishments. But this was the end of it. The last obstacle on his quest. If he got through this, he vowed silently, he'd stop punishing himself and try to live for what he really wanted.

At the top of that list was Mary Deveraux.

He bent to her; she lifted her face to his. At first their lips brushed almost hesitantly. Then the kiss deepened, trying to express what they should have had years together to say. That they really were a package deal. That he hadn't meant, in denying himself, to deny her, too.

When they leaned back from one another, caught their breath, he realized they had at some point embraced, tightly. He gave her a final hug.

Then he let her go.

Her eyes echoed fear back at him. He'd forgotten that she might not want to be on his list—that she might not love him, for fear of losing him. He wished he could turn back time—again—and keep her from those fears. But of course he couldn't.

He ran the backs of his fingers across and off her cheek— then shrugged off the rifle and lifted the metal box. D— Darn, but it was heavy. Still, he decided, hefting it as he walked to the gateway from the cemetery, he could do this. They had a plan. At least he knew, for the first time in a long time, that he was doing the right thing.

The heavy clouds parted farther, allowing more moonlight through, as if God himself—herself? whichever—approved of their intent. Guy grinned encouragement toward Mary, who stood with the lantern and looked stricken. "Be safe, *chère*," he instructed her. His throat tightened. "Please don't forget—"

But he couldn't ask her that. If the only way she could go on, should he not come back, was to forget him, then so be it. He'd be dead. It shouldn't matter to him.

He filled himself with the sight of her, one last time, and admitted that it did matter.

Then he held the box to his chest like a football—and ran.

Everything fell into slow motion around him, like a nightmare in which he struggled forward, only to be pulled back. He realized that he could navigate the roots and vines well enough in the moonlight. He saw nothing threatening, no flashes of white from the trees, no movements in the shadows, nothing to foreshadow the Grim Reaper's approach. But that didn't make him feel better. At least if he saw it, he could prepare.

The dog ran ahead of him, illuminated in a dancing white light—and he heard footsteps behind him, echoing his own. Small footsteps. Familiar footsteps. Mary!

He wanted to yell at her to go back to the assumed safety of the cemetery, but refused to split his concentration from his main goal—the water. The sound of their feet accompanied him past the sentinel oaks that had once lined a drive, and now merely guarded ghosts. He saw a flash of white, and movement! He recognized a fleeing white-tailed deer before he could panic.

His breath tore from his chest in a counterrhythm to his pounding footsteps. He hadn't actually run like this recently, not with this kind of load. What if he didn't make it?

But then he did. He ducked through the trees that crowded the bank. The water rose up to meet him, not a bony hand or gaping eye socket in sight. Unwilling to stop, determined to end this, Guy splashed into the water. Duckweed, an almost impossible green in the spotlight of Mary's lantern, sloshed away from him, showing darker brown water beneath it. His feet sank, deep, into mud, but he waded farther in. Knee-high. Waist-high.

"What are you doing?" screamed Mary, behind him.

"Nobody's going to find this thing again!" he shouted back, taking another gooshy step, then another. Water lapped his ribs, his chest. The sturdy leaves of a hyacinth brushed past his arm.

Enough. He'd done all he could; that had to be enough. With both arms and all his strength, Guy hurled the chest of coins outward, into the bayou. The lid flew open as it arced. Coins spilled out, catching halogen and moonlight before plunking into the water just before the box. More duckweed and hyacinth bobbed away in spiraling ripples from the treasure's splash.

It sank in the dirty water. "And stay there," Guy ordered, low. "You son of a—gun."

He stood in a pool of light, catching his breath. Farther across the oxbow lake, moonlight reflected more naturally off the water, which calmed quickly. He heard the *splash* sound of a fish, and the staccato call of a night heron. Then the other night sounds joined in, tentative at first, quickly swelling. Crickets, tree toads, *ouaouaron*. Guy found turning awkward, with silty footing and tangling, submerged roots to trip him, and so he merely lifted his feet from the bottom as he did a backstroke, then rolled onto his chest to check on Mary.

It waited.

He half feared he'd see a skeletal creature, dripping ooze and vegetation, standing right behind her. He didn't. She stood on the sapling-crowded bank, alone except for Drifter at her feet. She'd pressed a hand to her mouth, and now stared joyfully over it, as if she'd forgotten it was there, tears of relief catching moonlight, as well.

She couldn't believe it had been this easy, either, he guessed as he found purchase in the goo again, maybe ten feet from the bank, waist-deep in the water. Okay, he did worry that maybe an alligator or a water snake could still turn this into a lousy night. But that was paranoia, he knew. It seemed too easy. But it had been easy because it had been the right thing.

"It's all right, Mary Margaret," he assured her, and she slowly lowered her hand, smiled the most precious smile he'd ever seen. "We did it, *chère*. Lazare's at rest. The Reaper has his treasure—may it do him no good. Everything's taken care of." *Except us.* But they had time now to deal with them; all the time in the world. This time, he wasn't going anywhere.

The smile on Mary's face hovered, suddenly uncertain. "Did you get rid of that last coin?" she asked, as he struggled his way into water that only came hip-high. "The one in your pock—"

It struck.

A sudden loud splashing of water behind Guy drowned out the rest of her words. A skeletal arm fastened itself around his chest, another around his neck, and they pulled him backward. His feet lost purchase on the silty bottom as he fell, making another splash, yelling out instead of gasping a last precious breath.

The weedy surface of the muddy water closed over his head.

Yesss.

She screamed. Useless. Helpless. She knew that, but she screamed anyway. One moment, everything had been fine, more than fine, the beginning of a wonderful happily-ever-after. And then the Reaper had reared, shiny-wet and mercilessly dead, from the black water behind Guy, and yanked him under, so fast she'd barely seen it. She hadn't had to. A heavy sense of déjà vu suffocated her, drowned her. This had happened before, in her dreams, and this time she knew the ending.

Her, in the canoe, searching well into the next morning, fighting through the water hyacinths until finally a hand— a familiar, loving hand, now waxy and lifeless—caught her attention amid pale green leaves.

No! He had to survive. He had to!

Drifter barked frantically, running up and down the bank. Water churned, weeds splashing every which way. Mary ran several feet into the water before uncertainty and helplessness stopped her. Healer or not, she would fight to the death, fight Death, for Guy. But getting herself drowned would help neither of them. She had to call on her own strengths to help him. Centering herself, Mary concentrated with her whole being and cast protection in his direction.

Focus, concentrate. The power of water is cleansing, and protective—protect him. Water is buoyant—hold him up.

She doubted it would be enough. "Guy!"

The surface broke, and Guy emerged, hair and water streaming over his face with the weeds. He began to open his mouth—to shout? To breathe? A bony claw dragged him under again.

It really had looked like the Death card.

"No!" she screamed in horror, reaching out to Guy with all her magic.

As if to match the thrashing battle, her churning fears, the wind picked up. At least she heard a moaning, wailing sound.

"We tried to help you!" she screamed at the water. "You bastard, we tried to help you!" The wailing drowned her voice.

It felt them approach. No!

In a rush of water, Guy and the Reaper resurfaced, rolling. And then, miraculously, beneath the wind's howl—

The Reaper let go. The howls, she thought, and then realized she heard more than howling. She heard weeping, whispering, suffering, anguish, fury—all aimed at the horror in the water.

Guy fell back, flailing and choking. Yet the wave of misery, of countless tormented souls, washed over and through Mary, stealing her momentary relief.

She saw Guy grasp the Reaper's collarbone. Guy meant to fight this to the end, as if he really thought he could win— and that keening sound wasn't wind.

Mary raised her fists to her temples, as if that could protect her from the fog of agony and death—undeath—that bled from the very air around her. She recognized it, them, from last night, after the Reaper had vanished into the shadows.

After the Reaper had vanished? *They scared him. That mass of keening souls scared him!* They'd been chasing him, all along!

His victims. Too late? Perhaps not always, after all!

"Hang on to it!" she screamed, her voice lost beneath theirs.

The churning that marked Guy's battle spread unnaturally. Hyacinths turned over, slimy roots tangled across boiling water. Then, everywhere, even at Mary's feet, the bayou bubbled and roiled as the mournful cries of murdered souls filled the moonlit night. She couldn't have moved if she wanted to, which was how she saw it. The skeletal form of the Reaper, the pirate, reared from the bubbling brown surface, artificially white in the harsh halogen light, water and weeds pouring from it—and Guy doggedly clutching its collarbone. Then the water that poured from it morphed into...hands. Murky, liquid hands that joined Guy's around the skeleton's arms, its neck. Weedy fingers dragged at it. Its empty eye sockets stared upward at the sky; its mandible fell open, as if in a silent scream, as the swamp's churning reached a fevered pitch.

"Let go!" Mary shrieked through the howling. "Please!" Muddy waves splashed her as high as her waist; she barely noticed through her relief that Guy let go.

He backstroked frantically to escape the pull of rushing, vengeful water. She sent him more strength, tapping her deepest reserves. Behind him, countless watery hands pulled the Reaper down, inexorably down...

And a final, grasping bone claw caught at Guy's arm and dragged him under with it.

Mary reached out helplessly toward where he had been. Suddenly, the sky exploded with—thunder? Lightning? But the storm had ended! The blast of ozone knocked Mary to her knees in the waves, like a shock wave from the force of that much energy tearing from her world.

The wails faded into a sigh of...relief?

And then, it was over.

Almost. The water stilled, a mess of hyacinth roots and churned-up muck. The night sounds began, tentative, once more.

Mary shook her head, stared at the calming chaos in shock. Not over. Not yet. It couldn't be! She wouldn't let it be. She lunged for the shore, grasped the halogen lantern. She didn't know if it was waterproof or not. She dived under anyway.

The lamp continued to glow, under the bayou's surface, exposing a completely different world, a jungle of up rooted tendrils grabbing at her from the opaqueness of stirred-up water. She'd barely gotten her bearings before she had to surface, gasp, submerge again.

Slimy roots and leaves and pods oozed across her as she skimmed the murky bottom. She saw a whiplike form moving diagonally away from her—a disturbed water moccasin. Silt writhed in patterns all their own in the lantern's light, mocking her depth perception, taunting her sense of reality and time. Time! Every moment into the future brought Guy closer to death.

If he wasn't already dead.

She felt dizzy, had to surface. As she gasped a breath, she heard her own sob cut across the still bayou. Pain twisted in her chest, in her soul, more pain than she'd ever known. It wasn't worth this. Why not just give up?

No. She dived again, pushing displaced muck out of her way, realizing that she was as likely to find a corpse as—

She thought she saw a face through the thick brown water, and kicked toward it.

Then she nearly inhaled a lungful of water.

She forgot to kick. Her feet drifted toward the silty bottom as she stared into the translucent face of her baby brother Joey.

Seven-year-old Joey stared back at her, his expression even more angelic because of the inner glow that seemed to illuminate him. His hair wavered away from his head in all directions.

Not another ghost. Please, not another one. But he smiled, and at his smile the agony that twisted inside her eased away. A sense of joy filled the vacuum it left. A sense of peace. This wasn't the wandering spirit of a miserable soul.

Wherever he was, Joey was just fine.

He held out his small, childlike hand, kicking with babyish awkwardness to keep from floating right to the surface. She hesitated, then reached for him. Joey...

He receded, floating upward anyway. Someone was with him now. She recognized Lazare as he waved at her, then vanished with his best friend forever.

And Mary's flailing hand grasped the cold, lifeless hand of a man.

She grabbed on with a death grip—no, a life grip—and tried to stand. Too deep; his battle had drawn him too far into the water. With several powerful kicks, she managed to surface anyway, drawing her find with her. As she gasped a breath, she hurled the lantern shoreward with all her might, then turned all her attention and strength into drawing the man's—Guy's—head and shoulders above the water.

Remembering her Red Cross training, she checked for debris in his mouth, then pressed her lips to his—so cold!— and breathed into his mouth.

No response.

She used the water's buoyancy to turn his heavy, awkward form and latch her hands under his arms. Then, kicking desperately, she made her way toward the bank of the bayou. Twice she paused to give him more breath. Each time fear clawed deeper into her chest.

No response.

Her feet sank deep into the submerged mud as she continued to drag Guy's limp form inland; once she slipped and went under herself, but she struggled back out. Finally, she managed to lay his torso across the muddy bank, leaving his feet in the water.

She checked his breathing. None. Joey's peace had vanished with Joey, and she fought a second wave of agony as trembling, she checked his pulse. Faint. Far too faint. He visions had been correct, after all. Guy was dying.

She prayed without words, prayed to whatever divine being truly existed, be it Goddess or God. She tipped Guy' head back, pinched his nose shut, then lowered her moutl to his in a morbid mimicry of the passion they'd shared. Sh breathed a long, full breath into him.

His chest rose. She sat back. His chest fell. Nothing.

She tried it again, barely noticing Drifter at her elbow. Nothing.

She continued, struggling harder for each breath herself Why fight it? She'd seen this future, hadn't she? If his hear stopped this far from emergency facilities, he had littl hope. Misery choked her in the middle of a long breath, an she had to break her rhythm to gasp another one. His ches fell. She felt dizzy, and not just from lack of air. Sh couldn't bear any more. She'd tried to guard herself, trie to pull away this evening, but that had been too late, afte all. She'd fallen in love with him, foolishly, stupidly in love Loving him hadn't been worth this. Loving him could neve be...

Then Mary made it past the fear. It *was* worth it! She in haled deeply and breathed another lungful of air into him then another. It was worth even this. It had been wortl anything that might happen to her, ever again. At least she' learned how much more to life there was than merely no being dead.

She gasped another breath, pressed her lips again to th lips she loved so much—and his blue eyes fluttered open.

She reared back, so reconciled to his death that sh couldn't, for a moment, wrap her mind around this. Was h alive? Dead? Undead?

He drew a hoarse, bubbling breath on his own; she man aged to turn his head before he began to cough up water. H rolled, with her hands' guidance, onto his side on the bank

Alive. He gasped another breath, then another through his coughing, as he slumped back onto the mud. He didn't even seem to have taken in much water! He wasn't just alive—he was going to stay that way.

He hadn't left her, after all.

She sank into the mud and cried, Guy's ragged coughing music to her ears. She prayed a quick thanksgiving toward Whomever, not caring about names or genders. Maybe she couldn't change the past—but she'd changed the future. She listened to Guy breathing, and she loved him. But she reminded herself that they still weren't out of the water—so to speak. "Are you okay? I'll go get something for you to drink."

He nodded, sitting up himself, but when she started to stand, his hand floundered out and caught her arm.

She waited, absorbing every detail of his weed-strewn wet hair, his moonlit face with its still-bleeding gash, his so-very-blue eyes. "The—" He coughed again. "The Reaper?"

"The pirate?" she clarified. It had been a dealer of death but it had not, she knew now, been Death. Death had given them a second chance. Death wasn't evil, it just...was. "He's gone. Forever." She waited a moment, in case Guy wanted to ask anything else.

He cleared his throat, then managed to draw an uninterrupted breath. His voice still came out raspy, pained. But his eyes softened it. "Marry me?"

She sat back down in the mud. Hard.

The night songs had begun around them in earnest. Katydids, tree toads, banjo frogs. Birdcalls cut across the swamp.

"Too soon," Guy said quickly, looking down at his hands on the bank. "Never mind. Look—" He coughed a moment; caught his breath. "Forget I said it."

She shook her head slowly. How could it be too soon? They'd known each other most of their lives; lifetimes' worth, if instinct told true. She just hadn't expected...

"I love you, Mary Margaret Deveraux. I love that you're magic." He grinned a weary version of his hundred-watt grin. "I love that you have a pod of swamp weed on your head."

She swiped it off, blushing.

"I may not have a lot to offer right now, *chère*, I've wasted a lot of time. But I'm really good at construction and I'll do that until I can start my own company. I'll build us a future, I promise. I'll take care of you."

"You always have," she assured him, to ease some of the desperation in his gaze. Why should she ignore the past when it reminded her of that? "Always."

It worked. His eyes softened, and he cocked his head at her. "I know you won't want to marry in the church...."

"If they'll marry you to a Wiccan, then I'll be glad to marry you in the Catholic church," she assured him, and giggled. "My mother will be ecstatic."

He grinned. "I'll be happy to marry you in a Wiccan church, if you want."

She looked around her for a moment. The oxbow lake lay silent, its fields of water hyacinth, past the immediate battle zone, pale in the moonlight. A blue heron flew by, its neck bowed. The almost full moon dominated the sky above them, jewel-bright against the retreating storm clouds. The air smelled muggy and damp and warm, and the future felt—wonderful.

She suddenly, belatedly, realized that today was the first day of spring, the festival of Ostara. New beginnings...

"We're already in the Wiccan church," she told him seriously. "And I have the feeling that, as far as this church is concerned, we've been married all our lives. Maybe longer."

Guy leaned forward and kissed her. Long. Deep. She found herself sinking back down onto the mud, but this time in his arms, as his wet, heavy body rolled over hers.

He braced himself on his elbows, grinning down at her in the moonlight—then cocked his head away from her. "Look, *chère*."

Confused, she obeyed. Beside the protective roots of a tupelo gum sat one, two, three . . . seven baby rabbits, noses twitching. Drifter stood nearby, nose pointed at them, her tail whipping back and forth in double time until the mother rabbit appeared and the babies were bundled into what must be their burrow.

The dog looked back at them, ears perked. Mary looked back to Guy, her eyes wide and her soul stilled in wonder. She felt as if her bunny Sneezy, and his littermates, had returned to show her they were all right—like Joey and Lazare.

"I can't promise not to die, *chère*," he murmured, stroking her wet hair away from her face. "But I can promise to fight it with everything I have. That is the only way I'm ever leaving you." He continued to pet her hair, gazing lovingly—yes, lovingly—down at her, content just to be with her . . . and, probably, to catch his breath. Their being together felt so very natural, so very right. Could she risk the pain of losing it?

She decided she had to. Wanted to. Because that meant she had him in the first place.

"Hey," she murmured, tingling at his steady caress.

"Hey yourself," he answered, his grin incredibly sexy.

"I love you, *chère*," she whispered. Her eyes filled with happy tears. "I plan on loving you for a long, long time."

And the man she loved kissed her. "And I you, Mary Margaret. And I you."

And she believed him.

EPILOGUE

Father Ralph Poitiers married them—officially, that is—in mid-September at Ste. Jeanne d'Arc Catholic Church. They held the reception at the church hall, their largest and happiest family reunion yet. Children played and laughed in the background; in fact, Mary's oldest nephew looked a lot like Joey had, and Guy's younger nephew reminded everyone of Lazare.

So life went on.

Mary's two sisters and her three circlemates were bridesmaids, floating among the crowd in pastel gowns. Guy's groomsmen were his brother TiBoy, Rand Garner, Steve Peabody, and his two new construction partners, Mike and Stan. Re-New Construction, thought Mary with a proud smile as her husband shouldered his way toward her, through the congratulatory crowd. They specialized in renovating older buildings, but their first project had been her and Guy's new A-frame houseboat.

Guy caught her to him, brushing her ear with his lips. "Hey there."

"Hey yourself." She tried not to get too turned on by how incredible he looked in his gray tuxedo. It complemented the width of his shoulders, and brought out the blue of his eyes.

So did his obvious love for her.

The band struck up a Cajun waltz, heavy with fiddle and accordion, and Guy backed away from her, towing her toward the middle of the room with both hands. She smiled at the mischievous look in his eyes, but she definitely understood it.

This was their first dance—ever. Since they'd already made love, they'd decided to save *something* for their wedding day.

The official one, that is.

As soon as he swept her into the waltz, she knew they'd be as good at this as they were at the other. She laughed.

"Keep looking at me like that, *chère,* and I'll keep all the dances for myself," he warned her.

"But think how much money we're going to earn," she reminded him teasingly. Once she started dancing with relatives and friends of the family, men would traditionally pin bills to her veil.

Guy rolled his eyes. "Oh, yeah." He sighed dryly. "You know how important money is to me."

She snuggled closer against him, and the hand he'd rested on her shoulder slid across the white satin back of her wedding gown to keep her that way. Lady praise, but she did love this man.

"What are you smiling about, Mary Margaret?" he asked, his voice husky with curiosity.

"Just remembering a dream I had," she assured him, swaying in time with the music, smiling even wider. No reason to tell him it had been a premonition.

He could find out about their first son, Joseph Lazare Poitiers, when the time came. Because time *would* come.

They could count on that.

* * * * *

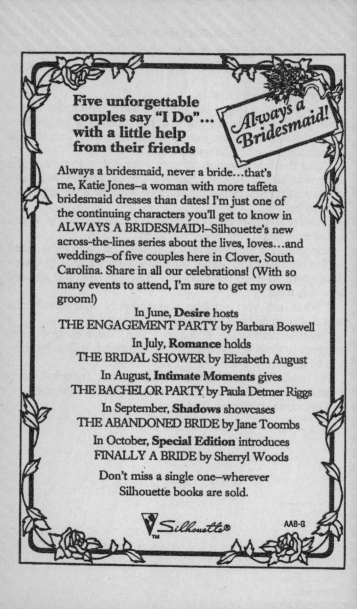

Five unforgettable couples say "I Do"... with a little help from their friends

Always a Bridesmaid!

Always a bridesmaid, never a bride...that's me, Katie Jones—a woman with more taffeta bridesmaid dresses than dates! I'm just one of the continuing characters you'll get to know in ALWAYS A BRIDESMAID!—Silhouette's new across-the-lines series about the lives, loves...and weddings—of five couples here in Clover, South Carolina. Share in all our celebrations! (With so many events to attend, I'm sure to get my own groom!)

In June, **Desire** hosts
THE ENGAGEMENT PARTY by Barbara Boswell

In July, **Romance** holds
THE BRIDAL SHOWER by Elizabeth August

In August, **Intimate Moments** gives
THE BACHELOR PARTY by Paula Detmer Riggs

In September, **Shadows** showcases
THE ABANDONED BRIDE by Jane Toombs

In October, **Special Edition** introduces
FINALLY A BRIDE by Sherryl Woods

Don't miss a single one—wherever
Silhouette books are sold.

Silhouette®

AAB-G

Take 4 bestselling love stories FREE

Plus get a FREE surprise gift!

Special Limited-time Offer

Mail to Silhouette Reader Service™

3010 Walden Avenue
P.O. Box 1867
Buffalo, N.Y. 14269-1867

YES! Please send me 4 free Silhouette Shadows™ novels and my free surprise gift. Then send me 2 brand-new novels every other month, which I will receive months before they appear in bookstores. Bill me at the low price of $2.96 each plus applicable sales tax, if any.* That's the complete price and—compared to the cover prices of $3.50 each—quite a bargain! I understand that accepting the books and gift places me under no obligation ever to buy any books. I can always return a shipment and cancel at any time. Even if I never buy another book from Silhouette, the 4 free books and the surprise gift are mine to keep forever.

200 BPA AWJE

Name	(PLEASE PRINT)

Address	Apt. No.

City	State	Zip

This offer is limited to one order per household and not valid to present Silhouette Shadows™ subscribers. *Terms and prices are subject to change without notice. Sales tax applicable in N.Y.

USHAD-595

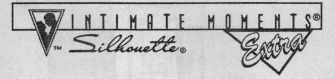

CODE NAME: DANGER

Because love is a risky business...

Merline Lovelace's "Code Name: Danger" miniseries gets an explosive start in May 1995 with

NIGHT OF THE JAGUAR, IM #637

Omega agent Jake MacKenzie had flirted with danger his entire career. But when unbelievably sexy Sarah Chandler became enmeshed in his latest mission, Jake knew that his days of courting trouble had taken a provocative twist....

Your mission: To read more about the Omega agency.

Your next target: THE COWBOY AND THE COSSACK, August 1995

Your only choice for nonstop excitement—

Announcing
the New Pages & Privileges™ Program
from Harlequin® and Silhouette®

Get All This FREE
With Just One Proof-of-Purchase!

- **FREE Travel Service** with the guaranteed lowest available airfares plus 5% cash back on every ticket

- **FREE Hotel Discounts** of up to 60% off at leading hotels in the U.S., Canada and Europe

- **FREE Petite Parfumerie** collection (a $50 Retail value)

- **FREE $25 Travel Voucher** to use on any ticket on any airline booked through our Travel Service

- **FREE Insider Tips Letter** full of fascinating information and hot sneak previews of upcoming books

- **FREE Mystery Gift** (if you enroll before May 31/95)

And there are more great gifts and benefits to come!
Enroll today and become Privileged!

(see insert for details)